LAST HEARTBEAT

---

a novel by

ROBERT LOUIS DIGIACOMO

REVERIE BOOKS

LAST HEARTBEAT
Published by Reverie Publishing LLC / August 2009
Wesley Chapel, Florida

This is the work of fiction. Names, characters, places and incidents are either the product of the author's imagination or are used fictitiously. Any resemblance to persons living or dead as well as locations and events is coincidental.

No classified information was used to create this book, and no member of any government agency was contacted in researching this book.

Cover image by julia forte
Visit her website at
www.anatomicalart.co.uk

Library of Congress Control Number: 2009905160

ISBN-13: 978-0-9840788-0-6

www.LastHeartbeat.com
www.ReverieBooks.com

Printed in the United States of America.

Acknowledgements

With appreciation and gratitude, the author wishes to acknowledge the invaluable assistance of Cherie' Korn and Mike Velat for the many hours they spent preparing this book for publication. Their hard work and attention to detail in editing as well as their developmental ideas were a welcomed contribution.

For Ruth Ann Edwards, a lover of books…

PROLOGUE

THE FOUR BLACK-CLAD FIGURES crouched down in the small patch of woods two hundred meters south of their target. Tim Falwell, the leader of the assault team, was concerned. The large house with its fortified walls stood downhill over open territory, and although it was a moonless night, he feared there was too much ground to cover in the open.

His intelligence was 36 hours old, and there was no sign of his contact. It annoyed him that the informant had not shown up yet. This was a risky operation, the blackest of all ops—an action not sanctioned by the United States government and unknown to his superiors. The team was on its own. If caught, the Bolivian authorities would prosecute them as criminals, and they would not get any help from the Justice Department back home. The DEA leader was also aware that there was a short window to get the job done and still rendezvous with their transportation in La Paz. A small plane was waiting on a private airstrip north of the city that would take them out of Bolivia. If their contact didn't show up soon, they would have to either abort the mission or go it on their own with the stale information.

This was Falwell's last operation in the field before he started his new assignment, training DEA recruits at Quantico. Their mission tonight was purely payback and personal. They would kill General Victor Eduardo Castillo. He was the man they believed was responsible for torturing and murdering three undercover agents. The dead agents were colleagues as well as friends of tonight's all volunteer squad.

"What can you see?" Falwell asked the agent whose weapon was equipped with a night vision scope.

"I've got two men inside. One is near the gate smoking a cigarette and another is walking the perimeter."

This squared with the information given to them several days ago by the paid informant. The man indicated that the general's protective detail was usually comprised of two men who changed every eight hours and would not be relieved until midnight. Tim looked at his watch. Midnight was still more than an hour away. Still, he was uneasy. Without good intelligence, he knew this was precarious business. Tim didn't know if the general was home and who else, if anyone, was in the large house. Their informant advised them that the general's wife with some other family members should be on vacation in Europe this time of year. However, General Castillo was fond of playing poker and frequently had visitors over on Friday nights. The team couldn't see much from their position, though all appeared quiet. The general's large black Mercedes sat on the circular drive along with two older cars, probably belonging to the guards. If the general had any visitors, it was unlikely that their cars would be in the large garage.

Falwell decided he could not wait for the contact any longer. The mission would go forward. Their plan was to cross the open area and make their way along the outside wall until they were almost at the wrought iron gates. The guards wouldn't be able to see them from inside the compound. There was a long driveway, and it would be unlikely for a passerby to spot them from the main road. The neighborhood was an enclave of large estates belonging to some of the most powerful and influential men in Bolivia. At night, the local police would stop and question anyone that they didn't know.

"Okay, let's move out."

The assault team made it over the open territory without any problems. Falwell was relieved. He considered this the most dangerous part of the operation. When the squad reached the wall, the agent with the night vision equipment peeked around the corner. "Tell me when the second guard comes into view," whispered Tim.

On his signal, the assault team would move to the front of the gates and take out the guards with their specially silenced weapons. The gate didn't appear reinforced so Tim knew that the four-man team could force it open enough to get through once they neutralized the men inside. If they were lucky, they could take the men down before they were able to fire their weapons. That way, no one inside the house would know the team was there. However, unknown to Falwell, the guard's schedule had changed. Their relief would be coming at 11:00 PM instead of midnight.

As they prepared for the attack, the squad was illuminated by a set of bright headlights coming up the long drive. The driver accelerated and started blaring his horn to warn the guards about the intruders. Tim realized he needed his men to spread out and not make such an easy target. He signaled two members of the team to move to the other side of the gates. As the men crossed, the driver tried to run them down and lost control of the vehicle. He rammed the gates creating an opening for the squad to enter.

Tim shot the driver through the windshield and yelled, "Let's move!"

The assault team dashed inside the compound and took cover behind a large fountain. The element of surprise was gone, but Falwell expected they still had a good chance of completing the mission.

The bodyguards inside were scurrying around looking for some protection when a second car pulled into the drive. Tim saw the occupant exit the vehicle, circle around and take cover behind the passenger door. He thought this was not good. The team was now vulnerable from the front and back. They would find themselves in a crossfire situation and would have to withdraw. The two bodyguards, who had now found cover, started to react. They began firing blindly at the team.

"Concentrate your fire on the guy in the driveway!" shouted Tim. He knew they had to take out the new guard first, and then they could make their escape.

In seconds there were bullets flying in all directions, although none hitting their mark. The guards apparently were not well-trained marksmen, and the team was not having much luck either. Tim thought this is incredible. They were all shooting at the guard outside the compound, and he was still returning fire. Finally, a bullet hit the man but not before his last shot went wild. The bullet ricocheted off the top of the wall and hit a large propane tank that served most of the home's fuel needs. The air was filled with shrapnel from the tremendous explosion. One of the bodyguards firing from inside the compound was killed while the other guard was wounded badly.

Since the team had taken cover behind the fountain wall, the explosion didn't injure them except for their eardrums. Tim signaled the men to withdraw.

"Let's get out of here. This way..." he yelled to his men.

With all the noise, the hope of a cross-country stealthy departure was now out of the question. Falwell judged that the second guard's car, although riddled with bullet holes and a broken windshield, might still aid in their escape. He figured they didn't have much choice.

"Move, move..."

They reached the car and piled in. The keys were in the ignition but the car wouldn't start. Apparently, a stray bullet damaged the engine during the firefight.

Senora Castillo and her daughter were watching her two grandsons playing with the new video game console in the large family room. It was past the children's bedtime, but it was Friday night, and there wasn't any school the next day. Senora Castillo's husband, the general, and her son-in-law were playing poker with some acquaintances at her daughter's home about a quarter of a mile away. The games usually broke up around midnight, so the general would be home in about an hour. Because of the two bodyguards that her husband provided, she felt safe in the large house. Besides, there were no drugs in the residence. They were kept in the mountain hideouts. There was also an unwritten rule among the rival drug organizations that you didn't go after families. However, kidnappings were on the rise in Bolivia, and her husband didn't want to take any chances. She thought that it was doubtful they would be a target. Almost everyone in Bolivia knew how powerful the general was, not because of his military rank but his status as the head of one of the countries largest cocaine producers. Still, she knew the poorer people in the southern part of the country were getting desperate, so it was good that her husband provided the family some protection. Therefore, it was a surprise when she heard the loud crash as the metal gate came down and later the shots. She quickly realized what was happening. She yelled to her daughter, "Kidnappers!"

They had a safe room on the second floor, but when the bullets started breaking the large windows near the staircase, she knew they wouldn't be able to make it upstairs. She figured it would be safer in the kitchen, which had smaller windows.

She pointed, "The kitchen, go..." She yelled at the boys, "Stay low."

They crawled to the breakfast nook area, which appeared to Senora Castillo to be the safest spot.

"Help me with the table," she shouted at her daughter.

The two women managed to overturn the small but heavy oak table. The Senora hoped this would add to their protection. They were now clear of the errant bullets that were still zinging through the family room. She was sure her husband and his friends would come to their aid, as the noise was horribly loud and would reach down the street. That was Senora Castillo's last thought as the propane tank on the other side of the kitchen wall exploded.

The general and his son-in-law, both having spent a good deal of time in the United States, were fond of playing poker. Along with several acquaintances, most Friday nights hosted a game at one of their homes. They played for relatively low stakes, as the men at the table were not wealthy like the general.

General Castillo anticipated the game would be over soon. Most of the chips were in front of his son-in-law, Alejandro. They were playing at his house tonight. The general had just lost another pot when a servant burst into the room. The men at the table were startled by the intrusion.

"General Castillo, there are shots coming from near your home!"

As the men jumped up to run outside, they almost knocked over the table. The servant was correct. The noise had to be coming from his estate, feared the general.

"Go to the car," he shouted.

The four men, three of whom were armed, jumped into the large vehicle belonging to his son-in-law and headed down the street. Then the general saw and heard the explosion.

"Hurry, hurry!"

His son-in-law was driving—the car almost out of control now. It took about three minutes to reach the general's home. As they turned into the drive, the general saw one of his guards on the ground. His car was blocking their way. Then four men armed men jumped from the vehicle. The general saw that they were all carrying assault weapons, so when they approached and demanded in English that they get out of the vehicle, he didn't draw his weapon. The men dressed in all black immediately pulled the general and his son-in-law from the front seats and clubbed them to the ground. The general's friends, who were sitting in the back, drew their weapons and managed to wound one of the attackers. They were killed when the gunfire was returned. The attackers, pulled their bodies out, jumped into the SUV and escaped. The general though dazed, tried to make it to his home. Fire had almost totally engulfed the large house by now. The heat and flames were unbearable 100 feet away. He knew there was little chance for anyone left inside. He hoped that his family had somehow escaped.

His son-in-law was up and at his side.

"My boys..."

Sirens were blaring in the distance. The authorities were on their way. The general learned later that a security guard at a neighboring residence had called them when he first heard the shots, and later to report the fire.

It took almost three hours to put out the flames. The general and his son-in-law, Alejandro, spent most of that time in silence. Even though the paramedics were concerned that both men might have a slight concussion, the general was not going to leave the scene until he knew about his family. Alejandro, who was a doctor, dressed his father-in-law's wounds while his own went unattended.

"Who would do this?" asked Alejandro, his hands quivering as he tried to apply the bandage.

"They were Americans," exploded the general.

During their wait, the police showed General Castillo a weapon that one of the attackers had dropped when the general's friends shot him. General Castillo recognized it as a modified AR-15 Tactical Carbine equipped with night scope and noise suppressor. This was a sophisticated weapon and he knew it would not be in any local kidnapper's arsenal. In addition, the attackers were all dressed the same way. It wasn't an official uniform of any kind. However, it was similar to the jump suits that many police and para-military use in an operation. The general also noticed the way the attackers moved. Some organization had trained them well.

On closer inspection of the weapon, the general recognized it as the standard issue assault carbine used by the DEA and American FBI. He told his son-in-law that the attack looked like the work of the DEA. But, he wondered why if the Americans were after him, why they didn't shoot him when they had the chance.

The captain of the fire brigade walked over to give the general the bad news. The firefighters had already carried two bodies from the compound. One man was dead but the other was still alive but badly burned. The general had recognized him as one of his bodyguards, a man named Bartolomeo.

"I'm sorry, General. We found four charred bodies in the kitchen area of your home. Two of them appear to be children."

The general watched as his son-in-law wept at the loss of his wife and two sons.

1

LELAND HUNT SAT in his real estate agent's small conference room waiting for Alejandro Reyes to arrive. The Bolivian doctor had called from the Jacksonville airport as he was leaving the rental car area. Leland figured the drive to Waycross would take the doctor a little over an hour. While he was waiting, Leland was making small talk with his real estate agent and the lawyer who would handle the closing.

Leland was feeling good. The old castor oil plant had been for sale for almost eight years with only a handful of people interested in the rural Georgia property. It was the last of its kind in the United States. Now, India produced almost all castor oil imported into America.

Leland's father had started the company in the early 1950's and the business prospered for the next few decades. The company property consisted of a large building surrounded by forty acres of farmland where the castor beans used to make the oil were grown. The processing facilities where situated in a three story corrugated metal structure of approximately 12,000 square feet. Most of the machinery was still in place.

When Leland's father passed away, he and his brother ran the company for about ten years. But, competition from overseas caused them to lose most of their business. When their last customer, a company making motor oil left them eight years ago, the brothers closed the plant, and it stood for sale ever since. His brother, Roger, continuously harangued him about his unsuccessful effort to sell it. They had lowered the amount fifty percent from the original one million dollar asking price. Still there were no takers.

Leland was happy but anxious about the sale. The last two prospects lost interest when they learned what was stored on the property. There were huge piles of waste mash. It was the refuse from the castor oil making process. This mash wasn't much good as fertilizer or animal feed because it contained an extremely toxic substance known as ricin. Leland estimated that the mash included between five and ten percent of this toxin. Although, it was relatively safe in its current form, there were some sensational news reports about incidents involving terrorists trying to use the substance. There were even a few well-documented incidents during the cold war about the Soviets using ricin to murder dissidents. The result was that nobody was willing to haul the waste mash away, and Leland was also unsuccessful in trying to get a permit from the county to burn it. Essentially he was stuck with over 100 tons of waste material, which was now turning to compost, and he had no way to dispose of it. Potential buyers didn't want to take on this burden either. Therefore, the result was 40 acres of good farmland left fallow, a building deteriorating and a lawsuit waiting to happen.

"Hey bubba, the day's finally here," announced Jeb, Leland's real estate agent and fishing buddy.

"It's not a done deal yet. Don't jinx it."

"I already put a deposit down on a new bass boat from the commission you're earning me on this sale."

"Watch out, your wife doesn't send the money to Brother Lucas instead."

"No chance of that happening again. We had a talk."

"Yeah, right. Neither of us might end up with any money anyway. Remember we still have the issue with the waste mash," noted Leland.

"I told you, the doctor's all right with it."

"He mentioned something about making bio-diesel. He explained it, but I didn't know what he was talking about."

Leland, who still received castor oil producer's trade journals, read that companies were experimenting with castor beans as a potential renewable fuel source. He remembered Brazil as the country where this was happening. Leland had even given the idea some thought and was going to approach his brother about it. However, this opportunity to sell came up.

"You said that Doctor Reyes is from Bolivia?" asked Leland.

"Yes he is."

"How far is Bolivia from Brazil?"

"I don't know. I had the same geography teacher you did," said Jeb.

"They border each other," stated the lawyer.

"So the Doctor indicated that he was planning to re-start the mill?" asked Leland.

"Yeah, he had me send photos of the machinery."

Leland knew the machinery was still in good shape. His father had purchased first-rate equipment, all stain-less steel, and even after several decades, the equipment showed little wear. The building's condition was an-other matter. It needed a new roof and a hailstorm this past spring smashed several windows. Some vandals had also sprayed some graffiti on one side.

From the conference room window, the men saw a car pull up. The driver seemed to be having a problem parallel parking the sedan. After several tries, he man-aged to get the car parked, got out and looked at the parking meter.

Leland told his fishing buddy, "Go put some change in the meter for the doctor."

Without argument, Jeb headed outside. After taking care of the meter, Jeb brought the doctor in, and they all introduced themselves. The doctor insisted that they call him Alejandro. "You don't pronounce the 'J'?" in-quired Jeb.

"No. That's how we get away with naming our kids Jesus," said the doctor smiling.

The men laughed. Alejandro Reyes seemed to Leland to be a nice fellow. But curiously, he spoke without an accent.

"Jeb told us you were from Bolivia. You sound like an American."

"I did almost all of my education here in the United States. My father was a Bolivian diplomat assigned to the embassy in Washington. Except for my last two years of high school, I was educated here," responded Alejandro.

"Have you been back here since?" inquired the lawyer.

"I returned for college and medical school. I received a degree from Johns Hopkins. I also did my internship and residency there. When my VISA expired, I had to go back to Bolivia."

"So you practice down there?"

"Not anymore. I stopped a couple of years ago."

Leland wished they would stop asking the doctor questions. He wanted to get on with the property matter.

The lawyer asked, "So why did you pick this town?"

Leland was starting to get impatient with the nosy lawyer. Yet, the doctor seemed okay with answering his questions so he didn't interfere.

"I was looking to return to United States and wanted to start a business. You can get a VISA if you deposit a million dollars to start a new business. However, if you choose a county where unemployment is fifty percent higher than the U.S. national average, you only have to deposit a half million. This county qualifies."

"I didn't know that," remarked Jeb. "Are you bringing your family with you?"

The doctor hesitated and then answered with a curt, "No."

Leland could see that the last question seemed to irritate Alejandro Reyes and declared, "Why don't we start going over the transaction."

The doctor seemed pleased with his suggestion that they get on with the matter at hand. After two hours, they concluded their business. Leland gave Alejandro Reyes the keys to the building, and the doctor handed the attorney a cashier's check for $476,000.

Leland and Jeb celebrated that night.

2

BRIAN BURKE WAS BUSY breaking down the illegal crystal meth lab that his employers had him move every five or six weeks. It was a huge pain in the ass, but he knew it was necessary to keep him out of trouble. He was glad his employers were careful and ran a tight ship. He was currently on probation and did not want to go to prison. So he took a dose of his medication and got on with the job. He expected his boss would be driving up within the hour and didn't want to make him angry again.

The meth operation was no mom and pop business. Since the DEA removed all the cold medicine containing ephedrine, which was a prime ingredient used to make crystal meth from store shelves, the big drug cartels took over the operation. They managed to smuggle the ephedrine into the United States alongside cocaine and heroin. Once the cartel took over, they distributed the drugs more efficiently than the tweakers, who were formerly making a sustenance living cooking the crystal meth as a backyard brew. Brian decided that the DEA must employ some of the dumbest people on earth not to realize what would happen by taking the little guy out of the picture.

Lately, Brian had distain for all government officials after what he regarded as an unjust arrest for soliciting sex from a minor on the internet. He wasn't heavily into porn but he did visit some chat rooms occasionally. On one occasion, he struck up a conversation with a 14-year old girl and things got carried away. When she asked for pictures, he sent photos of someone else's private parts he found on the internet. When she asked if he wanted to meet, he agreed. Unfortunately, the Florida Department of Law Enforcement ran the chat room, and they arrested him. The sting had cost him his place at the University of Florida, and instead of getting his PhD, he was now using his education in biochemistry to make illegal drugs.

Brian looked up as he was finished packing the old van and saw two cars pulling into the drive. He was not alarmed because he recognized the first vehicle as the pickup truck belonging to his boss, the man who recruited him. They had met in a group therapy session. In his plea bargain, Brian agreed to participate in a program for sexual predators. It was mandatory that he attend the bi-weekly sessions. During each meeting, when it was Brian's turn to speak, he would talk about how smart he was and how he would have a doctoral degree by now if he hadn't been kicked out of the program. The University, after finding out he was registered as a sex offender, asked him to leave. That was six months ago, and Brian lamented that he wasn't able to find a job once prospective employers did a background check on him.

One night after repeating his story, a scary looking Latino guy with a spider-web tattoo on his neck approached him. Brian usually kept a safe distance from the man when he chose a seat. He knew the man's name was Xavier but hadn't talked to him before. Xavier asked him if he wanted to make some money using his chemistry degree. At first, Brian was skeptical. When he told Brian that he could make up to $3,000 a week doing some part-time work, Brian jumped at the chance. He needed money because of his mother's problems. So now, almost a year later, he was one of the top producers for the drug cartel. His boss told him his yields were much higher than his peers. At first, Brian was surprised that these people talked in terms of yields and throughput, but then he came to realize that this was a business like any other.

As the vehicles came to a stop, Brian could see that his boss had a passenger with him. They got out of the truck and his boss grunted, "Give me the keys to the van."

Brian was alarmed and inquired, "Is there something wrong?"

"No."

As he was handing over his keys, the man in the second vehicle got out, approached him, and smiled. "My name is Doctor Reyes but please call me Alejandro. You are Brian Burke?"

Brian nodded.

"I'm told you do good work," stated the doctor.

"Thanks."

"We have a special project for you. It involves some-one with your background in biochemistry. It pays very well."

Brian finally relaxed. If they were going to kill him, they would not bother to go through this ruse.

"We're going to double your compensation. But you have to know that the work will be somewhat demand-ing and dangerous."

Brian wondered what could be more dangerous than cooking crystal meth. Since changing his medication, he was more willing to take risks. That's probably how he got himself in trouble with the law. When he doubled-upped his dosage, he tended to do stupid things. But the drug did make him feel good.

"Are you interested?"

"Sure."

Today was a double-up day for Brian. He needed the extra kick to motivate him to disassemble the meth lab.

Brian saw the doctor signal to Xavier. Then the pick-up followed by the van drove away.

"We're going to take a little trip together. On the way we can stop for lunch."

The two men decided on a small Mexican restaurant down the road from the meth lab, which was located in suburban Jacksonville in the city of Orange Park. After eating, they found their way to I-10 and continued west for a short way, then Alejandro exited the interstate. For the next hour, they snaked their way along several rural routes that ran between the Florida and Georgia border. Brian didn't ask many questions. The doctor did most of the talking. His conversation centered on his growing up in America and the differences between this country and his native Bolivia.

"If you don't mind telling me, where are we headed?" asked Brian.

"Across the Georgia border near a small town called Fargo."

Brian thought that was a good omen. Fargo was the name of his favorite movie. He must have watched it at least a hundred times.

"Another twenty minutes and we'll be there," responded Alejandro.

The doctor kept his word. A short time later, they arrived. Brian noticed as they pulled up to an old building, two men were sitting outside. Brian thought they looked creepy, maybe even menacing. The two men stood up and greeted the doctor in Spanish.

"These two gentlemen will be helping, but you are in charge," declared Alejandro. "I'm sorry they speak little English, but I'll be around often. You'll have to do the best you can when I'm not here." Alejandro reached into his brief case and retrieved a large ring of keys. After a minute or so of trying different ones, he managed to unlock the front door, and the four men entered. It was dark in the building. The group waited while Alejandro made his way over to an electrical panel and pulled down on a lever, which turned on most of the building's interior lights.

Brian looked around. The facility, whatever it was, looked like it hadn't been used for many years. In the corner was office furniture, some of it broken. File boxes and crates littered the area. However, what Brian could see of the machinery, it appeared to be in good shape. Brian couldn't place the strange but familiar smell. It wasn't noxious, but there was something unpleasant about it. Then he recognized it as castor oil. He remembered his grandmother had given it to him once as a child when he had complained about a stomachache. He hadn't complained to her again.

Brian was confused. Certainly, they weren't going to be making castor oil. However, he would be patient. Eventually he would find out what this was all about. The doctor had stated dangerous and difficult. So far, he didn't see anything ominous.

The doctor was talking to his helpers in Spanish, and they were nodding their understanding. When he was through, he walked over to Brian and handed him a piece of paper. It was a hand-drawn layout.

"I told Luis and Juan that I want the place cleaned up. I arranged for a large dumpster. It will be coming in the morning. After the place is in order, I want some of the machinery moved according to the layout. Also, there will be some additional equipment being delivered over the next couple of weeks."

"What kind of equipment?" asked Brian.

"When it gets here, I'll tell you more. Okay? For now, get the place cleaned up."

"Do you want to throw out all that furniture over there?"

"See what's in the office area. Bring some up there if it's needed. If not, then store it neatly out of the way."

The doctor gave Luis and Juan a few more instructions and then said, "It's getting late. Look around and tomorrow we'll continue with the clean-up. There's a small motel twenty miles down the road. It isn't much, but that's where we'll be staying for now. Later I might rent some RVs and put them on the property."

Brian asked, "Alejandro, do you have a second?"

"What's the matter?"

"The terms of my probation say I can't leave the state of Florida without permission. I have to register as a sex offender and also furnish my current address." Brian looked up as he mumbled this to see if the other men were listening.

Alejandro saw this and remarked, "Don't worry they probably don't understand. I'm familiar with your situation. The motel is actually back over the Florida line. Can you use that for an address?"

"I guess I could. It's over an hour commute each way if I have to go home everyday."

"Well, it may come to that. Actually, as I think about it, I'd prefer it. I don't want the government snooping around, checking addresses. We'll give you gas money to cover the costs. But for tonight you can stay at the motel without a problem?"

"Yeah, I can do that."

"It's Thursday, I can drop you off at your home tomorrow, and you can get your car and come back here on Monday."

"That sounds good."

Brian supposed the arrangement would probably work out. The commute wouldn't be that tough. There wasn't any traffic with which he would have to contend. It might even be pleasant. Thinking about pleasant, Brian reached into his pocket to retrieve the bottle containing his medication. Brian took another pill and started exploring the old building.

As Brian walked around, he noticed a lot of stainless steel. At one end of the structure there were large hoppers, which Brian figured most likely held the raw material. A series of conveyers carried the material to a line of presses and then to some filtering equipment. There were pipes leading to vats and large storage tanks. In the middle of the plant was the office area. It resembled a square house built on platform. A steel staircase led to a second level metal walkway, and Brian could see several doors from where he was standing. He estimated the whole office area was about 2,000 square feet.

Brian continued to look around until Alejandro signaled they would be leaving for the night. The men stopped at a grocery store that was located near their motel to stock up. Brian noticed that his helpers bought mostly beer and little else. He himself drank Diet Coke because of his medication.

3

BRIAN AWOKE the next morning thinking that the motel was not bad. It was clean and the bed was comfortable. They also served a free breakfast so he threw on his wrinkled clothes and headed for the small lobby for some coffee. A short time later, he was joined by Luis and Juan and soon after by Alejandro.

After breakfast, Brian rode with Alejandro while the two other men traveled in the pick-up. When they arrived, Alejandro gave Brian a spare key and told him to see if it worked in the door lock. It did, so Brian found the electrical panel and turned on the lights.

A short time later, a truck pulled to the side of the building and unloaded a large dumpster. Brian, Luis, and Juan began cleaning up the old castor oil plant. It wasn't long before Brian realized that he was working much harder than his two compatriots. But, for five or six grand a week, he wasn't going to complain about doing some donkeywork.

About three in the afternoon, Alejandro walked over to Brian. "Why don't we get going. I'll drop you off at your home. Luis and Juan can continue cleaning up."

The two men left and headed for Jacksonville where Brian lived with his mother.

On Monday morning, Brian arrived about 8:00 AM to see a truck unloading some welding equipment. When he went into the plant, he saw that not too much had changed in the way of clean-up after he and Alejandro had left the previous Friday afternoon. The remainder of the morning he and his helpers finished cleaning the place. The work went quickly and the men finished by noon.

In spite of the language barrier and their appearance, Luis and Juan seemed pleasant enough. They smiled at him a lot and even gave him a nickname, *cochino*, which they used when they wanted to get his attention. Brian didn't have too many friends. Other children bullied him when he was young, and he wasn't liked much as an adult, particularly after his arrest. So he appreciated that the men were friendly to him.

Brian noticed that Juan and Luis were skilled with a cutting torch and welding equipment. Alejandro was supervising them. They were in the process of moving some of the larger equipment to an area in the middle of the plant, close to the elevated office. The equipment was heavy and Brian worked hard helping the men move it. Soon delivery trucks began arriving. Alejandro told Brian that it was his job to unpack the crates and assemble the equipment. He didn't want Luis and Juan to damage it.

Brian borrowed some tools from Luis and started unscrewing the wooden crates. It didn't take Brian long to identify the hardware. Any biochemistry student would recognize it as chromatography equipment, which was used as a way to separate the different compounds in a substance. This piqued Brian's interest. He was speculating about what they were doing while driving from his home that morning. Obviously, whatever drug they were making was organic in nature and certainly not any kind of methamphetamine.

While he was uncrating, a brown panel truck pulled up with a much smaller set of boxes. Brian needed a break from the heavy work, so he decided to tackle those first. Once he unpacked all the crates and cartons, he was impressed. Brian was looking at a jet pulverizer, as well as a high performance liquid chromatography machine. Lab workers use the HPLC machine to analyze materials, and the jet pulverizer could take any solid substance and break it down into tiny particles— small enough where hundreds could fit on the head of a pin. These were sophisticated pieces of equipment and expensive. Brian figured this couldn't get any weirder. Then Alejandro walked over with some plans.

"I want you and Juan to go to the home improvement store and get the materials to build this."

Brian looked at it. It was an environmental barrier or temporary "clean room" similar to what companies use when they are removing old asbestos. It protected the workers and public against contamination by the asbestos dust.

Brian and Juan came back with the materials necessary to build the clean room. For the remainder of the afternoon, the two men built the enclosure around several pieces of the equipment including the pulverizer. On the way home that night, Brian thought the day's events bordered on the bizarre. Nevertheless, he knew why they needed someone with his training. They were going to synthesize some type of compound, probably something found in nature.

The next morning, he arrived at the same time as Luis and Juan. Alejandro's car was already there as well as a vehicle Brian hadn't seen before. Upon entering the old plant, Alejandro called to him from the metal walkway to come up to the office area. He also wanted to see Luis and Juan. They climbed the stairs and walked into a small room that they were using for a meeting area. Sitting at one end of the table was an older gentleman. Brian saw his two coworkers visibly stiffen at the sight of the man. They obviously recognized him and were uncomfortable in his presence. Brian didn't see anything threatening in his demeanor. He looked to Brian to be frail and in ill health. Luis and Juan acknowledged his presence in a reverential manner and addressed him as General. Then the general asked the men some questions, and they responded politely.

Alejandro then asked everyone to sit down. There were enough chairs for everyone. However, Brian got the broken one and almost tipped over when he leaned back.

Alejandro retrieved two thick manila folders from his brief case and put them in front of Brian.

"Take a quick look through the file on top," declared Alejandro.

Brian opened the folder and looked at the first page. It was a copy of a US patent. The title was:

United States Patent Office
3,060,165 Patented October 3, 1962
PREPARATION OF TOXIC RICIN

Brian froze. Now all the equipment made sense. He looked up to object, and then he saw that the general had put a large automatic pistol on the table. The message was clear. Brian reached into his pocket for his medication.

Alejandro probably seeing his discomfort coached, "Brian, I want you to become an expert in the process. I've done extensive research, and this is the best information that's available out there."

Brian didn't know much about ricin except what the media reported from time to time. What he did know was that ricin was one the most toxic substances found in nature and difficult to handle safely. Since he was stuck with the situation, he was going to ensure he didn't kill himself.

Alejandro indicated the meeting was over, and the men started leaving. Luis when saying goodbye to the older man addressed him by his name. Luis called him General Castillo. Brian made a note to do some research to find out who the general was. On the way out of the meeting room, Brian bumped into Juan who said something to him that included the word *cochino*. This drew a strong rebuke from Alejandro first and then the general. Juan looked visibly frightened. Brian made another note to himself to find out what they were calling him.

For the remainder of the day Brian did what Alejandro had asked. As he studied the information provided to him, he was surprised. It turned out to be fairly easy and straightforward to make ricin. He thought this was something any chemistry major could do. There was nothing exotic about the process, and he could make it in small quantities without all the specialized equipment that they had set-up. Unless Alejandro wanted a hundred pounds of the stuff, it seemed to Brian that the doctor might have wasted a lot of money on expensive equipment. Beside the jet pulverizer, he had uncrated and assembled industrial strength filtering equipment and special compound dryers used in making pharmaceuticals. Brian estimated that there was several hundred thousand dollars in equipment.

That last thought jarred Brian. He knew Alejandro was a medical doctor and certainly not stupid. Only the military or a terrorist organization would be interested in making a toxic substance like ricin in these quantities. This was getting scary.

Brian wondered where they would get the raw materials. Castor beans were not something one could buy from a local garden store. Brian approached Alejandro. Before Brian could say anything Alejandro asked, "How you doing? Are you getting a good understanding?"

"About the process yes, but…"

"Brian it wouldn't be in your best interest to ask too many questions now. You're here to make the ricin. You should not concern yourself with anything else. Do you understand?"

Brian understood perfectly what Alejandro was telling him but questioned, "About the process... Where are we going to get the castor beans, and do we have to refurbish the rest of the machinery here to remove the oils?"

"Those large piles of vegetation out back are actually waste mash from the castor oil making process."

Brian thought *wow*. There were probably hundreds of tons of mash in the those piles out back. He would bet most of the oil has already been extracted which leaves a great raw material for manufacturing ricin.

"How old do you think the mash is?"

"All of it is at least eight years old, and some of it could be much older. As a manufacturing base for ricin, it's as perfect as you can get. It's probably unique in the world."

From the research, Brian knew that the toxicity of the poison was due in large part to the amount of oil that one could remove.

"I know what you're thinking," predicted Alejandro. "Most of the residual oil left in the vegetation after they processed the castor beans for castor oil has leached out as it has sat in the hot Georgia sun for these many years."

"Do you think we can skip the first part of the process then?" asked Brian.

"I don't think so. Even if there's less than one percent of oil left, we want to remove it."

"Well everything appears to be in place, ready to go then," announced Brian.

"Okay, we'll begin tomorrow morning with a small test batch."

That night Brian found out two interesting pieces of information and both troubling. The general was indeed a dangerous person—certainly, no one you would want to cross. He read about what happened to the general's family almost three years before. The news articles told of an attack on the general's home, which killed his wife, daughter and two grandsons. The Bolivian government blamed the United States. There were rumors of an informer supplying the DEA with information about the general's residence before the attack. Brian thought, *holy crap* and wanted to take another one of his pills. However, the anti-depressant medication was giving him severe heartburn lately when he took too much.

The other piece of information was the meaning of the word *cochino*. It roughly translated to pig or dirty pervert.

4

THE NEXT MORNING, Brian arrived to find his two helpers filling garbage bags with the old waste mash. Alejandro was supervising and telling the men where to dig. When he entered the plant, Brian saw that the hazmat suits had arrived. He did not look forward to wearing the heavy gear. He had only donned the protective clothing once while a student and remembered what it felt like. The suit weighed almost fifty pounds, and when wearing the attached hood, it could easily get over 100 degrees inside. Since it was June in Georgia and the building wasn't air conditioned, he was going to be earning his money. However, he knew they could accomplish the first few steps in the process safely without the suits. The only way to cool the building was the old industrial fans that the former employees used on hot days. Brian checked to make sure the fans were still working.

Alejandro and the men came back into the plant as Brian was pouring ten gallons of distilled water, which he purchased at the local supermarket, into a large vat. The stainless steel tub had its own heating element, which was contained in a water jacket that surrounded a central tank. It also had a mixing arm with blades that would agitate the material. At the bottom of the tank was a three-way valve for removing material and later cleaning. Juan and Luis built a steel platform six feet high to raise the vat off the floor. They also welded a stainless steel pipe to one side of the valve. It led to a series of filters.

Brian then grabbed a large bottle of sulfuric acid diluted to five percent. He carefully poured the acid into the water and used a testing kit to find the correct pH. Brian knew he had to achieve a pH of around 3.5, which was equivalent to the acid content of apple juice. The temperature of the mixture was 77 degrees, which was perfect for the process, so there was no need to use the apparatus's heating element.

Brian had Luis pour a bag of the waste mash into the tank, and they let it agitate for a few hours until it became a slurry. Brian explained that this would force the remainder of the oil from the waste mash. Alejandro translated what Brian was saying for Juan and Luis.

Brian then released the mixture to flow into the filtering apparatus and then to a washing step, which would take place in another tub. After the washing, he filtered the material again and then poured the liquid into a large glass beaker. He then mixed it with a seventeen percent solution of sodium sulfate to form a precipitate.

Brian noticed that both Luis and Juan looked amazed to see what happened next. All the solids in the mixture fell to the bottom and the liquid went to the top. It looked like a fancy layered drink that someone would order in bar. Using a siphon pump, Brian drained the liquid and spread the solid material, which was now a combination of ricin and sodium sulfate into a layer along the bottom of a large baking dish. He carefully carried it into the clean room and placed it into the compound dryer.

When Brian came out of the clean room, Alejandro approached him and asked, "How much of the operation can Luis or Juan help with?"

"They can definitely do the first part. Mixing the water with the sulfuric acid is simple. Testing the Ph is no more difficult than getting your swimming pool chemistry correct. But I would suggest we get a second tub with an agitator though. The mixture can remain in a slurry for a number of days so I'd also suggest that we change the layout and pipe the mash slurry into one of the large holding tanks after it's filtered. Then Luis or Juan can draw it down when we need it. We'll set up a number of glass columns to form the precipitate."

"I'll have Juan or Luis change the plumbing," agreed Alejandro. "What about the drying time after it's mixed with the sodium sulfate?"

"That should be handled by the compound dryer."

Then Brian thought about it and said, "There's actually two drying steps in the process, and the dryer you bought is designed for laboratory applications not manufacturing."

"Can we use another oven of some kind?"

"Possibly, but remember that the ricin can't tolerate temperatures over 175 degrees without losing some of its toxicity."

"How about an electric conveyer oven like those they use in some fast-food restaurants?" asked Alejandro.

"That could work well. We can position it so the oven exits the trays right into the clean room."

"I'm thinking that's too much heat in the clean room. Brian, I'm a little worried about how long you can stay in the hazmat suit anyway. We have to be very careful of heat stroke here. Let's think about it, but I'll look into the oven. I think that's necessary. We can get one second hand, I'm sure."

"Okay."

"Why don't you head home for the day."

"Thanks, I'll see you tomorrow."

The next morning as Brian was donning the protective suit, he looked up and saw the general watching him from the railing above. The general spoke English but didn't have much to say to Brian. Brian surmised that the general knew about his arrest and didn't like him. However, the general didn't speak harshly to him as he sometimes did to Luis and Juan. Brian witnessed what happened when the general caught Luis smoking a cigarette inside the building. He chastised him severely. Brian didn't understand much Spanish but he recognized the words for stupid and moron.

It was only ten o'clock, and it was already hot in the building. It was going to be miserable in the hazmat suit, but he knew that without it, there was a good chance of exposure to the poison. Ricin in a refined state was toxic by not only breathing or ingesting it but by any contact through the skin or eyes. He expected the quality to be very high. This would not be any backyard brew, and the risk of exposure would be great.

Brian got into the hazmat suit. He would be using the filter mask built into the hood. Later, he thought it may be necessary to use an air pack. The experiment today would give him that answer. He entered the clean room and retrieved the glass dish containing the dried ricin along with the sodium sulfate from the compound dryer. Brian was surprised. The dried mixture didn't a-mount to much. There was a quarter inch of material covering the inside of the 8X10 baking dish.

Brian could see there was another problem. The next two steps called for grinding in the jet pulverizer. He would have to clean the machine between each step.

Brian used a spatula to carefully scrape the mixture from the dish and poured the compound into the pul-verizer. He pushed the button on the panel, and the machine did the work. His research told him that the particles had to fit through a forty-mesh screen, which was about a third of the size of a grain of salt. Brian emptied the powder into a clean glass dish and added an inch of carbon tetrachloride to cover the mixture. The carbon tetrachloride slowly separated the ricin from the sodium sulfate. After thirty minutes, he skimmed off the ricin, which was now floating on top. He put it in another glass dish to go back into the dryer. Brian then took the jet pulverizer apart for cleaning. They were going to need hot water and a place to clean the equipment.

Brian left the clean room, took off the suit and explained the problem to Alejandro. Alejandro told Luis and Juan to clean out the janitor's closet, install some metal counters and see if they could get the old hot water heater working. By mid afternoon, they managed to accomplish the task. Brian showed Luis how to put on his hazmat suit. He would hand him the glass dishes one at a time for cleaning. They could reuse the carbon tetrachloride many times before it had to be disposed of. Brian would clean the pulverizer himself.

After the jet grinder was clean, he reassembled it and poured the ricin into the unit. This resulted in an extremely fine powder, the grains minute enough to fit through the eye of a fine needle. But the yield was poor. Much of the powder remained as a residue on the metal surfaces of the grinder. He put the ground and purified ricin into a testing vial, added a measure of distilled water, and injected it into the liquid chromatography machine to test for purity. While he waited for the results, he set out to clean the pulverizer again. He saw right away that he would need a number of small cleaning brushes to remove most of the residue before disassembling the machine and bringing it to the large sink for cleaning. The powder was so fine, that he was sure that if he didn't remove it first, the act of carrying the metal parts to the sink would put powder in the air and eventually falling to the floor of the old building. Soon nobody would be able to enter the building without protective clothing, which would be unacceptable in the Georgia heat.

Brian had to get out of the suit. He was soaked with perspiration. This was going to be miserable work, but he knew he couldn't slough it off on Luis or Juan. After finding out what the men were calling him, he didn't like them much. Nevertheless, the work in the clean room was delicate, and any mistakes would ruin the ricin or may even kill Luis or Juan, the former being a bigger problem than the latter in Brian's mind.

Brian removed the suit and found his medication. As he was taking one of the little yellow pills, Alejandro asked him, "What are those?"

Brian handed him the small container and watched Alejandro read the label:

KYRI-LAISON

Take one three times a day.

Apparently, Alejandro recognized the drug and said, "Brian, this is a very strong anti-depressant/anti-anxiety drug. How long have you been taking this?"

"About a year."

"I was an oncologist back in Bolivia and frequently prescribed anti-depressants for my cancer patients, but I've never prescribed this myself. It has some harsh side effects. I thought they took it off the market."

"I'm not having any problems, except for some heartburn."

"I've also noticed that you're taking far more than the prescribed dosage."

Before Brian could respond, they were both startled and turned around as the general was yelling at Luis again.

Brian commented, "The general doesn't seem to like those guys."

"He's losing his patience."

"What do you want me to do with the ricin?"

"What was the yield?"

"About twenty-eight grams."

"So by my calculation, it took about eight hours to produce an ounce of ricin?"

"Most of that was slurry and drying time."

"Okay, we already have a plan to speed up the drying. Anything else we can do?"

"Another jet pulverizer would help."

"With the changes, what's your expectation in terms of production?"

"Once we get going, maybe seven to eight ounces a day."

Alejandro appeared to ponder that for a moment. Then he said, "That will work."

"How much do you want me to make?" asked Brian.

"You need not worry about that. I'll let you know when we have enough. Take what you have now and store it in the refrigerator."

"It doesn't have to be kept cold."

"It's a safe place, that's all."

"I'll get a new refrigerator we can use for food and drinks. I'll have Luis install a padlock on the one we'll use for the ricin."

Both Brian and Alejandro heard the signal from the liquid chromatography machine. Brian had hard-wired his notebook computer, so they could read the results without going into the clean room. The computer screen showed a level of purity much higher than they expected.

Alejandro looked at Brian. "Where's that chart?"

"Which one?"

"The one that shows toxicity levels."

"It's over there in that top manila folder," indicated Brian, pointing to the research that Alejandro had given him.

"See if you can find it."

Brian thumbed through the folder and found what he was looking for. The chart showed the purity level of their sample equated to a 500-microgram dose to be fatal to the average adult. Brian did some quick math. He had 28 grams in the vial so there was enough ricin to kill 56,000 people, and they had only started.

Brian handed the chart to Alejandro. After a few seconds, he smiled and declared, "Good job!"

5

BRIAN WAS SIGNALING his two helpers that there was lab equipment to clean, but they were ignoring him again. Whenever Alejandro wasn't there, they didn't do much work. And they began calling him *cochino* again. General Castillo went back to Bolivia two weeks into production, and as soon as the he left, Luis and Juan slacked off and began picking on him.

Brian didn't want to rat out anybody, but these guys were starting to make him angry. The other day Luis went after him. Alejandro had purchased an electric pressure washer, and it was Luis's job to wash Brian down before he removed the hazmat suit. The pressure washer was supposed to be on its lowest setting, but Luis turned it up to the maximum pressure, which hurt. Both he and Juan thought that it was funny. Brian contemplated that maybe it would be a good time to speak to Alejandro these two idiots.

Except for the bad behavior of his two helpers, everything else was going smoothly. They had made many changes since the test batch, ten weeks before and had managed to ramp up production to where they were now producing about seven ounces of the toxin a day. The quality of the ricin remained excellent. Brian kept track of the yield. His records showed he now had over thirteen pounds, or eleven million doses of the deadly poison from the 41 days of actual production. He had another pound of the powder, he considered waste, which was still deadly, stored in the clean room. This was the residue from dismantling and cleaning the jet pulverizer. Brian had tested the waste powder, and it had a high purity level. He would ask Alejandro when he returned, whether he should store it along side the ricin that was in the refrigerator. He had enough for another 896,000 doses.

While he was breaking down the pulverizer, Brian heard a loud argument break out between Juan and the security guard that Alejandro had posted the second week. He had no idea what they were arguing about, but he was sure either Luis or Juan had started it. He didn't like Luis and Juan, and he wouldn't mind seeing either of them getting their asses whipped. The *cochino* thing was starting to get old, and Luis and Juan reminded Brian of the bullies of his youth. Maybe he'd think of something to get back at them for their taunting insults and harassment.

Apparently, Juan had second thoughts about taking on the security guard with the horrible burn scars on his face. He was bigger and meaner looking. Juan turned to walk back to the loading dock area where the hazmat suits were drying and donned the one belonging to him. He then came over to Brian to retrieve the lab dishes and the pieces of the pulverizer.

Brian was anxious to get out of the hot hazmat suit, but he had to be careful. They had set up an area in the northwest corner of the building for cleaning and drying the suits. The protocol was to use the pressure washer on the suit while the occupant was wearing it and then employ a leaf blower to dry it before taking it off. They would then hang the suits in the covered loading dock area to fully dry. They washed the suits on a cement pad in the loading area, where there was a clear view of the access road leading to the property from the main road. As Brian was hanging the suit to dry, he saw Alejandro returning in the pick-up, which appeared to be loaded with some building materials.

Alejandro pulled the truck up to the loading dock and told Luis to unload it as Brian walked back to his work area to analyze the latest batch of product. Later, Brian watched for several minutes as Alejandro gave instructions to Luis and Juan. The men appeared upset at what Alejandro was saying. After some argument, Alejandro called to the security guard who was previously arguing with Juan and said something.

The security guard pulled out his pistol and put the barrel in Juan's mouth. Juan raised his hands in submission and without further argument, the two men went to work.

After Brian finished what he was doing, he walked over to Alejandro who was supervising Juan and Luis. The two men appeared to be constructing another temporary clean room.

Brian asked Alejandro, "What are we doing here?"

"Brian, this isn't something you need to be concerned with," answered Alejandro.

Brian thought that Alejandro seemed to still be angry. This surprised him because the doctor always had a friendly demeanor.

Alejandro asked, "How much ricin is in the refrigerator?"

"Almost thirteen pounds with today's production."

Alejandro's mood seemed to change immediately for the better, and he exclaimed, "Good, good!"

Brian was about to tell Alejandro about the powder that he had in the clean room when Alejandro said, "Brian you've worked hard for the last few months, why don't you take the next two weeks off with pay."

Brian knew when to give yes for an answer, so he quickly responded, "Sure." He would use the time off to rest and maybe try to get some of his mother's money back. Maybe he could even coax her out of the house.

Alejandro looked over at the progress Luis and Juan were making and announced, "You can go now if you want."

On the long ride home, Brian pondered about what he was doing for the last few months. Certainly, he knew what he was making but he hadn't yet figured out what Alejandro and the general were going to do with the substance. The best Brian could come up with in his mind was maybe the general was going to use the ricin on his competitors. However, it seemed to Brian to be a convoluted way to eliminate the competition when the general had access to some obviously dangerous people with guns to do his bidding.

Brian thought it more likely that they would sell the ricin, but although the process was similar to making crystal meth, it was more expensive and involved. He thought why get into the chemical weapons business when the drug trade was so lucrative? Even as a weapons system, ricin was not a good choice. Brian knew from his research that the military had experimented with ricin but it found that other agents were better suited to chemical or biological warfare. Substances like anthrax or saran gas were easier to make and deploy. Weaponizing ricin was not easy, and the military had abandoned the notion years before. Ricin was better suited as a terror weapon, and there were news reports that Al-Qaeda had used the substance in the past. Yet, Brian thought that was unlikely.

Today's odd events were adding to Brian's curiosity. Something was changing, and he wondered what was going on at the old plant. It seemed obvious to him that Alejandro wanted him out of there for some reason. However, he wasn't about to argue. It was the middle of August, and he would have two whole weeks where he didn't have to wear that hot hazmat suit. He could also sleep-in well past his 5:00 AM wake-up time. Nevertheless, it was strange that they were building another clean room. This one appeared to be considerably smaller than the one he was using everyday. No matter, he would find out when he returned. For now, he was going to enjoy the next two weeks.

6

IT WAS THE LAST DAY of the political convention and it wasn't very exciting. This was the convention for the party in power, and there was little in the way of controversy all week. The delegates would nominate a new vice-president tonight, but the press had known her name for a month. The news media was complaining in their not so subtle way that the gathering was dull in comparison to other conventions. No doubt, the political opposition was happy with this type of coverage.

It was close to 10:00 PM and as the 4,500 delegates gathered on the floor to confirm their party's nominee for vice-president, they were unaware of the biological time bomb that hung 265 feet above their heads.

"Ladies and gentlemen, let me introduce to you the next vice-president of the United States…"

The crowd went wild. They were looking for a reason to cheer. The balloons and confetti began dropping and people became jubilant in celebrating their popular VP nominee. The crowd began slapping at the balloons while a delegate from Fort Worth removed his vintage campaign button and used the pin to pop a red one. The boisterous crowd quickly followed suit and for the next few minutes, the little pops could be heard throughout the hall.

As each of the red balloons burst, the tiny explosions efficiently disbursed a small cloud of white powder in the air. With the confetti still dropping, no one noticed the tiny crystals that were enveloping them. Even if they had, there was nothing they could do about it. Floating in the air, circling around them was a thousand times the lethal dose of ricin, one of the most deadly poisons found on earth.

As the evening's festivities went on, delegates and guests left the Georgia Dome to go their various ways. The MARTA trains were filled to capacity with people headed to their hotels. Taxis carried people to local area restaurants for a late dinner. And an assortment of conveyances were used to take individuals to the airport to catch "red eye" flights. But despite their destination or mode of transportation, many well-meaning individuals helped the delegates remove the latent confetti that was still attached to their clothing. As they brushed away the little pieces of colored paper, the ricin became airborne for a second time. Those within four or five feet were now breathing and carrying around the deadly toxin. The MARTA trains would eventually carry the poison throughout Atlanta.

There were also private parties. A number of delegates decided to take some balloons back to their hotel suites in order to brighten the décor. Red was by far the most popular color. Those balloons would end up as little toxic explosions that night as well. And before the Georgia Dome went dark, a clean-up crew of two hundred would burst the remaining balloons before throwing them in the garbage.

One enterprising member of the crew filled a dozen trash bags with confetti with plans to later repackage it into smaller bags and sell them on eBay as convention memorabilia.

The first 9-1-1 call came at 6:00 AM. Several convention attendees were exhibiting severe flu-like symptoms. Fever, cough, tightness in the chest, and nausea was the common complaint. Most had difficulty breathing.

Shirley Mason-Knight, a delegate from Philadelphia, who hadn't attended any parties or gone to a restaurant after the final gavel fell on the convention, awoke about 6:30. She felt bad. At first, she feared she was having another heart attack because of the tightness in her chest. But, it wasn't like before. She felt hot and then started coughing violently. Her throat was sore and she was nauseous. She was also having trouble breathing. Shirley knew she needed help and dialed 9-1-1 on her hotel phone. She waited almost an hour before someone arrived at her door.

Over the next several hours, emergency services received thousands of calls for help. The EMS people and medical personal, still not knowing the origin of the sickness, were unaware that they were exposing themselves to the poison as they handled the patient's and their clothing. By 10:00 AM, hospital staff had admitted two thousand people into their various health facilities. All nearby hospitals were at capacity, and like the first responders, the attending medical staff were also exposing themselves to the toxin. Patient x-rays showed excessive fluid in the lungs. Finally, respiratory failure and low blood pressure started taking its toll. Several patients died. Shirley Knight was among them.

A young ER doctor, who suspected this was more than a series of un-related illnesses, made the first call to the CDC hotline at 10:30 AM. He described the symptoms to the duty officer who immediately notified his superior. For the next two hours, the CDC would receive almost 300 similar reports from worried medical personnel.

By noon, 273 people were already dead. Three thousand others were sick including 52 members of the news media. Doctors and lab technicians performed a myriad of medical tests on these individuals. Unfortunately, no one thought to test for ricin poisoning, and even if they had, there was no known cure or vaccine available. The nearby Centers for Disease Control, located in Atlanta, dispatched an environmental team to test for contamination. Because of the sudden onset of the symptoms, they suspected a biological or chemical attack. The head of the CDC investigative team, Dr. Mathew Palena, immediately suspected ricin. He had practiced various chemical and biological attack scenarios, and a ricin contamination incident seemed to be the most likely candidate. He immediately notified Kerry Sterling, Executive Assistant Director for the National Security Branch of the FBI, to activate the terrorism protocols. He told her this was going to be bad, and she agreed to head to Atlanta for a first hand look. Dr. Palena then called the local authorities and told them to mobilize the special teams that the CDC trained to deal with this type of crisis. He needed samples to determine ground zero of the attack, but he suspected that it was somewhere within the Georgia World Congress Center. Once they determined this information, he would be in a better position to deal with the contamination. Dr. Palena then called the state's governor. When the word leaked out that the teams were looking for ricin, there would be panic among the populace. They would need the state's National Guard to help keep order.

In the meantime, a network reporter who had earlier arrived on a flight from Atlanta to Washington collapsed in the airport terminal. Over the next several hours, similar events would take place in 43 additional cities. People were arriving sick in airport terminals all over the country. As the reports filtered into the CDC, Dr. Palena knew that this would be difficult to contain. Then a report came to him that two first responders who had attended to some early victims had become ill. This was the worst-case scenario. Since ricin wasn't contagious that meant the attack must have been airborne in nature and secondary contamination would be a major factor. He sent out the word that all first responders and medical personnel must wear protective clothing to deal with victims. Once the public saw this, there would be chaos.

Matt was preparing a press release when members of the media started calling him directly. He decided that a press conference would be more appropriate. He scheduled it for 3:00 PM when he expected Kerry Sterling to arrive from Washington. By then, the first results from environmental testing would be completed and could confirm ricin was used. He began preparing his opening statement. The public would need to know how to protect themselves. This was going to be difficult. He didn't want to create more panic. Ricin was not only a weapon of mass destruction but also a weapon of mass hysteria. Like radiation and anthrax, the word ricin would automatically amplify the fear factor.

7

IT WAS SHORTLY AFTER NOONTIME and General Castillo was waiting for his son-in-law, Alejandro, to arrive back from Atlanta. The general was alone in his penthouse condominium except for his two new bodyguards. He now lived in a fashionable part of La Paz, near the medical center where his doctors were treating him for his illness. He never rebuilt the large house the Americans destroyed in the raid three years before. Even though he was a hard man, it was too painful for him. After he and Alejandro buried his wife, daughter and grandsons, his grief turned to anger. The investigation turned up evidence that the Americans were behind the attack on his home, and he wanted them punished.

The Bolivian government also wanted answers. They had asked the DEA to leave their country years before and authorized no drug enforcement operations against citizens of their nation. When the Bolivian government

protested the raid, the United States government em-
phatically denied any involvement. DEA officials dis-
missed the physical evidence—the assault weapon left
behind—with an unlikely story about the firearm being
lost in a south Texas drug raid. This infuriated the general. No matter what his crimes, the general thought
killing one's family was never justified. Not even the
most vile drug dealers would do that. He needed to do
something about the lying perpetrators of this outrage,
and now he had.

His building had a satellite dish on the roof, and he
was watching the convention coverage on an American
cable news network. The convention was over, but the
huge story was the epidemic that followed. The authorities hadn't yet determined the cause but there was speculation that it may have been a terrorist attack. Some
offered anthrax as a possibility because of the symptoms.

He marveled at his son-in-law's ingenuity. The general thought if Alejandro hadn't chosen to be a doctor,
he could have been a fine military officer. The attack on
the convention was in the works for over two years, and
now they had successfully accomplished it.

After the raid on his house, which killed his family,
and the denials by the Americans, he and Alejandro had
decided that they would do what the Bolivian government wouldn't. For several months, they discussed
many ideas. The general wanted to strike the "heart of
the beast". He wanted an attack on the American
government, possibly the president of the United States.
They discarded this idea as being impractical. Alejandro

offered the suggestion of an attack on the president's political party. It was also Alejandro's idea for using ricin on the Americans. When he was a medical intern, six months of his training had gone into research. Since he had chosen oncology as a specialty, he worked in a cancer institute were various natural remedies were being researched. In the lab next to his, a group was working with ricin as a possible chemotherapy agent. Alejandro was friendly with one of the researchers who worked on the team and learned a lot about the substance as the men conversed frequently about their research. Before he finished his assignment, the institute eliminated the ricin program. They considered it as being too dangerous. Other organic substances were more promising. Still, as a weapon, it was possible to deliver ricin by injection, inhalation, or ingestion. This offered a myriad of possibilities.

Alejandro worked tirelessly putting the details of the plan together. The general thought it was brilliant and initially threw himself into the work as well. However, it was Alejandro who noticed the unusual lesion on his skin. Tests later would confirm the diagnosis of melanoma, the deadliest type of skin cancer. Unfortunately, further tests showed the cancer had spread to his pancreas and liver. Therefore, Alejandro did most of the work because of the treatment the general had to undergo. In the general's opinion, Alejandro did a superb job putting everything together. He had done the research, found the old Georgia castor oil plant and the people to do the work. So far, the general's only contribution was to bankroll the scheme. The general wanted that situation to change. He wanted more involvement for the next attack.

The general noticed that the news coverage he was watching bordered on hysterical. Two of the reporters who were on the convention floor became ill, and one had died earlier that morning. The general reflected that when the news people become part of the story, the reporting usually proceeded at a frenetic pace. This was no exception.

According to the media, local officials disclosed at the 11:00 AM briefing that the body count was now 1,300 dead and 9,000 sick. The general thought that had to be an exaggeration.

As he continued watching the coverage, he heard a knock. One of the bodyguards let in Alejandro. The two men greeted each other warmly. The general had left America shortly after they had begun the ricin production so he didn't know the details of the attack. He knew the where and when but not the particulars. For security purposes, they didn't speak of it on the phone, and the general was anxious to hear the details.

The general said, "The Americans do not know it is ricin yet." The general spoke English because he didn't want his bodyguards to overhear their conversation. He was sure neither of them spoke the language.

"It will be some time before the authorities figure it out," said Alejandro.

"Have you heard any of the news?"

"No. I came straight here after I landed."

They decided to watch some of the news coverage. They heard all the numbers reported by the media. The general asked, "Do you think that is possible?"

"I don't think so. But the toxicity of the ricin was off the charts."

"Did you anticipate this much collateral damage?" queried the general.

"No I thought there would be some, because it was an airborne attack. But if all the reports are true, things may be somewhat out of control."

"It was an airborne attack and nobody noticed? How did you do it? I thought ricin was hard to weaponize that way. There are no reports of an explosion."

"The ricin was in the red balloons. When the people popped them, it disbursed the poison among the crowd. I didn't anticipate that it would spread from the dome area as much as it did," noted Alejandro.

"How did you manage to get the ricin inside the balloons? How did you come up with that plan?" asked the general.

"There were several articles about making the convention 'greener'. The environmental wing of the party wanted to do away with the balloons altogether and only use confetti, which could be recycled. The organizers compromised and said they would keep it to six thousand balloons. I got the idea from that," responded Alejandro.

"So you had Brian Burke put the ricin in the red balloons?"

"Actually I sent Brian home for a while. I don't fully trust him with all the medication he's taking. Juan and Luis filled the balloons."

"How did that go?" asked the general thinking about the two morons that Alejandro had hired.

"At first, when I told them what they had to do, they tried to hold me up for more money. They didn't want to put on the hazmat suits and work in the heat. I think Juan was also afraid. I asked Bartolomeo to help convince them that it would be okay."

The general smiled, imagining how his former bodyguard Barto would convince them. "But how did you get the balloons into the convention hall?"

"It was easier than I thought," replied Alejandro. "I did some research on the internet to find out who had coordinated the balloon drop in the past. I called the company and posed as a reporter. I told them I was doing a story on the convention preparation. When I found the right person, I interviewed him and acquired all the details on how the balloon drop works and how the nets are filled."

"I find that to be brilliant."

"The company also had a website where they sold balloons and other party supplies. They actually identified the type of balloons they used at the conventions. They called them the 'Rolls-Royce' of balloons. I ordered two thousand of the red balloons and had them sent to one of those private postal places where I rented a box."

"Why did you choose the red ones?"

"I don't know. I like red, and they're the most popular."

"What did you do then?"

"I carefully opened the boxes and the inner plastic bags that contained the balloons so I could seal them back later without anybody noticing. Then I had Luis and Juan fill each one with two grams of ricin. It actually took ten days to fill them all."

"What did you use to fill them?" asked General Castillo. He wanted to know all the details.

"There's a special laboratory tool for measuring and filling vials. We used that."

"I think you can anticipate my next question," said the general.

"When I interviewed the balloon person, he told me that the balloons are filled by volunteers. So I called them back and asked about how one would volunteer. The person told me that the group would be meeting at Entrance B of the Georgia Dome. So, I drove 185 miles from the plant, waited until the balloon company was unloading their truck and carried our boxes into the convention hall. They had set up separate workstations to inflate the balloons. Each net held only one color: red, white or blue. So I went to the red balloon station and put our boxes on top. I guess they never noticed that they had extra red balloons after the nets were filled."

"Alejandro, it seems strange that no one noticed the extra balloons and nobody got sick prior to the convention. When did all this happen?"

"Three days before the convention started," answered Alejandro.

8

DR. MATT PALENA WAS LOOKING at the first results of the environmental testing from the patient's clothing. It was definitely ricin. He looked up when he heard a knock on his office door. It was Kerry Sterling from the FBI. They worked together many times before and were good friends. They would usually have dinner together when he visited Washington.

"Hey Matt," said Kerry.

"Boy this is bad!"

"What do you have so far?" asked Kerry.

"It's definitely ricin, so it's a terrorist attack."

Kerry immediately used her cell phone to call the FBI deputy director to give him the bad news. When she was finished, she went back to Matt who was reviewing some additional data that had arrived.

"This is worse than I thought," said Matt. "Samples came back positive from the Georgia Dome, MARTA and at least 14 hotels in the city. The highest concentrations of ricin are in the Dome and the MARTA trains."

"What's that tell us?"

"From the levels found, we can expect thousands of casualties."

"Do you think there was more than one attack?"

"We can't tell from what we have so far."

"We've got a press conference in less than an hour. What are we going to say? We have to tell the public something," said Kerry.

"We are breaking new ground here. We practiced this scenario but we didn't figure the lack of warning. We assumed that some explosive device would unleash an airborne attack. That didn't seem to happen in this case. So we didn't know about the contamination until people started becoming sick."

"How far do you think it's going to spread?"

"If I were to guess, I would say that anyone riding the MARTA trains last night, this morning or even now would be exposed."

"I'm going to tell the mayor to shut down the trains," declared Kerry.

"I believe that's the right course here."

Kerry called the mayor on his emergency number. Matt listened to Kerry fend off his questions because no one had the answers yet.

"The mayor said he would shut down the trains."

"What about the airport? Atlanta has one of the busiest airports in the country," said Kerry.

"I would suggest you call the governor also."

Dr. Palena listened to Kerry have the same unpleasant conversation with the governor.

"He's going to shut down the airport. He also said the National Guard would be deployed throughout the city. He needs some guidance on their mission."

"We'll have to think about that, but first let's craft the opening statement for the press conference," said Matt.

"Tell me about the ricin. I've read the briefing papers but I'm no expert. From what I read, ricin is an unlikely agent for a chemical or biological attack of any significance. I guess that's probably wrong." Kerry said shaking her head.

"I don't know why they would come to that conclusion. Ricin is extremely dangerous, and we don't have much information because we haven't seen many cases of ricin poisoning. It's true—it is expensive and difficult to make enough for an airborne attack—but if it did occur, it would be devastating."

"Worse than anthrax?"

"I believe it would be. First of all, anthrax takes longer for people to get sick. We've treated it many times with antibiotics, and there are drugs like Cipro to prevent infection after someone is exposed. Anthrax is also not usually contagious unlike some other biological weapons."

Kerry looked pensive so Matt continued, "Kerry, here's the problem with ricin. Exposure can take place by injection, inhalation, ingestion or even contact with the skin or eyes, and they all present with different symptoms. The result is the same, severe cell damage and then organ failure, but how it manifests itself is different. In the case of an airborne attack, not only are you inhaling the ricin, but it's making contact with your skin and eyes. However, the particles get on the clothing and other places that people may touch. Later, if they put their hands in their mouth, they could ingest the poison. That would give a different set of symptoms. A major airborne attack is the worst case scenario."

"And that's what we have here," uttered Kerry.

"From the samples we have so far, we would expect secondary exposure and people also getting sick from ingesting the toxin."

"Then how widespread can this get?"

"Look at it this way. Say the original attack was in the Georgia Dome. There were over 5,000 delegates, news people and others on the floor. However, there were over 15,000 hotel rooms booked for the convention. Therefore, it's possible that the convention goers interacted with many others. Also, thousands of people ride the MARTA trains daily."

"And then there were the air travelers," observed Kerry.

"Precisely. Expect what we call 'hot spots' to develop throughout the country, and we haven't even considered additional attacks. Maybe this isn't over."

"How do we warn the public?" asked Kerry.

"That's another problem. If you put the symptoms for inhalation and ingestion together, that could cover anything except maybe a hangnail."

Kerry smiled more from nervousness than the levity of Matt's remark.

"Kerry, combinations of those symptoms could point to anyone of three or maybe even four thousand different conditions. And remember, there is no practical physiological test for ricin unless you suspect it. You can find it in the urine but the test takes time. The easiest way is if you suspect it; look for it in the environment."

"So you're saying essentially there is no warning we can give?"

"None that I can think of, without causing a huge panic."

"How much exposure can a person tolerate?"

"Given the purity of the samples we've collected, five hundred micrograms may be enough to be fatal to an average size healthy adult," answered Matt.

"500 micrograms is how much exactly?"

"There are twenty-eight million micrograms in an ounce."

"Oh, my God!"

An assistant walked in to give Matt some more information. The doctor perused it for a while and then looked up. "We have 2,200 dead and more than 15,000 sick. We suspect ricin poisoning in 120 U.S. cities. Over 250 medical personnel and first responders are part of the death toll."

"How long can this go on?"

"Like radiation, ricin won't stay active forever. It's susceptible to high temperatures and it's water-soluble. In other works, hot soapy water and lots of it, can greatly reduce the risk."

"So we go out and tell the public to take a shower," grunted Kerry shaking her head.

Matt didn't take offense. He knew she was under a lot of pressure. She was the Executive Assistant Director for the National Security Branch of the FBI. Kerry was the government official in charge of investigating this attack and preventing further ones. The new WMD Directorate of the FBI also reported to her.

"Kerry, people are going to get sick and die. We have procedures in place for a pandemic like the Avian Flu. I would suggest we put those procedures in place. Our first priority is to protect our medical personnel and first responders. Tell the people that if they suspect they've been infected to stay away from medical facilities because there is nothing the doctors can do."

"You know the public won't listen to that."

"I know, but it may stop people from overrunning some of our hospitals and emergency rooms."

For the next half hour, Matt and Kerry worked on the opening statement. They made little progress and decided to postpone the press conference.

9

MATT PALENA'S ASSISTANT came into his office and said to Kerry, "Director Sterling, we have you set up in the small conference room next door when you're ready."

"Thanks, Jeanne."

Kerry picked up her brief case and other papers that Matt had given her and said, "I'll be next door."

"Why don't we get together again in about an hour," said Matt as he was handed more information from a summer intern.

"Sounds okay," replied Kerry.

Kerry walked into the conference room. The Special Agent in Charge of the Atlanta Office sent over an agent to assist her, who introduced herself. Kerry then got herself organized. She knew she had to call her boss but wanted an update on what the local FBI office was doing.

"Agent, where are we on the investigation?"

"The HEAT teams are here and collecting samples alongside the CDC people."

Kerry was glad the Hazardous Evidence Analysis Teams were already on station. These people had special training and were used to working offsite with partner laboratories like the CDC. Kerry supposed it was an efficient way to collect evidence in the field. There would be less duplication of effort.

"We also have more than two hundred special agents in the area taking statements," said the young women.

"Do we know anything yet?"

"So far, we're told that nobody saw anything suspicious."

"What about the locals?"

"They haven't found anything either," repeated the special agent.

"So far we have no leads? Is that what you're telling me?"

"Sorry ma'am."

"Turn on the TV please. Let's see how the media is covering the story. Maybe they've found something," Kerry said with a sarcastic edge in her voice.

Kerry saw the agent cringe and told herself to stop doing that. It was the second time today she took her feelings out on someone. After the agent turned on the television, it took Kerry all of thirty seconds to realize that the news coverage was already out of control. It would have been a blood bath if she and Matt had held the news conference as scheduled.

The media reported that a well-placed member of the FBI had confirmed that it was a terrorist attack, probably emanating from a radical Muslim group. Ricin was suspected as the substance that was making people sick. Kerry thought, so far they had two out of three facts correct. Kerry knew the truth was they didn't have any idea who was responsible for the attack—that piece of information she would have to relay to her boss in a few minutes. As Kerry changed channels to the various cable news networks, each one had a different set of casualty numbers. Kerry asked the special agent, "Who are we getting our numbers from?"

"The medical facilities are reporting the figures here to the CDC, and we're using those, ma'am."

"That's not reliable enough," said Kerry. "The medical people are busy and probably don't have time for reporting. Find someone in Homeland Security and see if they're collecting that information."

"Yes Director."

As she switched TV channels, she saw that the broadcast networks had suspended their normal programming and were covering the attack. That made sense to Kerry. This was a direct assault on the American government and if another country was involved it was an act of war. Many people who attended the convention were political leaders in America. This was huge, and they would soon be looking to her for some answers.

Cable news was showing that the highways leaving Atlanta were jammed. In retrospect, closing the airport may not have been such a good idea, she thought. That act telegraphed that the danger was coming from within the city. Kerry thought that if she had a family that would make her want to leave also. The news media started trotting out their terrorism experts who were talking about ricin. She had heard some of the same things from Matt Palena a short while ago, but the commentators added their share of drama so it sounded much worse as they explained it. One network had lost two reporters. It was memorializing those individuals every few minutes. This was adding to the tragic atmosphere.

Speculation as to who was responsible was running rampant. There were so many suggestions that Kerry told her FBI assistant to start writing them down. She was sure the bureau hadn't thought of some of these groups. Of course, the pundits had no evidence to support any of this conjecture.

One media outlet had the story that the president, who was present in the Georgia Dome with the delegates, was at Bethesda Naval Hospital. Doctors were checking him for possible ricin exposure. Kerry thought the president of the United States might have indeed been the target, which meant the Secret Service would be mounting their own investigation.

On the plus side, there were a number of physicians telling the public how they could avoid being exposed and what to do if they thought they were. She actually heard one doctor tell the listeners to take frequent hot showers. The way the doctor explained it, the suggestion didn't sound that stupid. The other plus was the advice to stay away from hospitals if possible. They explained that there is a higher likelihood of exposure in a medical facility as people go there for help. They used the example of infectious agents being more prevalent in a hospital than any other place. Kerry thought, *good advice!* She had put off calling her boss, the FBI Deputy Director, long enough and dialed his private number. The deputy director answered on the first ring. "Yes Kerry, what do you have for me?"

"Not much, Sir. I'm sorry."

"What do we know?"

"Not much more than I told you an hour ago. There are no leads, and we don't know who did it or even how they did it."

"For chrissakes, Kerry, we have eight members of congress and three United States Senators already dead. The president and his family are at Bethesda and the director is calling me every ten minutes for an update."

"I'm sorry."

"What's the story with the press conference?"

"We're waiting until we have something to say," argued Kerry, hoping the deputy director wouldn't go off on her again.

To her surprise, he didn't admonish her and said. "About the news conference, I think Homeland Security should take point on that."

Kerry thought that was a great suggestion. After Hurricane Katrina, they were used to the media slapping them around. She admired the political shrewdness of her boss. She guessed that's how he came to be the deputy.

"I think that's an excellent suggestion, Director," said Kerry who thought her friend Matt Palena would also be pleased when she told him later.

"Speaking of Homeland Security, I think we should form a taskforce to coordinate the information coming from the investigation."

Kerry thought, *oh no.*

"I want you to organize it so all the government departments are speaking with one voice, no back channels and no cross-talk. Homeland Security can chair it. We'll participate along with the Secret Service and the CIA."

"Do you think that's really a good idea, sir?"

"Just do it, Kerry."

"Yes Sir."

"Kerry, is there anyone else you would include?"

"I would think Dr. Palena here at the CDC should be part of that. I would also want to include Jeff Davis."

"You mean Dr. Goof?"

"He is the Executive Assistant Director for Science and Technology."

"Are you sure you want to expose him to people outside the Bureau?"

"Sir, he's good at explaining technical things."

"Kerry, I've been there when he's explained some of those so called technical things. I love the guy, but he can be over-the-top sometimes."

"We need someone like that. God only knows who Homeland Security will send," Kerry said, hoping that they wouldn't assign Nancy Noonan.

"Okay, get that moving and lose the attitude about the taskforce," said the deputy director. "And call me right away when you know something."

"Yes sir."

Kerry spent the remainder of the afternoon organizing the taskforce. They would meet the next afternoon at the Hoover Building. Matt Palena agreed he would be there after he chided her a bit on the uselessness of the taskforce. Then Kerry had her FBI assistant drive her to the executive airport where a private jet leased by the Bureau was waiting to take her back to Washington.

10

KERRY STERLING AND MATT PALENA were riding to the Hoover Building together. Matt had arrived the night before on the CDC's executive jet and Kerry had picked him up at the airport. They had dinner together, which was a euphemism for him staying at her place. Kerry made the dinner.

They were running a little late because of the traffic and extra security. The nation was on high alert. There were military vehicles and armed soldiers protecting every public building in the Washington, D.C. area.

When they finally arrived at the Hoover Building, Kerry and Matt proceeded straight to the conference room, which was set aside for the taskforce. Kerry and Matt walked into the meeting room and Jeff Davis was already there.

"Dr. Palena, *Como stai*?" said Jeff in Italian.

"Just fine and how are you doing, Dr. Davis?"

Kerry knew the two men enjoyed working with each other. Both Jeff and Matt were with the CDC as young researchers. Matt stayed and Jeff left to work in the FBI's laboratory, but they had remained friends over the last 16 years. When Matt came to town, Jeff would frequently socialize with them.

Kerry looked around, saw her CIA counterpart, and introduced everyone. Homeland Security hadn't yet arrived.

She heard Jeff say, "Oh Crap."

Kerry's back was to the door, and she turned around to see Nancy Noonan making her entrance. Before joining Homeland Security, Nancy was an outspoken critic of the FBI, CIA and Defense Department. Prior to taking a job with a liberal think tank, she was a constitutional law professor at NYU, wrote books and became a frequent guest on the cable news shows. She was vehemently against the Patriot Act, and believed that they should try terrorists as criminals and afforded all the constitutional guarantees. She didn't believe the government should consider them illegal combatants and fought hard to close Guantanamo Bay prison. Kerry figured the administration appointed Nancy to a position in Homeland Security as a token—a gift to the liberal wing of the current president's party. In her personal dealings with Ms. Noonan, Kerry noticed that Nancy could discover a right-wing conspiracy in almost every matter. As a professor at NYU, Nancy wrote several books on the subject.

Kerry did the remainder of the introductions, and they got down to business. Nancy took her place at one end of the table. Her director told her that she would chair the taskforce. Nancy said, "Why don't we go a-round the room, introduce ourselves and then summa-rize what we know so far."

Jeff Davis was sitting to her right so she said, "Dr. Davis why don't you start, and by the way whose bal-loon is that on the table?"

Jeff looked at Kerry and Matt who were sitting next to each other and smiled at them. "Well, we think we know how the terrorists disbursed the ricin." As he said this, he absently moved the balloon in front of Nancy, and it bounced off her ample chest.

"I'm sorry, can we get rid of this balloon," said Nancy. Not waiting for permission, she removed the pin from her navy blue jacket and popped the balloon.

At first the group was stunned, a white powder cov-ered Nancy.

"That's how they did it!" exclaimed Jeff pointing.

Nancy jumped up and yelled at him, "WHAT'S IN THE BALLOON?"

"Sugar substitute like you put in your coffee."

Nancy Noonan left for the women's restroom to clean herself up. As soon as she left, the group broke out in laughter. With the all the tension in the last day and a half, the prank did its work.

"Jeff, I think you went too far this time," said Kerry still laughing.

"Kerry, it's a good thing that Noonan showed up, that balloon was meant for you," said Jeff.

"I would've kicked your ass," said Kerry whose eyes were tearing from her laughter.

Nancy came back after a minute carrying her jacket and threw it on an empty chair. "I'm sending you the cleaning bill," she said to Jeff, trying to sound light-hearted.

Kerry could see that Nancy was angry and almost broke out laughing again. Kerry was sure her boss, the Deputy Director, was going to hear about this.

"As I was saying," said Jeff smiling. "When we did the environmental testing, we found the highest concentrations in the red balloons. One of our HEAT teams went into a hotel room that one of the victims rented. They saw two balloons, like the one we had here, sitting on the bed. Our technician accidentally popped one with his probe, and the team saw the powder. The technicians were wearing protective clothing, so no one was exposed. We took the remaining balloon back to the lab and carefully deflated it. It contained almost two grams of pure ricin."

"That amount of ricin—if injected directly into the bloodstream, could kill up to 4,000 healthy adults," added Matt Palena.

"How much was in the balloon you assaulted me with?" Nancy asked Jeff.

"Two packets of sweetener or two grams."

Jeff continued, "Our teams along with the CDC found residue in the Georgia Dome, MARTA trains and so far, in every hotel room we've tested. Dr. Palena, why don't you speak about the clean-up efforts?"

Matt started with, "Clean-up will be a nightmare." Matt stood up, grabbed Nancy's jacket, walked to the other end of the table, and shook it. "Okay, how many of you can taste the sweetener?"

After about fifteen seconds, one by one every member of the small group raised their hand. "If you can taste it, you're dead. Now look closely at the table. Now look at your clothes. This is what we're up against."

The CIA representative asked, "How much does it take to kill someone this way?"

"Take a sip of your coffee. Okay, now you're dead."

Except for Jeff Davis, everyone in the room appeared shocked to Kerry. She then asked Jeff, "How many balloons do you think contained the ricin?"

"So far every red one we tested."

"That means there could be thousands?"

"That's right."

Then Nancy asked, "Do you think it's possible there are more red balloons out there that haven't yet been popped?"

Jeff said, "Sure it's possible."

Nancy declared, "We have to warn the public right away!"

Kerry challenged her, "The reason for this taskforce is so we don't go out there and start a panic. The news media already has created a frenzy. We don't want to add to it. We have to be careful what we say."

"I don't want Homeland Security to be blamed for not warning the public," returned Nancy who rose from her chair to make the point.

"Sit down, Nancy!" declared Kerry.

The two women glared at each other and Matt said, "Did the CIA hear anything about a potential attack?"

"I checked with the NSA analysts as well as our own, and we don't have anything to make us believe that Al-Qaeda or other radical Muslim group was behind this. Usually before an attack, the NSA picks up a lot of chatter. In this instance, it's been quiet."

"Have you looked at the right-wing militia groups we have in this country? This could be another Timothy McVey incident," stated Nancy.

That question got under Kerry's skin and she said, "Nancy, you of all people should know that the CIA is not allowed by law to operate in this country and investigate American citizens. That would be the FBI who does that."

Nancy said, "What exactly is your problem?"

"Why don't we take a short break?" suggested Matt.

Everyone nodded and headed from the conference room. Matt pulled Kerry aside. "Take it easy."

"Oh she pisses me off. She's made a whole career out of tying the hands of law enforcement and the intelligence community, and then she asks a stupid question like that," declared Kerry.

"You're not going to hit her are you?" Matt said smiling. "She's a lot smaller than you."

Kerry looked at him.

"I meant shorter!"

Kerry finally smiled.

The short break turned into thirty minutes as everyone checked his or her voice mail and text messages. Nancy said, "Okay, we were speculating on who could be behind this heinous act."

Kerry said, "So far, we've turned up no leads on either foreign or domestic groups."

"Why don't we leave the 'who done it' for now," said Matt. "Let's concentrate on what we can control. I jotted down a list of recommendations for the next 48 hours."

Jeff said, "I'd like to hear them."

Everybody else nodded so Matt said, "First, we have to mitigate some of the damage from secondary exposure. I propose that Homeland Security order that all hotels in the metropolitan Atlanta area be shut down until each room can be cleaned by specialists."

Everyone agreed so Matt went on, "From what Jeff showed us, I think we can assume for now that the ricin was disbursed in the balloon drop around 10:00 PM. I would have Homeland Security contact the airlines to ground all aircraft that left Atlanta from 11:00 PM until the governor closed the airport. Those aircraft need to be cleaned."

Jeff said, "I'd do the same thing for the connecting flights for those passengers who began their trip from Atlanta. I'd also recommend that the departure gate waiting areas for those flights be cleaned before they're used for any other flights."

"What about MARTA, buses and taxi cabs?" asked Nancy.

Matt said, "As you know, I live in Atlanta and use MARTA frequently. They designed those trains for easy cleaning. They're all hard surfaces on the trains including the seats. I would have the maintenance people don hazmat suits to do their normal cleaning routine. They use automatic equipment. I believe they clean the buses in a similar manner. The taxis are going to be more problematic."

Nancy said, "I can start on those things as soon as this meeting is over. But what about the balloons we talked about before. What should we tell the public?" Nancy avoided looking at Kerry when she said this.

Jeff said, "Most likely any red balloons taken from the Dome ended up in hotel rooms. I would suggest that Homeland Security organize the locals to have a quick look in each room for balloons. The locals could probably have the entire search done in a few hours. If they find any red balloons, they can call one of our HEAT teams for disposal."

That proposal sounded reasonable to Kerry, and she looked over at Nancy who looked relieved that Jeff took her off the hook.

Nancy said, "Jeff, that sounds like a good idea."

"What do we want to tell the families of those who were in the Georgia Dome and were directly exposed?" asked Kerry.

"If the delegates made it back to their homes with their clothing and other possessions, I would tell them not to handle any of it until we can send a local hazmat team to remove the items," suggested Jeff.

Matt said to Nancy, "I would also have Homeland Security contract all the asbestos removal companies you can find to help with the disposal and clean-up. They have the right training and equipment."

"I'll talk to my director about that," responded Nancy. "Anything else?"

"It may be more productive if we assign some overall responsibilities for each member of this group," said Matt.

"What do you mean?" asked Nancy.

"For example, the CDC will determine what's contaminated and how we should clean it up. The FBI will do the investigative work showing how the terrorists were able to put the ricin in the balloons. Homeland Security will be the voice of this taskforce."

Kerry thought even Nancy could see through this transparent attempt to let Homeland Security take all the heat. Kerry looked at Matt and rolled her eyes.

Nancy asked, "Does everyone agree with Matt's proposal?"

The group looked at Nancy as if she had lost her mind. Nevertheless, there was quick assent around the table.

Nancy said, "Okay, when's our next meeting?"

The members kicked it around, then arranged another meeting time, and began to leave.

Nancy called to Jeff, "I need a minute."

Kerry figured Nancy was going to let him have it for the balloon prank, and she and Matt loitered at the elevator waiting for Jeff. While they were waiting Kerry said, "I can't believe she agreed to stand out there alone and let the media slap her around. Did you think she would agree to that?"

"Not really," said Matt.

"The Deputy Director is going to be so happy with me that is until he hears what Doctor Goof did to Ms. Noonan."

Jeff came out of the meeting room and joined his two friends as the elevator door opened, and they got on. "What did Nancy say? Did she rip you a new one?" asked Kerry smiling.

Jeff said, "She asked me out."

"What?"

"Yeah, she asked me if I would like to have lunch one day."

"What did you say?"

"I said okay. I thought that maybe the four of us could double date. What day is good for you, Kerry?" said Jeff pretending to reach for his PDA.

"The day you look out your window and see a flock of pigs flying by, trying to avoid that snowstorm in Miami."

11

BRIAN BURKE WAS HOME with a case of heartburn. He was almost at the end of his vacation when the
terrorist attack took place. He was intrigued like everyone else as he watched the drama unfold. He and his
mother were following the developments since the early
morning. He felt a gripping fear and became nauseous
when the media reported that the FBI now suspected
ricin. It took three doses of his medication to mellow
him out. Brian was telling himself that this had to be a
coincidence. Still,if the government was looking for ricin, they would eventually find the old plant in Georgia
and learn of his involvement. All those people dead, he
thought. His mother kept repeating every few minutes,
"Isn't that awful. Isn't that awful."

Brian knew he was screwed. He had about $45,000
hidden away but that wouldn't take him far. He didn't
know what to do. Then he heard the doorbell. He was
so scared now. It couldn't be that the authorities already

knew about him. His mother said, "Answer the door, Brian."

That was the last thing he wanted to do. Brian stood up and went to the door. When he opened it, the security guard he knew as Bartolomeo was standing there. Bartolomeo handed Brian a cell phone and an envelope. He then turned and left without a word. Brian closed the door. His mother yelled, "Brian, who was that?"

"No one, ma."

Brian opened the envelope and read the note. It said, *I owe you $100,000* and it was signed with a capital *A*. Ten minutes later, the cell phone rang. Brian answered tentatively, "Hello."

"You know who this is."

Brian recognized Alejandro's voice right away. "I'm sending you some photos. I'll call back."

Then Brian received a text message with some photos attached. The first picture showed a large Spanish style estate home. The second photo was of a beautiful young girl. The third was a private jet. Brian was puzzled. The cell phone rang again. "Hello."

"Did you like the pictures of your new home here in Bolivia? And your housekeeper is certainly pretty, isn't she?"

All Brian could say was, "yes."

"When the time is necessary, the jet is your transportation. Brian, do your job and everything will be okay. Think about it. Oh, and there's another photo I want you to look at. It comes from Bartolomeo. I'll see you at the plant next week."

Without waiting for Brian to answer, Alejandro hung up. A few minutes later, another picture arrived. It was a photo of an obviously dead person. The message was clear.

Brian thought about it. It was prison or death in the United States or living the highlife in Bolivia. When he was doing the research on the general, he learned that the country was poor, and a person could live like a king for around $5,000 a year. Alejandro had promised him a hundred thousand. Brian felt a little better, and his thoughts turned to the pretty, young housekeeper.

A few minutes later, his mother called, "Brian." This knocked him out of his reverie. "They're saying the president is in the hospital."

For the remainder of the afternoon they watched together. The experts were explaining all about ricin, how it was made, and how it could be used as a weapon. There was only one new piece of information for Brian. He didn't know they now had a medical test to determine if someone was exposed. Nonetheless, the experts did confirm that there was no antidote and no vaccine for ricin poisoning.

After eight or nine hours of watching the coverage, he and his mother were becoming numb to the tragedy. There didn't seem to be much new information and the media was interviewing an endless stream of victims and their families. The fate of the president was still an open question. One news outlet was reporting that the current vice-president, as unpopular as he was, would be addressing the nation at 8:00 PM. That was a couple of hours away, so his mother went to make them some dinner.

Later, Brian went back to the living room to join his mother. As they waited for the vice-president to speak, Brian picked up the cell phone that Bartolomeo had given him. Brian examined it closely. It was cheap, a prepaid phone that one could pick up anywhere. He told himself not to do it, but he found the picture of the young Bolivian girl and stared at it for a time. "Ma, how would you feel about living in a foreign country?"

"Brian, what are you talking about?"

"There may be an opportunity for me in my field in Bolivia."

"Brian, you don't even speak Portuguese."

"Ma, they speak Portuguese in Brazil not Bolivia. They speak Spanish in Bolivia."

"Brian, you don't speak Spanish either. Where did this crazy idea come from? What's wrong with where we live?"

"Since my arrest…"

"Brian I told you that I never want to talk about that. You shamed the entire family."

"Ma, what do you mean the entire family? It's only us."

"You don't think your father is looking down from heaven and is embarrassed for what you did?"

"No. I don't think Dad is looking down from any-where."

"It's a good thing we live way out here and there are no children around. If the neighbors found out what you did, I would never leave this house."

Brian thought, *you never leave the house anyway except to go to that sham of a church.*

"Brian, how would you like it if someone did to your sister what you did?"

"First of all, I didn't do anything. And second of all, Sissy is twenty-nine."

"Brother Lucas calls that denial."

"Don't start with that guy."

"Maybe you should call him and make an appointment. Maybe he can help you with your problem."

"I don't have a problem!"

Brian thought that maybe he *would* go to Bolivia and leave his mother here. Let Brother Lucas and the Divine Heart Unity Church take care of her.

Brian got up and left the room, he didn't feel like listening to what the vice-president had to say.

12

BRIAN HAD FINALLY SETTLED DOWN. The first week back was bad. Every time he heard the door in the old plant open, he was sure it was the FBI coming to get him. He was afraid, but strangely he didn't feel bad about the people that he had helped to kill. He wanted the money he was promised.

Alejandro hadn't returned from Bolivia yet, but they had talked several times on the disposable cell phone. Brian hoped that they wouldn't change phones on him because he liked looking at the photo of the hot young Bolivian girl. So far, they hadn't. Looking at that picture was the only thing that made Brian happy lately. He was lonely for some female company. When he was making crystal meth, he would hold back some of the product and barter for sex from the tweaker prostitutes that walked the streets of Jacksonville. He supposed he couldn't do the same thing with the ricin, but he had enough money to pay the prostitutes now.

Brian couldn't believe it could get any hotter in the old castor oil plant. August was bad but the September humidity in southern Georgia was killing him. He'd only been in the protective suit for fifteen minutes, and he was already sweating profusely.

Brian was doing most of the work. Although he was technically in charge when Alejandro wasn't there, Juan and Luis didn't listen to him. When he asked them to do something, they would pretend either to not understand or give him their middle finger. He supposed that Bartolomeo was the real boss. They would do whatever Bartolomeo asked without complaint. Brian hated doing all the clean up. Luis and Juan would laugh at him and call him *cochino*, and Luis had started screwing around with the pressure washer again. Brian thought that perhaps he would teach one of them a lesson. But for now, he had to finish so he could get out of the hot suit and take his medication. The Kyri-Laison was still working for his depression but the heartburn was now becoming almost intolerable.

Brian finished what he was doing and added the new production to what was already in the old refrigerator. The first time he opened it after he returned to work, he saw that Alejandro had used about nine pounds for the attack on the convention. Every night on the news, the media reported hot spots appearing all over the country. The authorities said that most of these were false alarms, and they expected the incidents of secondary exposure to diminish. Brian knew that would only be temporary given what he was doing. He had already made three more pounds of ricin.

Brian closed the old refrigerator and then signaled to Bartolomeo who told Luis to wash off Brian. Luis took his time getting to the loading dock area, and when he finally arrived, he used the maximum pressure setting on the washer. He pointed the nozzle right between Brian's legs when his back was turned. Brian never felt such pain, and he fell to the ground. Luis was standing there laughing. Bartolomeo, who had witnessed the incident, helped Brian up then slapped Luis in the back of the head, and cussed him out in Spanish. When Brian recovered, he removed the suit, retrieved his stuff and left for the day. On the way home, he thought about how he was going to pay back Luis for this last indignity. While he was thinking about it, his cell phone rang.

"Hello?"

"We'll be back some time tomorrow," said Alejandro.

Brian guessed that by Alejandro saying the word *we*, the general would be joining him. That to Brian seemed risky.

"Do you need me to do something special?" asked Brian.

"No. I've got it all covered, and I have a small surprise for you."

"Okay."

Alejandro hung up. Brian figured that if he were going to get back at Luis, it would have to be before the general arrived. On the way home, Brian hatched a devious plan.

The next day, before Brian suited up, he went to the new refrigerator and removed a box of baking soda. He poured some of the white powder into one of the vials he used for testing then put it in the pocket of his hazmat suit. Brian went about his normal duties, and when he was finished, he indicated to Luis that it was time for his clean up. Luis ignored him. Brian still in his protective suit removed the little vial from his pocket. Both Juan and Luis took notice immediately. Brian slowly removed the cap, walked over to Luis. The two men backed away, however they were against a wall. Brian poured the white powder into his gloved hand and then threw it in Luis's face.

Luis started yelling and jumping around. He looked to Juan for help. Juan moved away from Luis as fast as he could. Luis continued to scream and carry on until Brian produced the box of baking soda.

Brian was laughing so hard that he fogged up the face shield of his protective suit, so he didn't see the first punch that Luis threw his way. But Brian felt it. He immediately made himself as small a target as he could. He learned this trick having been beaten up so many times as a child at school. Most of the punches landed on his back, legs and arms. Brian thought that certainly Bartolomeo would help him, but so far, the man hadn't moved his way. Brian was now on the floor, curled up in a ball but could see the doorway. Alejandro and the general had arrived; both were now yelling at Luis. Brian didn't know what they were shouting, and apparently Luis was ignoring them. However with their arrival, he thought the beating would be over soon.

Then Luis stopped hitting him, and Brian was relieved until he saw that Luis had found a piece of pipe left over from the construction. The general yelled something, and when Luis ignored him again, the general grabbed Bartolomeo's gun from its holster and shot Luis four times in the chest. The general calmly walked over to Luis who was still alive and put another bullet in his head.

Juan helped Brian clean up and get out of his suit that day. Alejandro, who was looking down from the railing of the office area, signaled him to come up. The general was sitting there. He spoke to Brian in English. "Barto told us what you did, you stupid bastard. What the hell's wrong with you?"

Brian started to explain and the general said, "Shut up."

The general said something to Bartolomeo who grabbed Brian by the arm and dragged him down the stairs. Brian looked back at the railing where the general was now standing and said, "Stupid ass. Now you bury the man."

It was three hours later. Brian was hot and miserable. All his muscles ached from the digging. There were blisters on his hands. When he asked for some water, Bartolomeo said something Brian didn't understand but he knew the water wasn't coming. When he was finally finished, Bartolomeo pulled him from the hole. He had Brian roll Luis's body into the fresh grave. Brian refilled the hole, and Bartolomeo pushed him until they were back inside the building.

After Brian cleaned himself up, Alejandro walked over.

"Brian, you know that was a pretty stupid thing to do. I'm not going to replace that fool, so you're going to do all the clean-up yourself from now on."

Brian knew better that to argue. Alejandro went on, "You're lucky the general didn't shoot you too."

It was late and Brian wanted to go home. He was depressed and needed his medication. Alejandro noticing Brian's mood said, "I have something for you," and handed Brian an envelope.

Brian looked at the envelope that was addressed to him, written in a soft scroll. He opened it and found a photograph of the young girl in a bikini apparently taken at a municipal swimming pool. A letter written in simple English accompanied the photo.

For the next several days, Brian read the letter over and over. Her name was Roxanna, and she was seventeen years old, in her last year of high school. She hoped one day to study at the university and wanted to become an English teacher. Until then, she looked forward to working for him, and perhaps they could be friends. The letter went on for a few pages about her and her family and the things she enjoyed.

Brian could read between the lines. Roxanna said she wanted to be friends. He knew what that meant. Now, he couldn't wait until he left for Bolivia.

13

KERRY STERLING WAS FRUSTRATED. Two weeks had past since the attack, and they still have no idea who did it. The deputy director called her six times a day asking about new developments, and Kerry was running out of excuses. In her mind, this was one of the hardest investigations she could remember. It wasn't that they didn't have any leads, it was that they had too many. They had to investigate each newly suspected outbreak of ricin poisoning to determine if it was a false alarm or not. If it was a legitimate incident, they had to find out if it was another attack or secondary exposure. In any case, they sent agents to investigate and take statements. So far, the FBI alone had interviewed almost seven thousand people in the last two weeks. Kerry felt the whole process was spinning out of control.

The taskforce was supposed to meet the next day, and Kerry suspected that it wouldn't be very productive. Since the last meeting, membership had grown.

Once the different agencies determined that they were free of blame for not preventing the attack, they wanted part of the glory when the perpetrators were finally caught. Now the Secret Service, who initially declined the invitation to be part of the group, wanted representation along with eleven other agencies. Kerry was surprised to learn that even the Agriculture Department had an investigative wing. The only thing that brightened her spirits was that she knew Matt Palena was coming to town. She would pick him up at the executive airport in a few hours.

Kerry spent the remainder of the afternoon fielding phone calls and going over the pile of data that was reaching her desk. She looked at her watch, and it showed that it was time for her to pick up Matt. On the way through the lobby of the Hoover Building, she ran into Jeff Davis, who looked at her with a big grin on his face. That reminded Kerry that her boss had never said anything about the balloon incident with Nancy at the last taskforce meeting.

"Hey Kerry," said Jeff. "Going to get Matt?"

"Yeah, I'm picking him up, and we're going to have a nice dinner at Strega's. Want to join us?"

Strega's Italian restaurant was a favorite of theirs. It had great veal, and the appetizers and desserts were incredible. It was one of those old style Italian restaurants, and Kerry was sure the owners hadn't remodeled it since the 1970's. It had little alcoves with red leather horseshoe shaped booths that she liked. It afforded the diners some privacy.

"Sure, I'll come," said Jeff. He occasionally joined them when they went to dinner.

"Have you made the reservation yet?"

"No, not yet. I was going to call from the car."

"You go get Matt, and I'll take care of the reservation. It's a slow night. I don't think there will be a problem."

Kerry walked outside to where a car was waiting and headed to the airport. She usually cooked for Matt. Kerry was half-Italian and her grandmother taught her. She supposed that was one reason why Matt became attracted to her. Kerry knew she was far from pretty, especially as she got older. She wasn't overweight but she was big-boned and close to 5'10" in flats. She figured her size worked for her FBI career but not the dating scene.

Within an hour, she and Matt had arrived at the restaurant. The owner, who was always there and acted as the host, recognized them right away. He showed them to their booth and asked them if they would like to order an appetizer and drinks while they waited for their friend. Kerry and Matt took him up on his suggestion and asked for the night's special, a calamari appetizer. Kerry ordered a double bourbon splashed with diet cola while Matt had his usual Scotch. They talked as they waited. Kerry, who could see the restaurant's entrance, was watching for Jeff. When he entered, she waved at him and then stopped suddenly.

"I'm going kill him," growled Kerry.

Matt looked behind him and saw Jeff coming their way with Nancy Noonan following close behind. Matt started laughing. The scotch had loosened him up.

"Keep laughing Mister, and you can find a hotel for the night," said Kerry not amused at all. She was looking forward to a nice evening, and now she was going to spend it in the company of Nancy Noonan.

When Nancy came over, she actually gave Matt and Kerry air kisses on the cheeks. Kerry could see the big grin on Jeff's face and she wanted kill him. Now she knew why the deputy director didn't chastise her for Dr. Goof's behavior at the last meeting; Nancy hadn't complained. When the waiter came over to take Jeff and Nancy's drink order, Kerry ordered a second double bourbon, this time neat.

During dinner, the conversation naturally found its way to the investigation. It seemed that Jeff and Matt were also frustrated with the progress they were making. Both the CDC and FBI labs were concentrating on the origin of the ricin and had come to the same conclusion. It was different from the substances they retrieved from the government depositories who kept samples of biological and chemical weapons materials. The ricin found at the scene of the attack was weapons grade but more pure than anything that the United States or its allies had produced. The analysis showed it had traces of the same chemical compounds used to refine it, but the amount of oil left in the attack sample was far less than the government samples. This was puzzling. Kerry understood what they were saying but Nancy didn't seem to grasp it. As the men talked about chemical composition, the concept of parts per million was not part of her normal discourse. Wanting to be polite, Jeff and Matt explained the problem as simply as they could. Matt being on his third scotch, wasn't having much luck with Nancy, who was enjoying her second glass of expensive wine. It appeared to Kerry that Nancy, in trying to look smart, was making ridiculous suggestions about why the ricin was different. This was getting under Kerry's skin.

"Maybe the ricin came from new genetically engineered castor bean plants," offered Nancy.

Matt said, "We looked into that, but there isn't any research to support it. Castor beans are used for hundreds of products, so if a new strain was developed it would be in the literature."

Nancy looked down at her wine and said, "Maybe the ricin was aged."

"Unlike your wine or a fine cigar, ricin deteriorates with age," said Jeff politely.

Kerry was getting tired of this but Nancy persisted.

"How about drying the castor beans, like when they make raisins out of grapes? The flavor is concentrated. Raisins are much sweeter than grapes."

Jeff started to answer and then looked at Matt who was staring back at him.

Kerry saw the two men look at each other. There was an epiphany going on of some sorts.

Matt said absently, "We've been assuming that the castor oil was extracted from newly harvested castor beans. Then the waste mash converted into ricin using the usual chromatography method. The chemicals one would use for chromatography were found in trace elements in the ricin samples."

Jeff said, "I think that's where we became confused. We knew how they made the ricin but couldn't figure out why it was so pure. The oil content was less than one tenth of one percent."

Kerry could see that both Jeff and Matt were eager to test the hypothesis.

Jeff said, "That's a good idea, Nancy. However, it's more likely that the waste mash or the mash cake is aged rather than the beans. Nevertheless, you may have given us the answer."

Kerry couldn't believe it. She had to remind herself that this was good for the investigation. Yet, it pained her that Nancy suggested the idea.

The group left the restaurant, and a car was waiting to take Matt and Kerry back to her home.

Kerry said, "Maybe it would be a good idea if you stayed in a hotel tonight."

"Oh come on, Kerry."

"It pisses me off, that's all."

Kerry didn't mention the hotel again, so they went to her place. Matt ended up sleeping in her guest room. Kerry joined him about 4:00 AM.

14

KERRY STERLING WAS IN A BETTER MOOD. She shouldn't have taken her anger at Nancy Noonan out on Matt, and Kerry hoped her little visit earlier that morning had smoothed things over. Matt was with her now, and they were traveling in her car heading to the FBI's headquarters. On the way, Matt tuned the radio to an all news station. The top story was that the FBI was concentrating on homegrown terror groups as the likely source of the attack. Kerry became so angry, she almost drove off the road.

Matt asked, "Where do you think the media got that story?"

"From Ms. Noonan, who else?"

"Oh boy," mumbled Matt barely audible.

For the remainder of the ride, Kerry gave Matt a detailed accounting of all the ways Nancy had tried to hamper law enforcement and the FBI's anti-terrorism efforts with her activism.

Matt didn't say much and when they arrived at the building, Kerry let him out in front of the building. Matt went on his way to meet Jeff Davis before the taskforce meeting, which wouldn't take place for another hour. Kerry parked her car and went to her office. Her secretary was waiting.

"The deputy director wants to see you right away."

"Damn, it must be about that news report."

Her secretary gave Kerry a blank look, so Kerry explained about the news item, then headed to the deputy director's office.

When she arrived, the deputy director was standing in his doorway talking to another of his direct reports. He stood aside and motioned Kerry into his office with a wave of his arm. Kerry knew this wasn't going to be pleasant.

"Kerry, I told you I wanted to hear all the developments right away! Why do I have to learn about our investigation in the press?" He picked up a copy of the Washington Post and tossed the paper across the desk. There was a front-page story above the fold that the FBI was looking at right-wing groups for the attack on the convention.

"Boss, it's not true."

"What?"

"We're looking at everyone. We don't have any evidence that it was a militia group."

"Then were did they get the story?"

Kerry explained to the deputy director about Nancy and her boss said. "Kerry, I'm making it your responsibility to contain that woman."

"She's the chairperson of the taskforce."

"I don't care about that! We're through here."

Kerry left the deputy director's office. It was only a few minutes until the taskforce meeting was scheduled to start. With all the new members, they had outgrown the old meeting room, and now they were assembling in a much nicer space. Kerry's secretary had arranged for some refreshments, and Kerry saw Jeff standing at the small table outside the room talking to Matt. Apparently, Jeff saw Kerry too. He put his coffee down and quickly ducked into the men's room that was only a few doors down.

"You better run," shouted Kerry after him.

Nancy was the last one to arrive and sat down in her place at the head of the table. Kerry sat at the opposite end. Kerry then took it upon herself to bring everyone up to speed, making sure she covered the false information that was the day's top news story. Kerry looked directly at Nancy when she covered the subject.

Nancy seemed unfazed at Kerry's not so veiled attempt at intimidating her, which made Kerry angrier.

Nancy didn't wait for Kerry to finish her remarks and said impatiently, "If everyone is up to speed, why don't we get started on today's agenda."

For the next hour, the taskforce worked through a number of administrative matters, none of which concerned Kerry directly, so she had time to decompress. Then the group discussed the immense clean-up task, which was difficult and time consuming. The taskforce accepted Matt's proposal to enlist some asbestos clean-up companies to help with the effort. The taskforce then turned its attention to formulating a policy for preventing further attacks. By now, Kerry's anger had subsided, and she almost laughed aloud when Nancy suggested they should ban balloons to prevent further attacks. When Jeff asked her with a straight face, if she wanted to ban all balloons or only the red ones, Kerry did laugh aloud. Nancy didn't seem at all bothered by Kerry's rudeness and moved on to the next item on her agenda, which was the investigation.

Nancy looked directly at Kerry and said, "I don't like the way the investigation is going. I think the FBI is wasting its resources."

Before Kerry had time to react, Jeff interjected, "Now Nancy, with your total of twenty minutes of law enforcement experience, what might bring you to that conclusion?"

Kerry was surprised, so Jeff did have a hard edge. She had heard about it but had not seen it before. The expression on Nancy's face told Kerry that Nancy had not considered that she would be insulting Jeff as well when she attacked the FBI.

Nancy said, "I meant to say…"

Jeff cut her off and declared, "The FBI has been conducting investigations for 75 years without the help of the Department of Homeland Security. So far, your organization hasn't shown me much except for the holes in everyone's socks when they have to take their shoes off at airport security."

Nancy appeared to be flustered and said, "Perhaps I used a poor choice of words."

Jeff said, "You think?"

Now Nancy starting to recover from the verbal sucker punch thrown by Jeff, appeared ready for battle. "It's obvious to me that a right-wing organization is behind the attack. I don't know how you people can't see that. I've done everything I could to make my point on this."

Kerry said, "Yeah, including that stupid story in the press this morning."

"You all agreed that Homeland Security would be the voice of this taskforce," returned Nancy.

"Not to say whatever you please, particularly when the story isn't true."

"Are you saying that you're positive it wasn't a militia group who did this?"

"Of course not. We don't know who did it."

"Well that's a problem then, isn't it," alleged Nancy with a smirk on her face. "Then I was right in my statement that the FBI is wasting its resources so far."

The representative from the Secret Service said, "May I speak on that subject?"

"Please do," said Nancy.

"In the presidential protection detail we keep track of hundreds of individuals and all types of radical groups in the United States, both on the far left and far right. Because our primary job is protection and not prosecution, we don't always concern ourselves with the constitutional protections, rules of evidence and the rights of privacy. In other words, we do what we please in order to get information on people who might want to harm the president. Nancy, since the president of the United States apparently suffered injuries in the attack, I can guarantee that we've investigated every known right-wing organization. We take it personally when we fail to protect the president as we did in September."

Nancy looked surprised and said, "I didn't know the Secret Service was that aggressive."

"Trust me, we are."

"So you're saying it wasn't a right wing organization that attacked the convention."

"No. I'm saying that even if the FBI hasn't spent one minute looking at these groups, they've been investigated uncompromisingly. It still could be what you think, but it's unlikely if they've been around for any length of time. I'm talking weeks here and not months or years."

Nancy seemed somewhat satisfied with the answer, so the group moved on and spent the remaining minutes putting together a "to-do" list. After they agreed on the next meeting date and time, they left.

Kerry, Matt and Jeff walked out together. Kerry said, "Sorry Jeff. It looks like you may have to look for a new girlfriend."

Before he answered, they heard the familiar beep for an incoming text message. It was coming from Jeff's cell phone. Jeff looked at the little screen and smiled. Then he handed his cell phone to Kerry. She read the message. It was from Nancy Noonan, "Are we still on for the weekend?"

15

ALEJANDRO SEATED HIMSELF on the comfortable sofa in the general's hotel suite. The two men were in Jacksonville, which was less than two hours drive from the plant. Several months before, Alejandro had moved himself as well as the other men from the small motel because people were asking too many questions, and Luis couldn't seem to keep his mouth shut. Alejandro leased two large RV's and positioned them on the plant's property. Alejandro didn't mind sleeping in the RV with Bartolomeo, but the general in his condition, needed quarters that were more comfortable.

Alejandro turned the television to a cable news channel. He was hoping to hear the latest developments on the attack. He wasn't disappointed. Over the last two weeks, the media was slowly changing the focus from the plight of the victims to the ineptness of the investigation. But most coverage still remained centered on the suffering of the victims. The news outlets exaggerated the original death toll they reported days after the attack. Nonetheless, eighteen hundred people had succumbed to the ricin poisoning. Another sixteen hundred had permanent disabilities and over six thousand people received treatment including the president of the United States, who was still recovering. Healthcare facilities in the United States were suffering as hospitals and emergency rooms tried to cope with all the people afraid that they were exposed. In most cases, it was determined that it was a false alarm, but there were enough cases of secondary exposure to ricin to keep the panic going.

Alejandro was indifferent to the human suffering, in spite of him being a medical doctor. The empathy for people that motivated him to be a physician had all but disappeared with the death of his wife and sons. He still had his outwardly friendly demeanor, but inside he was seething with rage over the attack on his family. He no longer could find compassion for any human being. He quit the medical profession and rarely used the honorific, doctor, when giving his name.

The general, who was not feeling well, came out of the bathroom and joined Alejandro on the couch.

"Are you hungry, General? I can order some room service."

"I have no appetite. I should not have become so angry today. Alejandro, order something for yourself. If you wish, you can order something light for me. I may be hungry later."

Alejandro studied the expensive room service menu, and then phoned in his selections. He looked over at the general who seemed engrossed in some development the news station was reporting about the investigation.

The commentator was saying, *"A high placed source in the Department of Homeland Security told us that the FBI has all but ruled out any radical Muslim group for being responsible for the attack on the convention. Although several Muslim groups tried to take credit, the authorities say their claims are bogus. Homeland Security also said that the investigation is now focusing on right-wing militia groups located right here in the United States."*

That was interesting thought Alejandro. Unless this was a rouse by the authorities, they still had no idea who was responsible for the ricin attack. He thought that maybe they could use this information in planning the next operation and told the general as much.

The general looked up and said, "Alejandro, I believe you did a magnificent job. You almost crippled the entire American government, but the collateral damage was much higher than I expected. We want to be more focused on the next target."

Alejandro didn't care about the collateral damage but he wanted the media's narrative to be that it was an attack on the American government. Instead, they concentrated on the killing of innocents. So Alejandro said, "I agree, there should be no doubt that we're attacking the government of United States."

When room service arrived, the general's appetite must have returned, noted Alejandro. Not much food remained when he put the tray of dirty dishes in the hall outside the suite. Over dinner, they discussed some potential targets. The general suggested the obvious.

The next attack should be on the DEA. After all, they believed the DEA actually killed his family.

The American presidential election was coming up soon. Alejandro and the general agreed that the timing of the next attack should be as close to Election Day as possible. The president's political party was in disarray with the deaths of so many of its leaders, and the president was unable to campaign because of his injuries. The current vice-president, who the party ousted at the convention, didn't have his heart in the campaign. He was also busy trying to run the government. The attacks were not the only crisis that plagued the administration. The new vice-presidential nominee turned out to be a disappointment on the campaign trail, so the other party had a substantial lead in the polls. The general remarked that no matter what else they were able to accomplish, they had managed to make an impact on the American elections.

Over the next several days, Alejandro used the internet to research the DEA. He was amazed that for a law enforcement organization how little they valued their security. Alejandro thought that perhaps they considered themselves invulnerable. They would soon see.

An attack on the DEA headquarters in Washington was out of the question. However, the DEA had other facilities. Their largest was in Quantico, Virginia. It was the home of both the FBI and DEA's training academies. Although Quantico was also a U.S. Marine Base, he felt sure from what he read on the internet that he could penetrate it. Perhaps he could even get two for one; attack the FBI and the DEA in one operation.

Alejandro learned that the DEA formerly used the FBI Academy for its training function, but as the organization grew over the years, they wanted their own facility. Plans for the proposed DEA Training Academy were posted on the internet. After the building was completed, no one thought to remove the information. The building's layout was readily available for anyone who wished to view it online. As Alejandro studied the plans, he thought the best bet would be the cafeteria where a crowd would gather at meal times. Instead of an airborne attack, he hoped it might be possible to get the ricin into their food supply. In this way, there would be little collateral damage from secondary exposure. The general would be happier, he thought.

Alejandro discussed his plan with the general who gave his approval. He needed his approval because the general was the one who was bankrolling the operation. So far, Alejandro reckoned that the general had put out nearly three million dollars on their activities. Alejandro knew the general didn't care about the money because he knew he was dying and had no direct descendants with whom he could leave his fortune.

"Alejandro, how do you think you can gain access to the marine base?" asked the general.

"I was hoping you had an idea about that. You've commanded similar bases."

Alejandro watched the general thinking about it for a while. The general said, "Alejandro, as an individual trying to sneak into that marine base would be risky.

Using forged documents at the gate would be easier but I believe it may be possible for you not to have to go there at all."

Alejandro was puzzled at this. The general went on, "I would bet that the marine guards posted at the gate are not as vigilant checking the trucks that come to the base on a daily basis. Food and other deliveries have to be made everyday to support the thousands of people who live there."

"You don't think they check the trucks everyday?"

"I have a notion that the marine guards eventually recognize the drivers and wave them through without much scrutiny."

"Are you thinking we bribe or threaten one of the drivers to place the ricin?"

"Too risky, I would think not."

Alejandro said, "Let me work on your idea. I'll see what I can find out."

The general was going back to La Paz for another treatment, so Alejandro decided instead of returning to the plant, he would drive his rental car to Quantico and see for himself. On the long drive from Jacksonville, he used the time to kick around some ideas in his head. The main problem was how he was going to contaminate the food with ricin. He questioned in his mind what foods were the most popular and made a mental list. Nearing the end of the drive, he stopped at a fast food restaurant before renting a hotel room for the night. Alejandro used the drive-thru window, and the attendant who took his order asked over the scratchy speaker, "Do you want ketchup or salt with your order."

Alejandro said, "I'll take both." He had ordered fries along with his burger. Alejandro checked into his hotel that was a few blocks away and removed the food from the now greasy bag. He found the ketchup and salt. Then he stopped and starred at the little packages. The foil ketchup packet wouldn't work, but the salt might. Almost everyone uses salt at one point or another. In a cafeteria there would be salt and pepper available. Even if that didn't work, many items on the menu would be prepared using salt. He had the answer.

The hotel chain where he was staying had free WiFi internet access. Alejandro connected then used the software that he bought to make his internet browsing anonymous. He would need the name of the food supplier for the cafeteria, which he thought might be a challenge. He was wrong. It took all of twenty seconds. As soon as he typed in "DEA cafeteria" into the search engine and hit enter, several entries came back indicating that there were press releases on the subject. Alejandro clicked on an entry. He read that the company had won the contract to supply both the DEA and FBI dining facilities at Quantico because they belonged to a special program of giving jobs to the disabled. Alejandro found the companies' website and read everything on it. The next day, he would scout the company along with the marine base.

16

AFTER A FITFUL NIGHT'S SLEEP, Alejandro walked to the lobby of the small express hotel where he was staying in Quantico. The hotel provided a free continental breakfast with lodging. Alejandro poured himself a cup of coffee, grabbed a cinnamon roll and headed back to his room. When he passed the front desk, he informed the clerk that he would be staying a few more days.

After the light breakfast, Alejandro fired up his notebook computer and accessed the food distributor's website again. He needed an address. Alejandro took down the information and headed out to his rental car. Once in it, he used the GPS navigation system that came with the vehicle to plot the distributor's location. After a few minutes, he was there. When he arrived, he saw a truck leaving. No other trucks were at the loading docks, and he realized that he had gotten there too late. It was only 8:00 AM but he would have to arrive much earlier to get the information he needed. Alejandro was disappointed until he noticed a number of small vans arriving. Many of the individuals getting out were wearing white kitchen uniforms. Alejandro parked his car and followed several people through the large double doors. Apparently, the food distributor had a warehouse store on the premises. Caterers and restaurants owners whose businesses were too small for delivery came there to buy their food and supplies. It resembled a warehouse club that one could join to buy their family's food in bulk. Alejandro walked around a bit, and after awhile he learned the system. He used a small computer terminal that the company provided to locate the aisle and bin number for the items he needed. There were a few false starts, but eventually he found what he was looking for. Alejandro saw that a case of salt contained twenty-four round boxes. He grabbed three cases and put them on a cart. He then proceeded to the checkout area and paid in cash. He put the three cases in the trunk of the rental car.

Alejandro looked at his watch and then headed for a popular discount store. In the photography department, he bought a pair of binoculars that contained a digital camera. In another area of the store, he found some single edge razor blades and some glue. He then went back to his hotel. Alejandro planned to return to the food distributor later in the afternoon when the delivery trucks came back. In the meantime, he would do some experimenting.

Alejandro removed a case of salt from the car. When he was in the warehouse, he noticed that this particular brand was given four times the shelf space as any of the others, telling Alejandro that this was a popular choice, and there was a good probability that it was used in the DEA cafeteria.

Alejandro took the cardboard carton to his room and studied it. The carton was machine packed so the flaps were glued not taped. He carefully pulled on the top left flap, and it popped open without damage. The same went for the right one. He figured he could glue them back without any sign of tampering.

Alejandro then removed one of the two dozen round boxes that contained the salt and looked at it. It wasn't any different from the kind one would find in anyone's kitchen. It had a metal spout on top covered by a small paper label to keep the spout in place before opening. Alejandro thought this should be easy. He took a razor blade and carefully slid it under one corner of the sticker. It was about twice the size of a postage stamp. It ripped when he tried lifting it off. Alejandro grabbed a second box of salt and the same thing happened. After two more tries, he knew that he would have to come up with a better plan. He could get the stickers off without damaging the container but he would not be able to reuse the sticky labels again. He thought that possibly he could make one. He turned his notebook computer on, accessed the hotel's WiFi connection and found the salt company's website. The company displayed their logo prominently on the various pages. He reached for a new box of salt with an undamaged sticker and look-ed at it closely. It was a simple design, the company's logo with a colored border. The same logo appeared on the website. Alejandro moved his mouse to the logo and right-clicked. A menu appeared and he chose the copy file option. This action put the image in his "My Pictures Folder" on his computer.

Alejandro opened the PowerPoint program and created a new blank slide. He told the program to insert the image he had taken from the website. It appeared much too big on the slide, so he resized it. He then used the program's auto shape function to create the border around it. After about twenty minutes of adjusting the image and the border, it looked almost identical to the sticker. He saved his work and looked at his watch. It was time to head back to the food distributor.

On the way there, Alejandro stopped by a large office supply store and bought an assortment of different labels. The store also had an area selling books and software. Alejandro bought a popular program advertised on television for learning a foreign language. He picked up the Spanish version. He also bought a small pair of scissors that he would need later.

After he left the store, Alejandro went directly to the food distributors company. When he arrived, he saw some trucks had returned. Not wanting to be too obvious, he left and came back every fifteen minutes and parked in a different place outside the gates. Alejandro used the time sitting in the car to become familiar with the operation of the digital camera built into the binoculars. By 6:00 PM, no other trucks had arrived for at least an hour.

Alejandro counted thirteen trucks, each one now pulled up to a loading dock. From his vantage point, he knew he wouldn't be able to tell the drivers apart. They were all wearing the same company uniform. However, the trucks were several different makes and models. They all had the same color scheme but with some variation. In addition, some vehicles had damage. It was still light enough so he took seventy digital photos, which was the limit for the camera's smart card. Then Alejandro left for the night.

The next morning, Alejandro arrived at the food distributor at 5:30 AM as one of the trucks was leaving. He made a mental note of the trucks description and followed it until early afternoon. The truck didn't go to Quantico. The next day he would follow another one. Alejandro got lucky on the third day. The truck went directly to the marine base. Alejandro parked a discreet distance away and pretended to be changing a tire. The truck was inside the base for a little under an hour before he saw it leaving by the same gate. Alejandro went directly to the base the next day, expecting to see the same truck leaving around the same time. He wasn't disappointed.

Alejandro checked out of his hotel and started the tedious drive back to the old plant in southern Georgia. He was tired so he stopped midway through the trip at a small motel in South Carolina. That evening he opened the remaining cartons of salt and carefully removed all the sticky labels. The hotel had a business center which was no more that a computer, desk and an inkjet printer. No one else was using it, so he spent a few hours experimenting, printing on the different labels he bought. When he decided which one worked best, he printed 48 stickers, which he would later trim to the right shape and size.

Alejandro arrived at the castor oil plant in the early afternoon and found Brian at the computer analyzing a batch of ricin. Brian acknowledged his presence with a wave.

"I have something for you," said Alejandro with a smile. He handed Brian a bag. Brian opened it and took out the Spanish language learning program. Alejandro saw Brian smile and said to him, "I thought you might need this."

"Thanks. I was going to buy one for myself but I couldn't decide. This is the most expensive one. Thanks a lot."

Alejandro watched Brian turn the box over in his hands and read the printed material on each surface. The general's idea to invent the young girl was working well. Alejandro marveled at the general's intuitiveness about people. He certainly knew how to motivate Brian.

"Brian, how much ricin is in the fridge?"

"Almost five kilos."

"Okay, don't make any more for now. I have another job for you."

Alejandro told Juan to go out to his car and get the cartons of salt. When Juan returned, Alejandro reached for a box of salt and said, "I want the ricin mixed with the salt. What's the best way to do it?"

Alejandro expected some pushback from Brian and had a speech ready. He didn't need it. Brian picked up a beaker, poured some of the salt into it, and pushed around the grains.

"I now this sounds funny but the salt particles are much bigger than the granules of ricin," said Brian.

"I understand. I guess everything's relative when you think about it."

"If you pour out some of the salt and pour in the ricin it's going to be noticeable, said Brian as he continued to play with the salt in the beaker."

"I agree," said Alejandro. Neither man spoke for a while.

"I have an idea," said Brian.

"Okay, what is it?"

"We can use the jet pulverizer at the lowest speed. In small batches it could give us a good distribution of the salt and ricin."

"Can you give it a try?"

"What do you want the ratio to be?"

"Make it three parts salt and one part ricin."

Alejandro watched Brian suit up and retrieve a container of ricin from the refrigerator. He handed Brian a new box of salt on his way into the clean room. He observed Brian weigh the ricin and pour it into jet pulverizer. He did the same with the salt and turned the machine on. After about 15 seconds, he turned the machine off and looked in the catch container. Brian was nodding his head up and down and gave Alejandro thumbs up.

Brian reached for a paper towel, wrapped it around the empty round salt box and brought it to the worktable. He then took a funnel from a basket that held his lab equipment. Then Brian shook his head. Alejandro watched Brian staring at the salt container and wondered what was wrong. Brian then grabbed another paper towel, cut a small slit in the middle and draped it over the funnel. "Very smart," thought Alejandro. If Brian had tried to fill the container, he would have gotten some of the ricin mixture on the outside of the box of salt.

Brian used the funnel to fill the container to its original 26 ounces. He then sealed the box of salt in a Ziploc bag. That reminded Alejandro that he would have to take care in handling the boxes of salt. He thought to be safe, he should have Brian put the labels on the containers in the clean room as well as pack and seal the cartons. However, at some point, he would have to handle the cases of salt himself. There would be a risk to that. He would have to give it some thought.

It took Brian until Tuesday of the next week to fill the containers and repack two cases of salt. Alejandro had Brian wrap each carton in a durable 6-mil polyethylene bag. He would keep the cardboard boxes in the plastic bags until the last minute. He still hadn't thought of a way to protect himself when he finally had to touch the cartons. It was only early November and gloves would probably not be appropriate in northern Virginia at this time of the year. When Brian was finished, Alejandro told Juan to put the cases in his trunk. It was still morning so he decided to begin his return trip to Quantico, which was located in the greater Washington metropolitan area.

Alejandro made it as far as southern Virginia before he stopped for the night. He decided to spend one more day in surveillance before he would go ahead and attack the DEA and possibility even the FBI. The plan was simple enough but not without risk. He would have to show his face this time.

Early the next morning he drove directly to Quantico Marine Base. As expected, he saw the truck he followed the previous week leaving at the same time. He spent the remainder of the day preparing for the next day's work.

17

IT WAS FRIDAY MORNING, and Alejandro had arrived at the food distributor's parking lot. There were vans with people waiting for the warehouse to open, so he didn't think he appeared suspicious. The delivery truck drivers were busy loading up, so no one was paying much attention to the parking lot. Alejandro had already removed the plastic from the cartons of salt in the trunk. As soon as he could, he would change rental cars. Now all he had to do was wait until his driver finished loading. After about 15 minutes, which seemed much longer, he saw the driver grab the strap and pull down the truck's rear door. The driver made a notation on his clipboard and headed for the truck's cab.

Alejandro got out of his car and popped the trunk. He put on a pair of leather gloves and then wrestled out the two cases of salt. Together they weighed almost 83 pounds and were difficult to carry. He hobbled over to the truck.

The door was still open, but the driver had turned on the ignition. The cold diesel engine was loud as it warmed up. Alejandro said to himself, *this is it*. He would know within the next thirty seconds whether his plan would work or not. He approached the truck driver and yelled, "These go with the Quantico order."

The driver looked at him and responded, "FBI or DEA?"

"One goes to each."

The truck driver grabbed his clipboard, and Alejandro shouted over the loud engine, "Just take them…no need to add them to the invoice. They're samples."

"Okay."

The driver, now seemingly anxious to get going, put the cartons on the floor behind his seat. Since he didn't ask any questions, Alejandro thought adding something to an order at the last minute must not be an unusual occurrence.

Alejandro walked back to the building and waited for the driver to leave the yard. He then followed him to the marine base at Quantico. About an hour later, the truck emerged, and Alejandro headed back to Georgia. He made a mental note to exchange his rental car when he arrived back.

Ellis Cleveland heard the familiar buzzer telling him there was someone at the delivery door. Each morning at this time, the day's food and supplies would arrive from the various vendors. He opened the door and a driver he knew as Gabriel handed him a carton. It was windy so Ellis used the carton as a temporary doorstop.

Ellis stood inside the entrance and checked the items off as Gabriel used a hand truck to carry them in. Everything was there as usual, so Ellis poured Gabriel a cup of coffee and sent him on his way. He always offered the drivers some sort of refreshment because he liked his deliveries early. He had other duties at the DEA's cafeteria; he was always busy later in the day.

Besides handling the storeroom, Ellis also maintained the dining area. He made sure the tables were tidy and the floors remained clean. He filled the salt and pepper shakers as well as the napkin dispensers each morning. Ellis also put fresh flowers in the vases that matched the shakers. He did these things every day because his manager insisted upon it.

He also maintained the salad bar during the lunch service, moving the items from the kitchen to the serving stations as food would run low. Additionally, he would help in the kitchen when needed. Ellis considered himself indispensable to the smooth running of the cafeteria's operation. So he didn't feel guilty about taking some food and supplies from time to time.

Ellis removed the heavy carton and closed the delivery door. He had already checked-off all the items on his invoice, so he wondered if the driver had made a mistake. He opened the carton and it was salt, which was not an expensive item. He put everything away. The produce and other perishables went into the walk-in and the supplies went to the storeroom. Before putting the salt on the shelf, he pulled out two containers, which he would take with him to the potluck supper that his church held every second Friday of the month.

Since Ellis couldn't "cook worth a damn," as some of the ladies told him, his job was to bring the condiments. Ellis helped himself from the storeroom when he needed. He already had the salt. So later, he would get the ketchup, mustard and the other items from the list that Miss Isabel had given him at church this past Sunday.

At 5:00 PM, Ellis left the DEA cafeteria. He didn't work weekends so he wouldn't be back until Monday morning. He drove his car the eight miles to his church. He picked up the box of supplies and went down the stairs to the basement, which served at the church hall. It had a full size kitchen, and there were several women there preparing food.

Miss Isabel saw Ellis and said, "Did you get everything?"

"Yes ma'am."

She looked in the box and pushed things around to make sure Ellis had done what he was supposed to do. "Okay. Now don't get under foot."

Ellis liked her despite her brash behavior and inquired, "Is there anything I can do, Miss?"

"Go fill the salt and pepper. And stay out of the kitchen for heaven's sake."

And that's what Ellis did.

Ellis woke up at three in the morning with severe cramps. He started vomiting and he had diarrhea. He saw blood in both. He also had a burning pain in his throat with difficulty swallowing. He knew he had food poisoning. It wasn't the first time that the good ladies of the church had poisoned someone. However, it was usually in the summer and had to do with mayonnaise in the potato salad. As a government kitchen worker, Ellis was trained in safe food handling procedures, and he often noticed that the women weren't following the guidelines. He made the mistake of pointing that out to Miss Isabel one afternoon, and she almost took his head off.

Ellis tried to tough it through, but the pain was getting worse, and he was having trouble breathing so he called 9-1-1. The paramedics arrived and took him to the hospital where an hour later he went into convulsions followed by failure of some of his internal organs. Ellis then went into shock and died. If he had lived a few more hours, he may have seen the hospital admit over a hundred of his fellow church members with the same symptoms.

18

GABRIEL SOLICE, THE DRIVER for the food distribution company that served the DEA cafeteria, had a different route on Saturdays. The company would go through its warehouse and find those items that had an expiration date coming up soon, as well as the products that did not sell well for the week. The company would gather the foodstuffs, and on Saturday, would donate them to various soup kitchens and food banks in the metropolitan Washington D.C. area. Gabriel was one of the driver volunteers who normally would deliver the food.

Gabriel was on his last stop when he noticed that the box of samples he was supposed to leave at the FBI facilities was still on the floor behind the seat. It had moved to the passenger side so he hadn't noticed it before. So on his last stop, which was a soup kitchen that catered to the homeless, he included the case with the other donated items.

The minister who ran the kitchen was always happy to see Gabriel, who he called his "angel of plenty." Sometimes Gabriel would even help on the line serving some of the facility's patrons. And this was one of those days. Therefore, he left the truck in the loading area and went inside to see what he could do. It was close to 3:30, and the kitchen would start serving at five. Saturday night was meatballs and spaghetti, which was a favorite among the clientele. They would normally prepare 150 lbs of pasta and the kitchen usually served between 300 and 400 people.

Gabriel watched as the chef, placed large pots of boiling water on the giant gas stove. Each pot of water received a generous measure of salt. As the dry pasta cooked, the salt water infused itself into the noodles. Because many of the patrons had dental problems, the chef didn't prepare the spaghetti *al dente*. Instead, he would let it cook longer, so it would be soft.

Since Gabriel was serving, he ate with the kitchen staff before the facility opened for the evening. He then went out and helped serve the people until the last seating, sometime after eight. It was an unusually cold night for November in D.C. and he heard the minister say that they had served over 450 people, not a record turnout but close.

Gabriel left the soup kitchen and drove the truck back to the distributor. He found his car and headed home. He was feeling nauseous. His stomach ached and he had cramps. He collapsed at the wheel a short time later.

He would never know that even with the high cooking temperatures, there was still enough ricin in one strand of spaghetti to kill six people.

19

IT WAS SIX O'CLOCK on a Sunday morning in the Centers for Disease Control facility in Atlanta. Matt was at his desk talking to Jeff at the FBI laboratory at Quantico. They were working four separate events, an attack on three homeless shelters, and a Pentecostal church all in the Metropolitan D.C. area. Four hours earlier, the first of the medical facilities called the CDC hotline reporting a possible outbreak of food poisoning. However the symptoms of a burning sensation in the mouth and throat, coupled with the other symptoms, alerted the duty person on the CDC hotline of a possible ricin attack. She notified Dr. Matt Palena right away.

Within ninety minutes, the CDC had people on station along with some FBI investigators in each of the reported trouble spots. Because of the number of people who were sick with the same symptoms, Matt and Jeff Davis determined that each of the four events represented a full-on attack and not a series of secondary hotspots. Now Matt and Jeff were on a conference call with Kerry Sterling.

"I'm thinking we need an emergency meeting of the taskforce," said Jeff.

"How can that help at this point?" asked Kerry.

"This attack was different. This time we believe the victims ingested the ricin, so until we rule out that ricin has not entered the country's food supply, we may have to take some preliminary precautions. At the least, we have to get the FDA involved in this for any possible product recalls."

Matt said, "Kerry, I'm agreeing with Jeff on this."

"Okay, but I want to talk to the deputy director first. Once the other taskforce members learn of the attacks, there is no way we're going to keep it from the press. I don't want to start a panic again. The medical facilities are only beginning to recover."

Jeff said, "Let's meet here at the lab at Quantico instead of the Hoover Building. I'd like to stay close to what's happening."

Matt chimed in, "That's a real good idea."

"What about access to the base?" asked Kerry.

"Email me the names, and I'll have passes waiting for those who don't currently have access," responded Jeff.

After the call was over, Matt called his people in the field. They were using the stations of robotic monitoring mobile unit. The STORM unit, built by the United States Army, existed in case of an anthrax or similar biological attack. The CDC modified it to help in searching for ricin. They could test three to five hundred samples a day at any location. It had cut down the time it took to confirm ricin exposure in humans and the environment by 85%. Since the Army based the mobile STORM unit in nearby Maryland, it was on station at the Pentecostal church within an hour after Matt and the FBI investigators determined that many of the victims attended the same church function the night before.

Matt was not optimistic that they would immediately turn up anything useful because unlike the attack on the convention, this one was not airborne in nature. Residue would not be as ubiquitous as what the investigators found in the Georgia Dome. So Matt was surprised when his lead investigator told him they found the ricin in the salt shakers as well as some unopened round containers of salt. Matt knew this was bad news. Product tampering cases were difficult. His investigator told him the FBI forensic lab now had the tainted containers and were looking for trace, fingerprints and any other evidence.

Matt called Kerry, and when she answered he said, "We found the source of the ricin. It was in the salt at the church hall. I'd suggest you have your investigators find out if the victims from the homeless shelters somehow ate at the same place."

"I'll get on it right now," said Kerry.

A half-hour later, Kerry called back. "We think the victims all ate at a soup kitchen called Holy Shepard."

"I'll have the STORM unit move to that location," said Matt.

"What's the soonest you can get to Quantico?"

"The aircraft is standing by. I can be there by 3:30."

Kerry said, "I'll set the taskforce meeting at that time. By the way, the deputy director will be there."

An FBI special agent met Matt at the executive airport to take him to Quantico. On the way, Matt received a text message stating that the STORM unit personnel had found traces of ricin in the cooking utensils at the Holy Shepard location. There was also a half case of unopened containers of salt. The carton also had traces of ricin both on the inside and outside surfaces of the cardboard. They sent the entire contents of the carton to the FBI lab for processing.

Matt's FBI driver had him at the Quantico lab with twenty minutes to spare. Matt went looking for Jeff and found him supervising the analysis on the unopened boxes of salt.

"Did you find anything?"

"We're trying to lift some prints from the cardboard carton but it's difficult. The containers themselves were clean."

"What's that tell you?"

"Well it's potentially bad news. If the containers had fingerprint smudges, we could imagine that whoever did the tampering did it after the factory packaged the product. This way we can't tell if the salt was contaminated with the ricin before or after it went into the individual containers."

"If it was contaminated before packaging that would be our worst case scenario!"

"You bet. If it was, then we can assume that there'll be more events."

Matt knew that was going to cause much consternation among the various members of the taskforce, and he was sure that the meeting was going to be difficult and contentious. There was bound to be another clash between Nancy and Kerry. Matt hoped that the presence of Kerry's boss, the deputy director, would temper some of the discussion.

"Were you able to reach somebody at the Clearlake Salt Company?" asked Jeff.

"Yeah, the CDC keeps a database of contact information for all the major food manufacturers. The company said they're sending someone to help. He or she will be here tomorrow morning. In the meantime, they claimed they would email me a list of customers who use their salt in food processing. Their representative said that almost 70% of all packaged or canned foods on a supermarket shelf contain one or more grades of their salt."

"It's almost time for the taskforce meeting," said Jeff looking at his watch. "Let's head down there."

On the way out the door, a worker handed Jeff the preliminary results of the analysis of the ricin found at the scene of both events.

"Bad news?" asked Matt.

"Our guy is at it again."

20

THE GROUP ASSEMBLED in the large conference room on the first floor. When Kerry walked in, true to his word, the FBI deputy director was there introducing himself to the other members who hadn't yet met him. Kerry also saw a person she didn't recognize and supposed that this was the representative from the Food and Drug Administration. Since, this attack involved the nation's food supply, her inclusion in the group was both needed and timely.

In her usual role, Nancy asked the group to sit down so they could start dealing with the situation. They dispensed with the administrative matters and got right down to business.

Nancy said, "Jeff, why don't you begin with what we know about the latest attacks."

Jeff looked at Kerry. She signaled him that it was all right. She thought this was not the appropriate time to stand on protocol. Kerry would normally be the person to summarize the investigation.

"Here's what we know so far about the attacks. There were two separate events this weekend. One was at the Calvary Pentecostal Church, only a few miles from here and the other was the Holy Shepard soup kitchen who serves mostly the poor and homeless. In both cases, we found ricin contamination in the salt on the premises."

"So what you're saying, the two events are connected?" asked the representative from the FDA.

Kerry spoke up, "We haven't found any link between the church and the food kitchen yet."

"Except that the victims were mostly the poor and African-American," added Nancy under her breath but loud enough for Kerry and the group to hear.

Kerry looked at Nancy. With the deputy director in the room, she wasn't going to let Nancy bait her into an argument. "We don't know the socio-economic makeup of the Calvary Pentecostal Church members. There isn't any data that suggests they're poor, said Kerry. "Jeff…"

"There is a connection but of a different nature. The ricin is the same as that used in the first attack on the political convention in Georgia. The analysis of the ricin used in that attack showed it to be of high quality. Even with our state-of-art equipment, we weren't able to duplicate the purity in small batches, never mind in the large quantities needed for an airborne attack. Also, the individual particles were extremely small, leading us to believe that the ricin was indeed weapons grade. On the way down to this meeting, I was given information that all but confirms the ricin from the convention attack is the same as what we are dealing with here."

The deputy director asked, "Jeff, have you and Dr. Palena theorized why the ricin is so unusual?"

"Actually the idea came from Nancy that perhaps the waste mash used to make the ricin was aged in some way."

Kerry thought, *that's right, Jeff—give her all the credit.*

"Our computer simulations show that it is possible and may be the answer."

The CIA representative asked, "Where would you find old castor bean waste mash?"

"Maybe in a landfill," answered Matt.

"Or outside a castor oil processing plant," added the agriculture representative.

Kerry made note of the last remark, she would have her agents search for such places in the United States. She would also ask her CIA counterpart to do the same for foreign countries.

Jeff said, "Matt, why don't you speak to the possible repercussions of the contamination."

"Okay, I've contacted the manufacturer."

"You contacted the manufacturer?" interrupted the FDA representative.

"Not to arrange for a recall but for information."

"Okay."

"Anyway, here's the problem we face. Undoubtedly, the salt manufacturer will recall the boxed salt themselves. However, we have not yet determined where the contamination took place. In other words, at what stage of the salt production and packaging was the ricin introduced."

"Why is that important in terms of a recall?" asked Nancy. "Have the FDA recall it all."

Matt responded, "If the salt was tampered with after it left the factory, further outbreaks would be much easier to contain. If it was contaminated at the production facility, then we have real problems."

Melissa from the FDA said, "That is definitely an understatement. I'm familiar with the company, and they supply salt to industrial customers as well. Many food processing companies use different grades of their salt in making their products."

Matt said, "I have the company emailing me a list of food processors they supply."

The deputy director asked, "Does the new information bring us any closer to the people responsible for the ricin poisoning?"

Nancy responded to the deputy director's question, "I think it should be obvious to everyone. Look who they attacked...poor black people. I believe I was right all along. The FBI should be looking at right-wing nut groups, and not spreading its resources all over the place."

Kerry finding it difficult to control herself smiled and said, "From what Drs. Palena and Davis have told us, all we have evidence of is product tampering and no evidence yet that the church and food kitchen was specifically targeted."

Nancy frowned and said, "I disagree."

The deputy director said, "From what I've heard so far here, I have to agree with Assistant Director Sterling. I don't believe we can rule out any terrorist group, foreign country or deranged individual at this point."

Nancy, looking straight at the deputy director, declared, "I would expect the FBI to close ranks around its own and defend its lack of success in investigating these crimes."

The deputy director didn't seem to react to Nancy's statement at all but asked the FDA person what she thought about recalling some or all of the products containing the salt manufacturer's ingredient.

"I'm not sure it's even possible to do an effective recall. For the sake of argument, let's say that the salt was contaminated at the plant before it was packaged and sent to the food processors. If they haven't used it yet, we can take it from their storerooms. If they have, where is the salt now? It could be anywhere in the supply chain—on a truck, in a customer's warehouse, in process of being converted, at the retailer, wherever. It could be anywhere. We would end up discarding millions of tons of food unnecessarily and creating huge food shortages and possible famine."

Nancy smiled and remarked, "I don't see that happening at all. Maybe it might be an inconvenience for some people who buy many processed food items. On the other hand, fresh foods should be safe. The public can eat the right way for a change."

Jeff Davis smirked and said, "Nancy, not everybody can get along on nuts and twigs like you. It might not be as dire as our friend from the FDA portrays it, but I think it's going to be a hell of a lot more than an inconvenience."

Matt interjected, "I should have the list of companies who do business with the salt supplier by now. But when I was talking with the rep, he said it was close to one hundred companies, some of them pretty large."

"I think at the least we would want to model some basic scenarios before calling for a massive recall like the one we're contemplating. I would also want some empirical evidence. Remember also, a large product recall like this would bankrupt many of the companies who supply this type of food," advised Melissa from the FDA.

Nancy said, "It's been my experience that the FDA has a history of dragging its feet in forcing recalls while they study the problem. How many times does the public have to suffer?"

Melissa responded, "Nancy, I think your comment is out of line. Everyone's trying to do what's best here."

The Defense Intelligence Agency taskforce member, who had not uttered one word up to now in any of their meetings said, "I'd like to propose something that could give us some insight."

The deputy director said, "Go ahead."

"It's almost 6:00 PM, and the food commissary here at Quantico will be closing soon. It's as large as a supermarket and carries many of the same goods. As you know Quantico with its base housing is like a small city. The commissary supplies that city. We can try removing the items from the shelves for those companies that do business with the salt manufacturer. This way we

can gain some perspective on what some of us are pro-
posing here."

Jeff said, "That's almost brilliant."

"How long do you think it will take us to remove the
items?" asked Nancy.

The deputy director said, "For us, not long. The FBI
training academy is located here at Quantico, we'll have
the recruits in the current class do it."

Matt Palena said, "Let me put together some instructions and get some copies of the list of food processors."

Forty-five minutes later, they had all the appropriate
calls made. Matt Palena, Kerry Sterling and the deputy
director took the short ride to the commissary together.
On the way, the deputy director said to Kerry, "That
woman, Nancy Noonan from Homeland Security, can
be difficult."

Kerry couldn't help herself and said, "Really Boss, I
hadn't noticed."

"Don't be a smartass."

When they arrived at the commissary, they saw that
the FBI had mustered eighty recruits, who were now
waiting in front of the building. The rest of the taskforce
members were also there. Matt was already giving instructions.

"Can everybody hear me?" yelled Matt.

"Okay, what we want you to do is take the list of
manufacturers I'm going to give you, find their products and then read the ingredient label. If one of the
ingredients is salt, I want you to remove the entire stock
of that item from the shelves and place the items neatly

in a shopping cart. When the shopping cart is full, leave it in the middle of the aisle, so later you can return the packages and cans to the shelf...any questions?"

No one raised his or her hand, so the deputy director said to Matt, "I'd like to add something.

"Okay."

"My name is Deputy Director Callaway of the FBI. You all work for me, so I want to stress this point. What you are doing tonight is part of an ongoing investigation concerning a possible terrorist attack. So be thorough now and later be discreet when asked what you were doing. Is that clear to everyone?"

The deputy director looked around and then said, "Go ahead."

The recruits immediately went about the job, while the taskforce members went to dinner. Two hours later, Matt received a call saying that the FBI trainees had finished removing the goods from the shelves, so the taskforce members reconvened inside the building.

After entering the commissary, Kerry and the other taskforce members were shocked. Almost all the shelves were empty. Only a few can goods remained and the cereal aisle was bare except for the oatmeal. She had no idea that so many products contained salt. When she walked down the cookie aisle, it was the same thing. She heard one of the taskforce members in another area say, "All that's left is a farmers market."

The trainees had filled nearly two hundred shopping carts. They piled them until they were overflowing.

The leader of the recruits walked over to Matt and told him that they had run out of carts so some items remained on the shelves. He also asked Matt for further instructions. Matt thanked him for the good work and asked him to replace the items.

Since it was after 9:00 PM, the group decided to re-convene the next afternoon. They would have to make some hard decisions. Kerry and Matt left together and headed for her home.

21

TIM FALWELL LOOKED DOWN at the tray he was carrying—scrambled eggs, dry toast and coffee—this new diet was killing him. He took his customary seat near the flat-screen television mounted high up on the wall. Today an all news channel was on instead of the usual sports programming. He figured it was probably because of Ellis. Tim learned while paying for his food that Ellis was a victim of the ricin attack at his church over the weekend. That was too bad, he thought. As a DEA training instructor at Quantico, he had talked to Ellis almost every day for the almost three years since the DEA assigned him to the academy. Tim considered Ellis a nice fellow, and they chatted frequently, mostly about sports. Tim looked up at the TV as a reporter was talking about the attack, so he listened. Tim reached for some sugar substitute for his coffee and there wasn't any. The little vase that usually had flowers was missing along with the glass salt and pepper shakers. One side of the napkin dispenser was also empty.

The commentator was saying, "We have reports from a person close to the investigation that it appears the terrorists have targeted African-Americans in the latest round of attacks, two of which have occurred in the last 48 hours. One was at a Virginia Pentecostal church and another at a Washington, D.C. food kitchen. Our source has told us that the FBI has confirmed the ricin was the same type which was used in the attack on the political convention in September."

While Tim was listening, he watched the cafeteria manager pushing a little cart around. When she got to Tim's table, the manager refilled the square container with packets of sugar substitute. She also replaced the salt and pepper shakers with full ones and said, "Sorry, no fresh flowers today."

Tim looked up and saw her eyes start to tear. She said, "That was Ellis's job."

Tim sighed, "We're going to miss him."

"You don't appreciate people until they're gone. I didn't realize how much he did around here. It took me twenty minutes to refill the salt and pepper. I remember he used to complain—actually, he never complained about anything—but he wanted me to buy the plastic shakers, which he didn't have to refill. It's funny that's what I'm going to do now."

Tim said, "I'm sorry."

"What is wrong with those people going after the innocents?"

"I don't know."

After the manager left his table, Tim thought, *what is wrong with those people*. They're cowards, going after old men, killing women and children. The thought made Tim sad. It reminded him that he also killed women and children. On his last day in the field, that's exactly what he did, but it was an accident. His recruits looked up to him as some hero type but he knew he was a fraud. He didn't even kill his intended target that day. The man was sitting in the passenger seat of the car, and he didn't recognize him when he pulled him out and clubbed him to the ground.

Now Tim was depressed by the memory. He placed a forkful of scrambled eggs in his mouth while he listened to the news program. He put down the fork. The eggs were terrible. Without his usual bacon, they were tasteless and bland. He reached for a shaker to spice things up. The doctor told him he had to cut back on his salt intake, so he only used pepper. He tasted the eggs, then thought, *screw it, you only live once*. So he picked up the other shaker and sprinkled the eggs liberally with salt. He tasted them and thought that was much better. He figured he would start his low sodium diet next week.

The commentator was saying that although the authorities believed the ricin was the same, the attack differed in some ways and may have involved product tampering. The victims had all ingested the ricin this time. Tim wondered if the symptoms were the same when the commentator switched to one of their medical professionals. "The symptoms of ingestion differ from inhalation. Four to six hours after exposure, a person would feel nauseous—have severe cramps and bloody diarrhea. There would also be blood in the vomit. If enough ricin was eaten the victim would feel a burning sensation in the esophagus and throat."

Tim listened and thought that would be ugly. He couldn't eat anymore after listening to the details. Then he heard the commentator say, "We have some breaking news. We have now learned that Clearlake Salt Co. has recalled all of their 26 ounce round boxes of salt. Their statement says that if the bottom of the box has a date code from the last sixty days, do not use it."

The commentator asked her reporter, "Do you think this has anything to do with the recent attacks?"

The reporter indicated she didn't know.

Tim didn't think too much about what he heard. He supposed that restaurants used a commercial brand and not the type one would buy in a supermarket. About three minutes later, he noticed all the cafeteria workers had left the serving line and were going from table to table. When the worker arrived at his table, he removed the salt shaker. Tim asked, "Aren't you people being a little over cautious?"

"No sir, this is the same salt they mentioned on the news."

Tim thought, *shit!* But, it was probably a coincidence. Maybe some worker dropped a wing nut in the salt, or they found a piece of glass. It probably had nothing to do with the ricin attack. Tim stood up and bussed his own table. On the way out, he grabbed a jelly donut.

By 1:00 PM, the sickbay at the Marine base was jammed with DEA recruits. Twenty-two people had arrived with gastro-intestinal distress. The doctor on call, who was alerted to watch for signs of ricin poisoning, put in an emergency call to the Centers for Disease Control hotline. The duty person called Matt Palena who was driving onto the base along with Kerry for their afternoon taskforce meeting. Matt, who had been listening to Kerry's non-stop rant about the latest series of leaks from the taskforce was at first grateful for interruption until he heard what the CDC hotline operator told him.

Matt said to Kerry, "Do you know where the sickbay is here on the base?"

"Yeah, I used it once when I was at the FBI training academy, a thousand years ago. Why?"

"There may be a ricin outbreak here at Quantico."

"No way!"

Matt and Kerry headed over to the base hospital and it was bedlam. An additional sixty people had come in with similar symptoms. As they were passing one badly ill person, Matt saw the man grab a doctor's arm and heard him say in a weak raspy voice. "The salt…I used the salt."

The doctor, who was busy, ignored him but Matt stopped.

"Did you hear what that man said?" asked Matt.

Kerry said she did as they both saw Jeff Davis entering the building. Kerry waived him over, "I think you have to listen to this."

They walked over to the sick man. "Excuse me sir, my name is Doctor Palena. This is Doctor Davis. I heard you say something about the salt."

The man didn't answer. "Tell us about the salt," Matt said again.

"They said it was the same salt."

"Who said it was the same salt?"

"The cafeteria girl…"

Kerry asked, "Sir, where were you?"

"DEA cafeteria, this morning," said the man as he turned his head to vomit again.

Jeff immediately used his cell phone to inform his lead technician to go over to the DEA cafeteria and secure it, then test everything for ricin exposure. They wouldn't need the STORM unit. They had the testing equipment right there at Quantico in the FBI lab.

Kerry called for a team of agents to take some statements from the cafeteria workers as well as the victims in sickbay.

Jeff then stayed at the hospital while Matt and Kerry went to the cafeteria. They were there before either of the FBI teams had arrived. Matt told the first worker he saw, "I need to see the manager."

The worker pointed to a middle-aged women standing near the television. Matt and Kerry walked over.

"Excuse me, ma'am. My name is Doctor Palena. I'm with the CDC. This is Assistant Director Sterling with the FBI. We would like to ask you some questions."

"Okay," said the women. Clearly, she seemed upset to Matt.

"A man in sickbay said something about the salt here in the cafeteria," said Matt.

"I saw it on the news. The company recalled the salt so I pulled it from the shelf and off the tables."

"How much salt was there?" asked Kerry.

"I counted eighteen round boxes that were in the carton."

"Do you know where the other six boxes went?"

"Well, I used four packages this morning filling the salt shakers."

"Where are the shakers now?" asked Matt. "Do they still contain the salt or did you pour it out."

"They still have the salt in them. I didn't know what to do with it."

"Okay, keep everybody away from them now, and I want you to find all your workers here that may have handled them. Are any of them sick?" asked Matt.

"No, not that I know of...this is awful, first Ellis and now this."

"Who is Ellis?" asked Kerry.

"He was one of the people killed in the church attack the other day," said the women.

"Did you know him?" asked Kerry.

"He worked right here. I've known him since the time I first started. He was a good man."

"Could Ellis have handled the salt?"

"I'm sure. He was in charge of the storeroom, and he usually filled the shakers."

"You said there are eighteen boxes of salt left. You used four this morning. That leaves two missing. Is it possible Ellis could have taken them?"

"I'm sure Ellis would never steal. I told you he was a good man."

"Okay, thanks for the help. There will be some other agents that will talk to you later."

By then the FBI technicians from Jeff's lab arrived. In a short time, they had the situation under control, so Kerry and Matt left for the taskforce meeting.

On the way, Kerry said, "At least this shows that the attack the other day wasn't targeting only poor black people. Maybe this will satisfy Nancy, and she'll stop leaking her theory to the press."

"I don't know, Kerry. This might make her point. If this was an intentional attack on the DEA, then she could make the same case."

"How is that?" Kerry asked with a frown.

"The DEA hires a large percentage of Latinos because they do much of their work on the U.S./Mexican border. I don't know if you noticed but many of the victims in sickbay did look Hispanic."

"That would be a real reach," responded Kerry.

"Kerry, remember this is Nancy Noonan we're talking about."

"What do you think about the cafeteria worker called Ellis?"

"I don't believe in coincidences in this type of investigation. These attacks are associated in some way. We have three known instances of product tampering and one person has a connection to two of them. This needs investigating."

22

WHEN KERRY AND MATT ARRIVED at the meeting room, most of the taskforce members were already there. Some, including Nancy, were watching a cable news station on the huge monitor that the lab personnel normally used for video conferencing. The news show had a panel made up of civil rights advocates, and the discussion centered on the reasons why black Americans were the target of the latest attacks. It was the first time many of the guests appeared on the news show for some time. The civil rights business was slow since the election of an African-American president and an economy that seemed bad for everyone. Kerry could see that the guests were making the most of their opportunity. Some of their remarks were over the top. Kerry recognized the person talking now as one of the few people still alive that marched with Dr. Martin Luther King. He was saying, "I'm not a bit surprised. African-Americans are the favorite target of white hate groups. In addition, for the last fifty years that I've been involved in our struggle, I've witnessed the ineptness of the authorities in stopping these people from hurting us. Frankly, I've had it. Enough is enough. If this was a white group that was attacked, don't you think the authorities would have caught them by now."

"Don't you think that's a little unfair?" said the host of the show in a half-hearted attempt to play devil's advocate. "What about the political convention attack? How were African-Americans the target there?"

"Look at the people who died. Sixty-one percent of them were African-American. If the attack was on the other party, there would be far fewer black folks in the grave."

"Good point," said the host.

Kerry thought that wasn't a good point. It was stupid.

Another guest broke into the conversation. "I think Homeland Security is more interested in protecting the white folks than people of color."

Nancy Noonan was hanging on every word, and she jumped when she heard the last remark as if she were stung. She yelled at the television, "Why are you blaming us?"

Kerry couldn't resist and said, "Nancy, you brought this on yourself because you couldn't keep your big mouth shut."

"Who in hell do you think you're talking to?"

The FBI deputy director upon entering and hearing the exchange yelled, "That's enough!"

An awkward silence enveloped the room. The group then turned their attention to the television. It appeared to Kerry that everyone seemed embarrassed witnessing the exchange between Nancy and herself. It was immature and she chided herself for doing it.

The host was asking a hip-hop rap artist that went by the name of FourJ what he thought. Kerry was familiar with the singer. The former administration asked the FBI to investigate him for the anti-government lyrics of his songs that they thought came close to sedition. The FBI refused the request.

He was saying to the host, "The U.S. govment' is behind the attacks on us black folk and ya'll knows it, like when they killed Dr. King and Malcolm X, ya-no-what-um-sayin? The convention attack was for the black man in the White House and the folks on the MARTA, ya-no-what-um-sayin?"

The show's producer finally had the good sense to deaden his microphone.

The deputy director sat down in Nancy's place and said, "Okay, let's get started."

There was no question in Kerry's mind that the deputy director had just ousted Nancy as the head of the taskforce.

"Kerry, give us a rundown on today's situation at the DEA academy," said the deputy director.

Jeff said, "Director, let me break in here for some information we received a short while ago. The lab has confirmed that indeed there was a ricin attack on the DEA Training facility emanating from the cafeteria. The ricin is consistent with that found at the political convention, the Pentecostal church and the Holy Shepard soup kitchen. As you know, the first ricin attack was airborne in nature, but all the others were the result of some sort of product tampering."

Kerry said, "Thanks Jeff, we suspected as much."

The deputy director said, "Let's discuss the results of last nights experience at the commissary. Speaking for myself, I was shocked that so many items contained Clearlake Salt."

Melissa from the FDA added, "This morning working with a representative of that company, we did some further calculations. If we were to recall all the items in question, 80% of the nation's food supply would be impacted in one way or the other."

"For how long?" asked Matt.

"For at least six weeks. We have to clear the entire channel of distribution for all the goods, re-manufacture the products and then create new labels for the packaging indicating to the public that the item is now safe to eat."

One of the newest members of the taskforce representing the EPA asked Melissa, "Did your analysis give any thought to where we might put millions of tons of this tainted garbage?"

"We didn't give that any consideration. Although, I'll concede it would be a problem."

"What are our options here?" asked the deputy director.

Melissa answered, "So far the Clearlake Salt Company has recalled their product without any urging by us. By now, all the round boxes of salt should be off the store shelves and put aside in the warehouses. However, the company will not accept shipment of the salt back to their processing plants until we tell them what to do with it. We also must tell the public what to do with the salt that they already purchased."

Jeff said, "I think our best option is to dump the boxes of salt in the ocean. The packages are made of a paper product that will deteriorate in a short time. The ricin will be diluted and rendered harmless."

The representative from the DIA who came up with the last night's commissary experiment said, "We can use ordinary depth charges to hasten the process, and not have to wait for the containers to deteriorate."

Matt asked, "You mean blow them up on the way to the bottom of the ocean?"

"Yes."

The deputy director said, "That seems to adequately address part of the question. But, what about the salt that is already in the hands of the public?"

"We can have the local first responders pick it up at the individual residences," offered Jeff.

"Okay, is this our recommendation then?" asked the deputy director.

There were no objections so he looked at Nancy and said, "Have Homeland Security take care of it."

Kerry snorted trying to keep from laughing aloud. Then the deputy director gave her a little wink.

Kerry mouthed, "Thank you."

"Now what do we do about the…"

"Sorry to interrupt," said a technician that came in and handed Jeff Davis a piece of paper.

Jeff looked at it and said, "Thank God."

Every one of the taskforce members looked at him expecting to hear some good news.

"The representative from Clearlake Salt, who is now working with us at the FBI laboratory, noticed that the contaminated boxes of salt have a paper seal that is slightly different from what their company uses. We also found that the adhesive is different. So now we can state that the product was tampered with after it left the manufacturer."

Kerry could see the relief on everyone's face.

The deputy director said, "This is a good time to take a break."

During the break, both Jeff and Matt checked with their respective labs for any updates. Matt found the CDC's hotline was quiet. No one phoned in any additional problems. Jeff's team was still collecting evidence at the DEA cafeteria, and Kerry's agents were busy taking statements from the people who were present at the location of the three recent attacks.

Matt heard the deputy director call the group back to the table. He too had noticed that the deputy director had taken over the taskforce. Matt didn't get into the politics of such things. He preferred to be a good soldier and do his job.

The deputy director was saying, "The news media is running with the story that a white supremacist group is responsible for the attacks. I personally don't buy it, and up to now, the evidence hasn't shown it."

Nancy said, "You don't see it?"

"If your theory is correct Nancy, how does the attack on the DEA Training Academy fit in?"

Kerry Sterling interrupted, "It doesn't. I think the attack was aimed at the DEA and somehow things went awry."

"It seems to me that the evidence doesn't support your hypothesis either," argued Nancy. "Maybe it was the other way around. The church and the soup kitchen were the targets and the DEA attack was the mistake."

The CIA representative asked Kerry, "Have you're agents made any connections in the three latest attacks, other than the ricin was produced in the same place?"

Jeff announced, "You're making an assumption. We don't know that the ricin was made in the same place. What we know is the ricin in all four attacks was the same but we don't know where and when it was produced."

The CIA representative said, "Well, from what I've heard so far, it seems to me like we are making another assumption here."

The deputy director asked, "What's the other assumption?"

"We are assuming the same people are behind all the attacks. But it could also be true that the ricin was produced and became available to a number of different terrorist organizations all with different agendas."

Kerry said, "I hear what you're saying. Still, we did make one connection. It seems a DEA cafeteria worker was a victim of the ricin attack at Calvary Pentecostal Church."

"Did he have access to the salt in both places?" asked the deputy director.

"We know he had access to it in the cafeteria, and we think he may have pilfered two boxes of salt from there to bring to his church," answered Kerry.

Melissa from the FDA offered, "For the sake of argument, we could conclude the attack on the church may have been unintentional, and the intended target was indeed the DEA."

"Then how do you explain the soup kitchen?" asked Nancy.

"We don't know yet," responded Kerry.

"Jeff, what else do we know about the ricin and the paper labels?" asked the deputy director.

"We already talked about similarity in purity of the ricin and the particle size. Further analysis shows the same trace elements appear in all samples. We can now say unequivocally that the ricin is the same. We can also say that at least 48 separate boxes of salt were produced containing the ricin, housed in two 24 count cases, and they all came from the same manufacturer."

"Did they come from the same food distributor?" asked Melissa from the FDA.

"That's a good question," said Jeff. "We also know that the product tampering took place after the salt left the manufacturer because of the bogus paper seals on the packages."

"So the ricin could have been put in the salt at the food distributor's location?"

"That's possible."

"Kerry, do we know if any of the victims at the soup kitchen worked for a food distributor?" asked Melissa.

"Give me a second here. Let me look through my interview summaries." Kerry shuffled through her papers. "Yes, we have a Gabriel Solice. His occupation is listed as a truck driver for a restaurant supplier."

Nancy asked, "Does your paper indicate his ethnicity?"

Kerry sighed, "He's African-American."

"I thought so."

23

BRIAN BURKE WAS SITTING in the upstairs office of the old plant studying his Spanish. He had his back to the door, and he didn't hear anyone come into the room until Alejandro corrected his pronunciation of the Spanish word Brian was repeating.

"How's the lesson going?"

"I don't know. When I say something in Spanish to Juan or Bartolomeo they laugh."

"If we have time later, I'll work with you some."

"Thanks, I'd appreciate it."

"I want you to make two more pounds of ricin. Then I think that will be it," said Alejandro.

Brian debated whether he should mention the almost three pounds he was keeping in the clean room which was the cast-off from the jet pulverizer. He decided he wouldn't. So he said, "Okay, I'll start right away."

For the next four days, Juan and Brian worked to produce almost a kilo of ricin, which was more than

Alejandro had asked for. After they cleaned up everything, Brian climbed the metal stairs and looked in.

Alejandro had several newspapers on the old desk and was highlighting certain sections. Brian assumed it was something on the attacks from a few weeks before.

"I've finished making the ricin. There's a little over 40 ounces in the refrigerator," said Brian.

"Go get Juan and Bartolomeo."

After Brian found the two men, Alejandro spoke to them in Spanish for about five minutes. They were asking questions and then Alejandro appeared to be finished.

"Did you get any of that?" asked Alejandro.

"I know you said something about the water."

"That's all you picked up from the conversation?" asked Alejandro shaking his head and smiling. "Time's getting short my friend."

"It is?"

"This is what I told Bartolomeo and Juan. I want you to break down the clean room and all the equipment. I don't know if you noticed, but there is an old irrigation pond at the back of the property. I told Bartolomeo to find out how deep it may be. If it's not too shallow, then that's where I want you to dump the equipment."

"It's pretty expensive stuff to dump."

"It can't be helped. Then I want you and Juan to remove any trace of ricin. Take as long as you need, but I want the job done well."

Brian understood what he was supposed to do. He donned his protective suit and started breaking down the equipment. About a half-hour later, he heard laughing. Brian looked out and saw that Juan was soaking wet and shivering badly. December weather in southern Georgia wasn't exactly balmy. Later, Brian learned that Bartolomeo pushed Juan in the pond to see how deep it was. It turned out to be over his head, not far from the shore.

Carrying the individual pieces of equipment almost half a mile in the soft ground turned out to be a chore. The pick-up truck Juan was using was not four-wheel drive. The truck became stuck in the mud frequently. Brian and Juan did the pushing as Bartolomeo drove. It took two days to finish the whole job. The next day they would dismantle the clean room. Brian had to make a decision about what he was going to do with the ricin that was still there. He decided to keep it. Brian found an old cooler, the kind designed to hold a six-pack of beer. It had indentations molded in the plastic to keep the cans from banging around, and it fit the ricin containers perfectly. Brian loaded the cooler. He also had several small testing vials of ricin. He wrapped those and placed them in the cooler, which he then put in the trunk of his car. He would think about what to do with it on the way home.

When Brian arrived at the plant the next day, he saw that a large dumpster was in front of the building. He walked in and saw that Juan was already busy at work breaking down the clean room. Bartolomeo was sitting in an old desk chair supervising. When Brian walked closer, Bartolomeo signaled Brian to help, which he did. By noon, the room was gone with all the pieces now in the dumpster. For the remainder of the afternoon, Brian and Juan moved the old furniture back to where they found it on the first day they visited the old plant. After finishing, Alejandro inspected their work. He looked around, didn't seem satisfied and then said to Brian, "The place looks too clean, doesn't it?"

"It's how we found it the first day except for all the dirt."

Alejandro said, "What we need is some dust."

Brian looked up at the ceiling. The building's construction was metal. There were I-beams and cross braces that held the roof in place thirty feet above them. Brian pointed to the ceiling and said, "How about blowing the dust off the beams up there?"

Alejandro looked up, seemed to think about it and said, "That might work. Let's give it a try."

He turned to Juan, pointed to the roof and said something. Apparently, Juan didn't care for what Alejandro told him from the animated way he was responding. Brian saw Alejandro point to the roof again and repeat what he said, this time more harshly. Juan resisted again. Bartolomeo kicked Juan between the legs from behind, which sent Juan to the floor. Bartolomeo was going to punch him in the face but Alejandro grabbed his arm.

Alejandro looked at Brian and remarked, "Scared of heights," then walked away.

When Juan recovered from his distress, using a ladder from the second floor office area, he crawled onto the beams. He used a dry mop, and the dust came off in big clouds. By the end of the day, the area they had used to make the ricin was filthy. Alejandro inspected the work and said, "Good enough."

Bartolomeo and Juan drove the RVs away while Alejandro got into his car. "We'll talk soon," he said to Brian handing him an envelope with his pay for the week.

Brian watched Alejandro leave and then headed for his car. On the way home, Brian added up all that he had made including the last payment. After expenses, he had almost ninety-thousand dollars hidden away. In his note, Alejandro had promised him another hundred thousand dollars. Now Brian finally had a plan for his life. He realized he hadn't even taken his medication today, which was all right. That meant no heartburn either. Maybe some day he could get off it completely.

As he drove, Brian remembered that he still had the ricin in his trunk. He had to find a safe place to put it. There was a self-storage facility not far from his house so he decided to go there and rent a unit. But, when he arrived, he found the office closed. He would have to wait until the next morning. As he drove from the parking lot, he made an illegal left turn. He thought no one was around. Two minutes later, he saw the flashing lights in his rearview mirror. He didn't know what to do now. Brian thought this was how the police caught Timothy McVeigh after he bombed the federal building in Oklahoma City. If they search his car, they'll find the ricin in his trunk. Should he try to make a run for it? He remembered seeing those pictures of high-speed chases on the cable news channel. The driver never gets away. When he heard the siren, Brian decided to pull to the side of the road. Although it was dark, he could see by the color of the patrol car that it was a sheriff's deputy and not the Florida Highway Patrol.

There were actually two deputies. One stood near his rear fender on the passenger side, the other tapped on his driver side window. Brian had turned his ignition off so he reached toward the key so he could activate his power window button. As he did that, the deputy sheriff removed his gun and yelled, "Put your hands on the wheel." Then the deputy opened Brian's door, "Get out of the vehicle, now!"

Brian did what the deputy told him. The deputy on the other side of the car growled, "Brian Burke?"

Brian looked over and recognized the deputy immediately. It was one of his tormentors from his high school days. The guy had beaten him up several times in his sophomore and junior years. Brian figured he was in for it now. The deputy walked over and slapped him hard on the back of his head. "The sign says 'Right turn only'. Don't you know how to read?"

The deputy then said to his partner. "He's harmless. Somebody would kick his ass everyday when we were in school. Isn't that right?" he said to Brian.

Brian nodded and then the deputy said, "Get going dickhead."

Brian heard the deputies laughing as they went back to their police cruiser. Brian's hands were shaking as he drove away. This is the one time in his life that he was glad he was a nerd in high school. Brian continued on the short trip to his home. As soon as he was inside, he double-dosed himself with his medication. Then his mother said to him, "Did you get the milk?"

"No ma, I forgot."

"Honestly Brian, sometimes you can be so irresponsible."

24

AT THE DIRECTION of Kerry Sterling, all FBI field offices were searching for defunct castor oil manufacturing facilities in the United States. Their counterparts in the CIA were performing a similar function outside America. In that effort, the FBI's Supervisory Special Agent in Charge of Counterterrorism in the Jacksonville Field Office had two such facilities to investigate.

SSA Beverly Ruddy was leading a team to a site a short distance from the Florida border in Fargo, Georgia. She received a report from the FBI's analysis group in Washington that a castor bean farm with a castor oil processing plant had existed there but had not operated for over nine years. Besides herself, SSA Ruddy traveled with her team consisting of four experienced special agents. They were in a four-wheel drive Chevy Suburban and had arrived at the property shortly after 11:00 AM.

Beverly noted two things riding up the long driveway to the old building. The actual structure wasn't visible from the main road. It was in a slight depression and a row of poplar trees acted as a windbreak for the fields, which were now devoid of any crop. This afforded a high degree of privacy, thought Beverly. The second thing Beverly noticed was the large piles of old vegetation. This she supposed was the waste mash from the castor oil manufacturing process. Her instructions from Washington were specific on this issue. They were to look for signs of activity showing someone had recently carried away some of the mash. They were also to take samples and send them to Washington.

Beverly left the car and looked around the area. The old building appeared unused for some time. However, there were subtle indications that people were there recently. A few cigarette butts littered the parking lot near the front door.

The team spread out to look around the property. They would stay in touch with each other via the push-to-talk feature on their cell phones. Beverly walked to the front door of the building. There was a small window. However she couldn't see much inside but some office furniture piled near the door. Her cell signaled that one of her agents wanted her attention.

"We have signs that someone was apparently digging in the piles recently," said the special agent.

"Okay, I want you to do a grid search of the entire property then."

"Bev, that's going to take us awhile, I bet there's twenty acres here."

"Hey, whatever it takes."

"Okay, Boss."

Beverly then walked the entire perimeter of the old building. On one corner near a loading dock, she noticed that someone had thoroughly cleaned the cement pad area—maybe with a pressure washer, she thought. That seemed strange to her. A little ways from the cement, Beverly saw a number of fresh tire tracks in the muddy ground. There were so many it looked like a convoy of military vehicles had traveled through there. She called the agent who had the keys to the SUV and told him to bring the vehicle around back.

Beverly got into the passenger side of the Suburban and told the driver to follow the tracks to see where they would lead them. On the way, she saw her other agents laying out a grid for a search of the property.

The five-minute drive showed the ground to be heavily disturbed in some areas with deep ruts and many footprints. Beverly pointed to the track in front of them and said, "What do you make of that, Jim?"

"When I was in Afghanistan, our humvees would get stuck frequently on the bad roads. This looks like that, people trying to push a vehicle out of the mud."

"Yeah, that's exactly what it looks like."

"I'd also say that from the depth of the tire tracks, whatever the vehicle was, it was definitely carrying a heavy load."

Beverly saw they were coming to a pond. The tire tracks showed that this is where the vehicle had turned around and backed to the edge of the water.

Beverly said, "Dump site of some kind?"

"Looks like it to me."

She and her driver Jim got out and looked around. "I don't see much," said Jim.

"Me neither."

Her cell phone rang. The special agent on the other end wasn't using the push-to-talk. This meant someone found something and wanted their communications to be more secure. "Bev, I think you should come here and look at this."

"Where are you?"

"About fifty yards from the southeast corner of the building," said the agent.

"We'll be there in a couple of minutes."

Five minutes later, Beverly was looking at what the agent found. She had seen this many times in the past—a depression in the ground about six feet long and three feet wide—gravel on the surface instead of top soil.

"I'll bet it's a grave," said Beverly.

The two other agents agreed. "Notify the local authorities, and call the field office to send out a forensic unit. Also, see if they can find a diver. I want a look in that pond at the back of the property."

"Got it."

Three hours later, several more vehicles were in the parking lot in front of the old building. The Clinch County Sheriff had a small front loader ready to excavate the area they thought might contain a grave. There were about twenty people now standing around watching the equipment operator begin to dig.

The local Sheriff yelled to the operator, "Mitchell, be careful. Go slow."

The equipment operator made four shallow passes. After each, an FBI technician would probe the ground with a long metal pole. On the fifth pass, he signaled the equipment operator to back off.

"There's a body."

The local coroner had his assistant along with a FBI forensic technician carefully remove the remains from the grave. The technician collected what he thought might be evidence. It took two hours to remove the partially decomposed corpse. It was almost dark, so they decided to suspend operations until the next morning. The sheriff agreed he would post a deputy to guard the area until they returned.

Beverly sent the FBI forensic team back to the field office in Jacksonville with the evidence they collected and told them to return the next day.

Beverly then asked the sheriff, "Is there a nice motel in the area?"

Beverly wanted to get an early start and didn't want to make the drive from Jacksonville the next morning. The sheriff was kind enough to escort them to a small motel, gave his siren a short toot to say goodbye and drove off. Beverly went into the motel's office. It was December. The clerk who was also the owner and manager said they had plenty of available rooms, so Beverly rented five. This made the owner happy, and he said as much. The man was chatty and said that didn't happen very often. Then Beverly had a thought. "Do you know of any activity that went on at the old castor oil plant up the road?" she asked the motel owner.

"I think is was about six month's ago I rented three rooms to a group that was working there. They stayed for a few weeks."

"You haven't seen them since?"

"No. Although somebody—I don't remember who—said they saw some RVs on the property."

Beverly called her other agents into the small office and repeated what the owner had told her.

The men starting taking notes as Beverly asked more questions. The motel owner probably liking all the attention he was getting seemed to want to be helpful. So, he began searching the database on his computer for information. He said, "All the rooms were registered to one person, Alejandro Reyes, who paid in cash. He also used cash instead of a credit card for the damage deposit. We usually ask for a credit card in case we find damage to the room after a guest leaves. If they don't have a credit card, we ask for a $150.00 deposit for each room up front. We inspect the room while the guest is checking out. If there isn't any damage, we will return the deposit."

"Was there any damage?" asked one of the special agents.

"Yeah, there was a $75.00 charge. I think it was for a cigarette burn in the bedspread."

Beverly asked, "Can you describe the men who stayed here?"

"Oh wait a minute. The first week they stayed here, there were four people, not three. Two shared a room. I think they were Mexican or somewhere south of the border. They didn't speak much English. One was always trying to hit on a Spanish girl we use sometimes to help with housekeeping."

"What about the other two?" asked Beverly.

"One was a younger man. He had a slight southern accent. He was the one that only stayed the one night. The other was a middle-aged man. He may have been American but he spoke Spanish too."

"Did you ask for an I.D. from the person who paid for the rooms?"

"Yeah, that's the law here in Georgia."

"Does it say on your computer what he used for identification?"

"He used a passport."

"Did you make a copy or get the number?"

"Sorry."

The last question Beverly asked was where they could get something to eat. The motel owner said there was a nice little café that the locals liked about twelve miles up the road. The agents who hadn't eaten since breakfast headed that way with no concern for local speed limits.

Early the next morning, Beverly and the other agents met the sheriff at the old plant. They hadn't anticipated an overnight stay so they were still wearing the same clothes from the day before. "Did you get the warrant?" asked Beverly.

"I was waiting for you all to arrive before I went in."

"Thanks sheriff, I'd like to also wait until our forensic team returns. I spoke to them, and they're on the way and should be here within the hour."

"That sounds good. I'm not sure how long we'll be out here today, so I asked my cousin who owns a catering truck to stop by. Is that okay?" offered the sheriff.

"Believe me sheriff, that's appreciated," said Beverly thinking that these people in southern Georgia were so nice.

While they were waiting for the forensic team, Beverly spied another FBI vehicle coming up the long drive. It looked similar to a plumber's truck. It had wide sides with compartments for tools and gear. This was probably the divers thought Beverly. She was right. Beverly asked one of her agents to show the divers the pond in question.

A few minutes later, an ordinary pickup truck pulled into the parking lot. Beverly asked the sheriff, "Who's that?"

When the driver got out, the sheriff said, "That's Leland Hunt. His father used to run this plant before he died. He left the property to his two sons."

Leland walked up to the sheriff and said hello. They chatted for a while about their families. Then Leland said, "I heard something was going on here, I came up to take a look around."

The sheriff introduced Beverly as FBI Special Agent Ruddy, and she shook hands with Leland. She didn't correct the sheriff about her proper title.

"The sheriff said you used to own this property?" asked Beverly.

"My brother and I until we sold it last July."

"Who did you sell it to, Mr. Hunt?"

"A Bolivian doctor said he was going to use it to make bio-fuel."

"Bio-fuel?"

"He said that some companies were experimenting with castor bean waste mash to make ethanol instead of using corn."

"Mr. Hunt, did you find that to be surprising or unusual?" asked Beverly.

"No agent, I had actually read an article in a trade magazine about it."

"What is the new owner's name?"

"He was a doctor. I believe his name was Alejandro Reyes."

This squared with the information that the motel's owner told Beverly the night before. "And you said he was from Bolivia?"

"That's what he told us. The attorney who handled the closing has all the information."

Beverly saw the forensic team coming, and she pointed to the door and said, "Let's break it down."

Leland said, "Agent Ruddy, I still have a key if they didn't change the locks."

Beverly took the key and slipped it in. It worked. She said to Leland, "Mr. Hunt, I don't want you to go in but if you could stick your head in the doorway, and tell us what you see."

Leland walked up to the doorway, looked in and then said, "It's pretty much the way we left it. I'd want to take a closer look, but it doesn't look like the doctor did much with the building."

Leland Hunt looked at the sheriff and asked, "What's going on here?"

The sheriff pointed and said, "We found a body buried on the property."

Beverly didn't want the information about what they were doing to get out. She was about to send Leland Hunt on his way when she had another thought. She called the special agent who reported the day before about the pile of waste mash being disturbed to show Mr. Hunt the area.

The agent took Beverly and Mr. Hunt to the place where he thought the waste mash had been disturbed. Leland pointed out, "Somebody's been digging in the pile."

"You think someone has removed some of the waste mash?"

"You bet."

"A lot?" asked the agent.

"I don't know if you know that castor bean mash contains ricin, which is potentially toxic..."

"We know that Mr. Hunt."

"I was always afraid of an accident so I kept close tabs on the mash stored here. I'd say that at least a ton is missing, maybe more."

"Thank you for all the help, Mr. Hunt. If you could leave some contact information with the special agent, I'd appreciate it. We may want to talk to you again."

"All right then, I'll do that. Good luck in your investigation, Agent Ruddy."

"Thanks."

As Beverly and her agent walked back toward the building, the agent asked, "Do you think he's involved in some way? He arrived here awful fast."

"I doubt if he's involved, but we're going to check him out anyway. Let's see if the forensic people have found anything interesting."

Beverly found the head of the forensic unit standing outside the building. "Did you find anything, Chet?"

"You bet. Someone went through a great deal of effort to make the place look unused. At first glance, it appears filthy in there, dust everywhere. However, in the office and the area surrounding it on the plant floor, there isn't one fingerprint."

Beverly's cell phone rang. The caller was the special agent who had accompanied the divers down to the irrigation pond. "Beverly, the divers have come up. They said there is a bunch of equipment at the bottom of the pond."

"How old is it?"

"Hold on, I'll ask them."

Beverly waited for about a minute. Patience was not on her list of virtues. The agent returned to the phone and finally spoke. "They said it appears new. Most of the surfaces are still shiny. They managed to bring up one item. But they said they're going to need some special rigging equipment to get the rest."

Beverly gave the order for all the teams to halt their work until she received some further instructions. There was obviously something here. SSA Ruddy called the Special Agent in Charge of the Jacksonville FBI Field Office, her boss, who then contacted Kerry Sterling in

Washington. The three of them were now on the call. Beverly explained what her team had found at the old plant. Kerry complimented Beverly on her effort and then told her that stopping the work was the right call. She told Beverly to wait for further instructions and expect more people from the FBI and CDC to join her team. They may have found the origin of the ricin.

25

IMMEDIATELY AFTER KERRY STERLING finished the call with the people in the Jacksonville FBI Field Office, she telephoned both Matt Palena and Jeff Davis. They all decided to go to the scene in southern Georgia instead of waiting for updates from their people. Matt had returned to Atlanta the day before, so he said he was leaving in a short while and would drive to the site near Fargo. Kerry arranged for a seat for herself and Jeff on one of the FBI's executive jets. It would leave the executive airport in one hour.

Beverly Ruddy had given Kerry a name of a Bolivian doctor they thought might be involved. So Kerry called Larry Simmons who was the CIA representative on the taskforce. Larry said he would get right on it and could probably have something for Kerry by the next afternoon or earlier.

Kerry then called the deputy director with the information about the castor oil plant. The deputy director

wanted to accompany Kerry to Georgia but Kerry per-
suaded him not to come. She didn't need him second-
guessing her investigation. She promised to give him
updates every hour.

Kerry and Jeff didn't arrive in Jacksonville until the
evening. She and Jeff were heading to their airport hotel
when her cell phone rang. She was surprised. It was
Larry Simmons at the CIA.

"That was fast," said Kerry.

"It turns out that we have quite a bit of information
on Doctor Reyes. Or I should say his father-in-law."

"Go ahead, I'm listening."

"Kerry, this is going to take a few minutes."

"Okay, I'm in a rental car with Jeff Davis, let me put
my cell on speaker, so Jeff can hear too."

"Are you there?"

"Yeah, I'm here. It seems that Alejandro Reyes is the
son-in-law of retired Bolivian Air Force General Victor
Eduardo Castillo. We know General Castillo very well.
Besides being a member of the diplomatic community,
he is also heavily into the Bolivian drug trade. About
four years ago, we believe he ordered the murder of
two undercover DEA agents."

"What do you mean diplomatic community?"

"He frequently visits the Bolivian Embassy in D.C.
But we don't know what he does there. In the past, he
served as military attaché. Now we don't know why he
comes here. The general still holds a diplomatic passport and uses an official Bolivian government aircraft, a
long-range business jet—the same one the ambassador
uses. Supposedly, he is a friend of the current president

of Bolivia as well as a heavy contributor to his political campaigns. That's probably why he has access to the jet."

"What about the son-in-law?" asked Kerry.

"Doctor Alejandro Reyes was married to the general's only daughter. She was killed along with Reyes's two sons in an attack on the general's residence in La Paz. The general's wife also died in the same incident."

"They were murdered? Do we know who was responsible? Was it a rival drug organization?"

"We don't know. At the time, the Bolivian government blamed the United States. They claimed the DEA attacked the general's home. Of course, we denied it."

"Did they offer any evidence to support their allegations?"

"According to the report, a weapon was left behind at the scene, which was issued to the DEA."

"What do you think?" asked Jeff.

"I don't have an opinion," answered Larry.

Kerry thought that answer was evasive. The phrase, 'I don't have an opinion' was 'CIA speak' for I don't want to tell you.

"Larry, what do you know?" asked Kerry.

"What I'm going to tell you can't be shared outside of the FBI, if you know what I mean."

Kerry knew exactly what Larry was saying. Do not share the information with the rest of the taskforce, specifically Nancy. "I understand," said Kerry.

"A pilot of a plane, the CIA uses to covertly go in and out of some South American countries, mainly Bolivia and Brazil, told us that he picked up four Americans in a small airport outside of La Paz. One of the Americans was injured."

"So you're saying it's possible that the DEA was behind the attack on Castillo's family? Why would the DEA kill his family?" asked Jeff.

"I don't know."

"I can't believe all this ricin business for the last several months is part of some elaborate payback scheme," said Jeff, who was probably thinking aloud.

"What else do you know about Alejandro Reyes?" asked Kerry.

"It says here, that Reyes was the son of a career Bolivian Diplomat that spent most of his time posted in the United States and Canada. Alejandro, the son, was educated in the United States from the time he was a young boy. He went to college here as well as medical school."

"Is that all we have?" asked Kerry.

"One more thing, the general is currently being treated for cancer. When I get more info, I'll call back."

"Okay. Thanks, Larry."

Both Kerry and Jeff were quiet and didn't comment on what Larry had told them. Kerry didn't want to think that all the people killed over the last few months was the result of some stupid drug raid gone bad. That was too much to fathom. There had to be more to the story.

Kerry and Jeff spent the night at a Jacksonville airport hotel and headed to Fargo, Georgia the next morning. When they found the site, the parking lot was full of official cars. Curiously thought Kerry, there was no media. That was a break.

As she was getting out of the car, a woman approached her. "Director Sterling, I'm Beverly Ruddy."

Kerry recognized her as one of the participants in a conference on terrorism that she chaired in Washington the year before.

"This is Dr. Jeff Davis," said Kerry.

"Nice to meet you."

"Is it alright if I call you Beverly?" asked Jeff.

"Bev's fine."

"Please call me Jeff. I think we'll be spending some time together, at least for the next several days. Later I want to tell your team personally what a fine job they did."

"Thank you, Jeff."

"What's going on since we spoke last?" asked Kerry.

"We arranged for a hoist and a flatbed truck. They've arrived, and they're down at the irrigation pond I told you about. Dr. Palena from the CDC is there also."

Jeff said, "I'd like to go down and see what's going on."

"Let's take the SUV. The ground is somewhat better, but you still need four-wheel drive. The flatbed also serves as a tow truck, which had to winch itself out of the mud several times this morning."

They rode the short distance to the pond. Several times Beverly got the SUV sideways in the mud. When they arrived, they saw a small crane dropping a piece of equipment on to the flatbed truck. Jeff said, "That's a portable high performance liquid chromatography machine. It's an expensive piece of equipment. We have three like it back at the Quantico lab."

Matt approached Jeff, "You see it?"

"Yeah."

One by one, the pieces of equipment emerged from the pond. Jeff and Matt were on the flatbed looking at them. Jeff put on gloves and started assembling some sort of apparatus. He yelled down to Kerry, "It's a jet pulverizer."

"What's that?"

"It's a fancy grinding machine. It can grind material into micro size particles without adding additional heat from friction."

Jeff hopped off the truck and slipped in the mud. Muck covered one whole side of his body. This broke the tension and everyone laughed. Kerry said, "Good going, Dr. Goof."

Jeff made a move like he was going to rub up against her. She declared, "I'll shoot you!"

Matt climbed down from the truck more carefully. Jeff went behind the flatbed and took off his muddy coat. He removed his pants, and one of the technicians threw him a hazmat suit, which he put on.

Kerry said, "Now you look official."

Jeff went back to get his coat when he heard his cell phone ring. It was still in his coat pocket. He answered and spoke awhile then rejoined the group. He seemed excited to Kerry who asked, "What's up?"

"That was the lab. We found traces of sulfuric acid on the clothes of the corpse."

Matt Palena said, "Okay. That does it for me then."

"What's the significance of the sulfuric acid?" asked Beverly.

"The first part of the ricin making process calls for extracting the remaining oil from the waste mash. A solution of sulfuric acid would be my first choice."

Matt said, "In my mind, from what we've seen here so far, I would conclude that this is where the ricin was produced."

"I concur," said Jeff.

Kerry said, "I'll call the deputy director."

When they arrived back at the parking lot, the sheriff approached Kerry. "The coroner called and said the man we found in the grave was killed approximately 4-6 weeks ago. The cause of death was a gunshot wound to the brain. He was also shot four times in the chest."

"Sounds like someone was pissed off," said Jeff.

26

GENERAL CASTILLO WAS NOW the only passenger on the Bolivian government owned business jet. The Aircraft was one of three used by the Bolivian Department of State and usually flew diplomats and other government officials to various destinations in North and Central America. The Jet was waiting to take-off after dropping off a Bolivian commerce official who was attending an import/export conference in Miami.

The pilot of the plane, a captain in the Bolivian Air Force, was waiting for take-off clearance after amending his flight plan and requesting a new Diplomatic Clearance Number. He needed a new DCN so the foreign aircraft could make an unscheduled stop in Jacksonville before going on to Washington. This change of itinerary was at General Castillo's request. He had told the pilot that they would be spending the night in Jacksonville.

The pilot received his take-off clearance and in less than an hour, he was taxiing to a stop at the new location. The general disembarked and found Alejandro waiting for him. The co-pilot handed Alejandro the general's carry-on bag, and Alejandro led the general to the nearby parking lot where he had left his rental car.

The sedan was equipped with a satellite radio so he found a Spanish language all-news station at the general's request. Alejandro let the general listen to the latest developments on the recent attacks. The news station reported that almost every hospital, emergency room, urgent care facility and doctor's office was being overrun with people who thought they were exposed to the ricin. Most of these cases turned out to be false a-larms. The authorities were warning people about internet scams offering a vaccine against ricin poisoning. The officials wanted the public to know that ricin was not a virus but a poison, and no vaccine was available. They were also warning parents not to give their children castor oil. Somehow a rumor had started that castor oil would act as an antidote since production of ricin called for the removal of the oil from the castor beans. The news reports claimed that some children had already died taking the oil. Unfortunately, one of the symptoms of ricin was severe diarrhea. Castor oil acted as a laxative prompting some of the parents to give their children more and more, thinking this would cure the diarrhea problem. Many children were suffering from dehydration due to the overdose of castor oil.

When the news was over, the radio station switched back to a talk format. The host was discussing with the callers whether the latest attacks targeted people of color. As Alejandro and the general listened, the consensus among the show's callers was that they were indeed.

The general asked, "What do you think happened?"

"I don't know. I gave the truck driver two cases of salt as we planned. I told him to drop one off at the DEA and the other at the FBI academy."

"How did it end up in soup kitchens and churches?"

"I have no idea, but that's certainly not what I intended."

"I know, Alejandro. Yet, this is the second time we let things get out of control. We are not about killing innocent children like the Americans have done."

They had reached the hotel. Alejandro already had a luxury suite overlooking the river. He registered under an assumed name. On an earlier visit, the general had arranged for some false identity documents, including a new passport from his colleagues at the Bolivian embassy. Alejandro had used the passport for identification when he checked-in to the hotel eight days before. The suite had two bedrooms, and the general would be using one of them. Therefore, there was no need to stop at the front desk when they arrived.

On entering the suite, the general collapsed onto the couch in the living area. Alejandro thought the general didn't look well. Over the last few months, his medical condition had worsened, and the prognosis didn't look good for his father-in-law. Alejandro was surprised that the general even made the trip and thought he probably should have stayed in Bolivia.

"Do you want me to turn on the television?"

The general nodded. So Alejandro turned it on and asked, "Spanish or English?"

"English, I want to watch CNN."

Soon after, the general fell asleep for a few hours and awoke as Barry Singer's show was starting. His guest was FourJ, who Barry introduced as a hip-hop rapper, civil rights activist, and staunch proponent of reparations for African-Americans.

Before Barry had a chance to ask any questions, FourJ took control of the interview with a diatribe on how the government wanted to annihilate black people. He said that US officials developed the AIDS virus as a way to wipe out the people of Africa. Then he went on to repeat the charge that the U.S. government was behind the recent attacks at the Pentecostal church and soup kitchen. He predicted that more attacks on the African-American community would be coming. Amazingly, he made all these assertions using a rhyming scheme, which took some of the vitriol out of the accusations. It was entertaining if not ridiculous.

Instead of challenging FourJ's ludicrous assertions, Barry Singer went right to the callers.

The general remarked, "They let you say anything in this country."

Both Alejandro and the general listened to caller after caller agree with the rapper.

"People will believe anything," said Alejandro.

"Well, remember who killed your family."

Alejandro was silent and didn't comment to the general about his last remark but instead pointed to a tray of food sitting on the table. "I ordered some room service while you were sleeping. It may be cold by now, so I can order something else if you wish."

The general had difficulty rising from the couch to walk the few steps to the table. He removed the metal lids that were covering the plates. He returned the covers and said, "I have no appetite."

"You should eat something."

"Then order me some soup...and something sweet."

After Alejandro ordered the food, he came back as Barry Singer's show was coming to an end. Barry asked FourJ, who still did rap concerts if he was appearing anywhere soon. FourJ said he was on his way to New Orleans to host a conference on reparations due to black people because of slavery. On the last day of the conference, he would give a performance. Then FourJ provided the audience with the address of the conference's website and urged others to attend. Barry then did a promo for the next night's guest. He would interview a popular preacher named Brother Lucas.

The general said, "You can turn that off now."

Room service showed up within a few minutes and as the general sat down to eat he asked, "How much ricin do you have?"

"Over a kilo."

"Have you decided where you are going to use it?"

"Not yet."

"This time, we should not let things get out of hand."

"I agree," said Alejandro. "What are your thoughts?"

"The American people seem to want to blame their government for the attacks," said the general pointing at the television's blank screen.

"I'm not sure Barry Singer's audience is representative of the American people, but many do seem to want to blame the government," said Alejandro.

"Maybe we can help that along," said the general.

"What are you thinking?"

"The black man on the television show...what is his name?"

"You mean FourJ?"

"Yes. He seems to have a big mouth and a following among his people."

"You want to attack FourJ?"

"He said he was having a conference soon in New Orleans."

Alejandro stood up, turned on his notebook computer and signed on to the hotel's WiFi network. He then googled, "FourJ AND conference" which brought back a website. Alejandro accessed the website, and he had the information.

Alejandro looked over his shoulder at the general. "It's a three-day symposium titled: The Case for Reparations. It's being held at the River Park Hotel & Convention Center starting tomorrow."

"What do you think?"

"There isn't much time to plan."

Alejandro then found the hotel's website. It showed an array of photographs of the hotel and its facilities. There was also some information about the staff.

"It says here that the hotel has a chef who won an award for his gumbo recipe. They say it's free with every meal in the dining room or room service."

"That is nice of them. How much did the soup cost here?"

"$7.95," said Alejandro. "I'm sure at least one meal served to the conference attendees will have gumbo as one of the courses."

"It is a possibility," said the general.

Alejandro went back to the conference's website to look at the schedule.

"There's a sit-down dinner planned for tomorrow night in the grand ballroom."

"How would you put the ricin in the gumbo? You are not doing that salt business again?"

"No, no. Let me think about it."

After a minute or two, the general laughed and said, "How is your Spanish?"

The general used to tease his son-in-law, saying he spoke Spanish with an American accent.

"My Spanish is getting much better," returned Alejandro with a smile.

"Can you wash dishes?"

"I see where you're going with this, pretend to be kitchen help?"

"It may work. If it does not, you can try something else."

"A big problem is timing," said Alejandro. "Getting to New Orleans by tomorrow may be a problem."

"Not when you have a multi-million dollar jet sitting down the road at the airport. Get me my cell phone."

Alejandro listened as the general called the pilot and told him to arrange for two people to fly to New Orleans at 9:00 AM tomorrow.

"It is done."

"How much ricin do you think you will need?" inquired the general.

"Certainly less than the three kilos we now have. Although the spiciness of the gumbo should mask the taste of the ricin, I don't want to use too much."

"Do you foresee any other problems?"

"The temperature of the gumbo...if it's boiling, the ricin gets unstable—some of the toxicity is lost."

For the next hour, they worked out the details of the plan. Then they decided to go forward.

27

AFTER THREE DAYS ON SITE at the old castor oil plant, the FBI and local authorities had finished their work. The FBI forensic team searched every square inch of the building, only finding one partial fingerprint. On the other hand, toxicologists were able to reproduce the ricin used in the attacks with the samples of waste mash taken from the piles outside the building.

Kerry Sterling was now almost sure that Alejandro Reyes was at least one of the perpetrators of the vicious ricin attacks. She suspected that his father-in-law, the general, was also involved somehow in the crime. Unfortunately, the FBI had no idea of the whereabouts of either at this time. This worried her. According to Matt, if the former owner of the property was correct and a ton of waste mash was missing, several more pounds of the poison could potentially be out there.

Her primary focus was finding Alejandro Reyes and General Castillo. The FBI was able to acquire photos of both men and was in the process of disseminating the photographs to the local authorities. The deputy director informed her that both Alejandro Reyes and General Castillo would be included on the "Ten Most Wanted List" if they couldn't be found in the next few days. There inclusion on the list would focus greater magnitude on the search. Kerry hoped these additional efforts would expedite the Reyes and Castillo capture.

Kerry who was now working out of the Jacksonville FBI office, made a call to Larry Simmons at the CIA. When Larry answered, she brought him up to date on what they were doing and then asked, "Can the CIA help us determine if General Castillo and/or Alejandro Reyes are in Bolivia?"

"Absolutely...consider it done. We've been looking for both men since you requested the information on Alejandro Reyes the other day. However, one thing I can tell you now is that we haven't been able to find Reyes in Bolivia. I'll let you know about the general's current location."

While she was waiting for the information, she made calls to the taskforce members, giving each a synopsis of what they've found so far. Nancy Noonan told Kerry she wanted more involvement in the day-to-day activities of the FBI investigation. Kerry assured her that she would involve her more, never intending to do so. After making the last call, Kerry checked her voice mail again. There was a message from Larry Simmons to call him back, which she did.

Kerry, anxious to get the information, didn't even say hello when Larry answered.

"Larry, this is Kerry Sterling, do you have something for me?"

"Yeah, the general left Bolivia on one of the government's executive jets. The flight plan showed a stop in Miami and then was going on to Washington. During the stop in Miami, the pilot amended the flight plan to land in Jacksonville. That's all we have."

"Thanks Larry, I'll get back to you."

"Oh, a couple more things Kerry, you may want to write down some of this. It's a 16-passenger, Embraer Legacy 600. They manufacture them in Brazil. It also has a Bolivian government crest painted on the fuselage. Here's the tail number."

Kerry took down the information and signed off. She thought to herself, *is it possible that the general and Alejandro Reyes could be here in Jacksonville?*

Kerry walked from the office she was using, found SSA Ruddy and said she wanted every hotel in the vicinity contacted to see if Alejandro Reyes or General Castillo was staying there.

In a few minutes, Beverly Ruddy had every available special agent in the office calling motels, hotels, bed & breakfasts and any other place that accepted lodgers.

Kerry was hopeful until Beverly returned in ninety minutes and told her they didn't have any luck.

Beverly asked, "What do you want to do?"

"Listen, I want to be sure these subjects aren't in Jacksonville. Copy the photos of Reyes and Castillo, and send an agent to each hotel to see if anyone recognizes them."

"Will do."

Hours later, Beverly rushed in to Kerry's temporary office. "We have a hit!"

"You found them?"

"No. We just missed them though. The front desk manager at the hotel said that Alejandro Reyes was a guest for the last eight days. He said Reyes checked-out this morning with an older man who was with him. He didn't get a good look but he said it could've been the general."

"Did you search the hotel room?"

"Yes. The housekeeper hadn't got around to cleaning it yet. We were able to check for fingerprints. We also retrieved the trash. We're looking at the evidence now. I'll call over and see if there's any indication of where they were going."

Beverly made the call from Kerry's temporary office. "They didn't find too much. There was a piece of paper torn from a pad by the phone. It had a few doodles and only the words 'New Orleans' and 'conference', nothing else."

Kerry thought for a moment, and then decided to inform the ASAC in charge of counterterrorism in the New Orleans FBI field office what they found. She said to Beverly, "Call your counterpart in New Orleans and tell him what's going on, then 3-way me into the call."

Kerry's telephone rang a few minutes later. "This is Sterling."

"Good afternoon, Director."

"Listen Peter, I need you to do something right away. I've reason to believe that there may be another attack, this time in New Orleans. Beverly told you about the note?"

"Yes Director, I'm thinking the conference could be at a hotel or a convention center. January is a busy time of the year down here."

"My suggestion is have your agents visit most of the larger venues, and get the locals involved for the other ones. Do you have the photographs of Alejandro Reyes and General Castillo that were sent out?"

"We have the photos."

"Start showing them around."

"That's going to take some time, Director. I'm thinking we may want to call ahead to the hotel managers telling them we're on the way to look around. Until then, they can look for anyone acting suspicious."

"That's a good idea. But be careful what you say, we don't want to start a panic where everyone tries to leave the city all at once, especially in New Orleans."

"I hear you," said the ASAC.

While Kerry was on the phone, an assistant passed her a note, which Kerry read. "Peter, I got a note saying that cable news is running pictures of Reyes and General Castillo, referring to them as 'persons of interest'. Maybe that will help us, too."

"I hope so."

"I'm on my way to New Orleans. I should be there in about three hours."

"Okay, Director. I'll have someone meet you at the terminal," said Peter and hung up.

"Beverly, are you still on the line?"

"Yes, Director."

"Get someone to call the airport, and see if there is a business jet on the tarmac with this tail number."

"Okay."

"And double-check with the FAA. See if the general's jet is still around or where it may be heading."

SSA Ruddy returned in a few minutes. "Director, the FAA said that the pilot filed a flight plan to New Orleans, and should be on the ground by this time."

"Castillo's on a diplomatic aircraft, they need a new Diplomatic Clearance Number before they can change their itinerary. The State Department requires a three-day notice. The FAA won't let them fly without it."

"I asked about that. Apparently, there is a State Department exception for VIP's."

"Who do they consider a VIP?"

"I was told cabinet ministers and three star generals and above qualify."

"General Castillo is a three star?

"Yes"

"Damn it!"

"What's Peter's number in New Orleans?"

Beverly gave Kerry the New Orleans ASAC's number.

Kerry got his voice mail when she tried to reach Peter Bounanno. She pushed the star button to get the attendant.

"Can I help you?"

"This is Assistant Director Sterling, patch me through to ASAC Buonanno or give me his cell number, whichever is faster."

The attendant patched Kerry through.

"Peter, this is Kerry Sterling again."

"Yes director."

"Send someone to the airport, and look for a business jet with a Bolivian crest on the fuselage. Also here's the tail numbers."

When Kerry was through giving him the information, her next call was to the deputy director to fill him in on the developments. Kerry told him she would be out of the loop for the next several hours while she was flying to New Orleans on a commercial jetliner. She suggested he could call the New Orleans Special Agent in Charge for any updates.

Kerry was getting her things together when her cell phone rang. The caller I.D. said it was Nancy Noonan. Kerry thought she would let it go to voice mail, but then she decided to take the call.

"Yes Nancy."

"What's happening down there in Jacksonville?"

"I'm on my way to New Orleans. We think that there may be another attack. We believe that's were Castillo and Reyes are."

"I'm coming to New Orleans."

"Nancy, what are you going to do down there?"

"I'm Assistant Director of Homeland Security. That's where I should be if we think there's going to be an attack!"

"No need to raise your voice, Nancy."

"I'll be down there. Where are you going to be?"

"How should I know. I'll be where they need me. Nancy, go to the New Orleans FBI field office. I'll find you."

Nancy hung up without saying goodbye, and Kerry was off to New Orleans.

28

GENERAL CASTILLO WAS LOOKING out the window on final approach to the Louis Armstrong International Airport. Landings were always his favorite part of the flight. He himself had logged thousands of hours in the cockpit as a pilot in the Bolivian Air Force before he joined the diplomatic corps. He even had a hundred or so hours in the right seat of the Embraer jet they were flying in now. Upon landing, the pilot taxied to a FBO, which provided services to general aviation. In New Orleans, like many other airports, the FBO operator had set aside a special waiting area for private aircraft passengers where they could arrange transportation and rental cars. The jet came to a stop after finding the place on the ramp designated by the ground controller.

"What do you want to do?" asked Alejandro.

"I will stay with this aircraft until you see what is happening at the hotel. Or, maybe I will go to the main terminal to get something to eat."

Alejandro walked to the rear of the plane, removed one of the eight-ounce vials of ricin from the impact resistant storage container, and put it in a small gym bag.

"I'll call later when I know more," Alejandro said as he walked down the jet's folding stairway. The general watched Alejandro enter the building.

The co-pilot interrupted him, "General, sir."

"Yes."

"We have a problem in the cockpit, our center display is flickering. I'd like to call for a technician, if it's all right with you?"

The general being a seasoned pilot himself would never take an aircraft into the air that wasn't 100%, so he told the co-pilot to go ahead. The cockpit door was open, and he heard the pilot radio the FBO operator. The operator told the pilot to, "Wait one". After waiting, she explained, that a technician at Apex Aviation Services agreed to look at it right away. Apex Aviation was located at the other end of the airport. The operator gave him the location of the building. The pilot radioed the ground controller who gave him taxiing instructions to the repair facility, which was almost two miles away. When they approached Apex Aviation, the general saw that they had a hanger, and a ramp worker was signaling the pilot to stop. When the plane came to a halt, and the pilot shut down the engines, a maintenance worker showed up with an old CJ7 Jeep. He hooked a tow bar to the nose wheel and then tugged the plane into the hanger.

A few minutes later, a technician was on board with some testing equipment looking at the display. The general seeing that the pilots were trying to stay out of the technician's way while not disturbing him in the back said, "Captain, you and your co-pilot can leave the aircraft if you wish."

"Thank you, General."

The general watched the two men depart the aircraft and go their separate ways. The co-pilot headed into the men's restroom while the pilot kept walking toward a break area. From his vantage point, General Castillo could see that there was a small area set aside with two tables and some vending machines. There was also a television mounted on the wall. The general watched the pilot walk over, stop abruptly and head back to the aircraft. The pilot looked agitated. He came aboard, made sure the technician was busy, then bent down and whispered in the general's ear, "Your picture is on TV."

Damn it, thought the general. He asked himself what he should do. His first instinct was to phone Alejandro and call the thing off, and then get the hell out of there. Instead, he said to the nervous pilot, "You will follow my orders."

"Yes sir."

"I'll stay with the aircraft. Go find out what is going on."

As the general was saying that, the technician interrupted.

"I'm going to have to remove the display. It's a fault on the video controller. We have them in stock for this model display, but it will be at least five hours to do the whole job. Three of that is going to be overtime."

The general nodded to the pilot and then said, "Go ahead."

Since they were stuck there anyway, the general decided not to call and alarm Alejandro. He sent the pilot out to watch the television to get more information. If they had a photo of him, most likely it was one people wouldn't recognize. He had lost forty pounds since the doctors had diagnosed him with cancer.

Alejandro was almost at the hotel. He had arranged a rental car to be at the general aviation terminal the night before. He would have to stop at a uniform store to pick up a set of kitchen whites that he would have to change into later.

When he arrived, he parked his car in the parking garage close to the River Park Hotel. He paid a premium to get a spot near the exit in case he would need to make a hasty departure later on. Alejandro got out, took the gym bag containing the kitchen uniform as well as the ricin and walked the two blocks to the River Park Hotel & Convention center. The hotel lobby was crowded with mostly African-Americans and a smaller number of Latinos. They were milling around and talking to each other, so no one gave Alejandro a second look.

Alejandro spent the next twenty minutes looking around. He found the central kitchen area was bustling with activity even though it was after lunch and before dinner. He estimated there were at least fifty people in the kitchen working. He called the general and told him he was going ahead with their plan. The general informed him about the problem with the cockpit display, so Alejandro knew he had at least five hours. He would take his time. He found a small locker room near the pool area, that if it were summer, guests would use to change out of their swimsuits. Alejandro removed his street clothes, left them in one of the empty lockers and put on the white uniform. He proceeded to the kitchen area. Everyone was busy, so he was able to walk around unobserved. Far away from the door and close to the scullery, he saw a giant kettle. He estimated it held at least thirty gallons. The giant pot had a self-contained heating element in a water jacket that surrounded the outside. It also had a probe thermometer with a digital readout. An older man, probably the chef, was giving instructions to another worker who was also wearing a chef's white tunic. Alejandro walked closer so he could hear the conversation. As he got nearer, he could read the temperature on the small display. Alejandro knew immediately that whatever was in the kettle was too hot for the ricin. He was disappointed.

The *sous* chef was apparently training the younger man. The chef was saying, "The executive chef likes the gumbo to be very dark so we use less flour when we're making the roux. We use tapioca later as a thickening agent because it works at a relatively low temperature. We keep the gumbo at 180 degrees for two hours and then lower the temperature to 168 degrees. That's when you add the tapioca. The gumbo will hold up for at least two hours for serving that way. Understand?"

"Yes, chef."

Alejandro heard the chef explaining something about the crawfish *etouffee*. He waited until the two men walked away and then looked into the large kettle.

A man wearing a black suit accosted from him from behind. The nametag he wore had the title of Executive Chef. "What are you doing?"

Alejandro pretended not to understand and implied through sign language that he was a dishwasher. The man pointed to the scullery and said, "Start on the pots and pans."

Alejandro figured he was lucky the executive chef hadn't told him to start on the dishes. He had no idea how to run a commercial type dishwasher. He was also fortunate he would only have to look around the corner to see the kettle's thermometer. He grabbed the first of the two dozen pots that were on the metal table waiting cleaning and went about the chore. The eight ounces of ricin was in his apron pocket. It was more than enough to dispatch several hundred unlucky people who ate the gumbo.

29

JACKSON JULIUS JORDAN JR. better known by his fans as FourJ was signing autographs in the hotel lobby. He was happy with the turnout. The conference organizer said that the attendance was almost double of what they expected. FourJ wasn't surprised. He was getting free publicity for the conference from all the television interviews he was giving about the recent terrorist attacks. He was surprised what they let him say.

In front of him was a long line. He was sitting at a small table, piled high with copies of his best selling rap CD called, "Reparate". It was also the title song. The lyrics were about African-Americans demanding reparations from the government in payment for the slave labor of their Negro ancestors. FourJ himself descended from immigrants from Nigeria. His grandparents came here in the 1950's. His father was a renowned doctor and his mother an English teacher. This was a problem for Jackson at first because the cadence of his speech and his accent didn't exactly fit that of a hip-hop rapper. He sometimes reverted into the King's English when he wasn't careful or had too much to drink.

He was trying to talk to a fan while another kid in line was singing a bad rendition of his famous song. The kid was listening on his MP3 player. He was using earbuds so his singing was without the rap beat. FourJ named the song Reparate. The kid sang:

We worked yo' lands, beaten down by yo' hands.
Our blood ran red from yo' bash in the head.
It was an abomination, for yo' subjugation.
From that we got little salvation.
We toiled in yo' soils, not even for spoils.
We sweat from our brow, as we pushed yo' plow
It was an abomination, for yo' domination.
From that we got never a vacation.
No mo' hate, then reparate.
No mo' hate, then compensate.

Separate but equal, we got from yo' people.
The burning cross made you the boss.
It was an abomination, for yo' segregation.
From that you got your separation.
You fill the prisons full of black citizens.
Justice is blind when it's only yo' kind.
It's an abomination, for our incarceration.
For that you got, no safe white nation.
No mo' hate, then reparate.
No mo' hate, then compensate.

No way yo' not going to pay for those you lynched every-
day.
The whips and chains caused us much pain.
It was an abomination, for yo' annihilation.
For that you got, our God's damnation.
You chose the way, now it's time you pay.
Because of Jim Crow, you pay us our dough.
But for raping our women, you won't be forgiven.
It's an abomination, for no compensation.
But now we get our remuneration.
Reparate or suffer the fate.
Compensate or meet yo' fate.

We hold these truths to be self-evident.
We get no help from our president.
It's an Obama-nation, for no appreciation.
For that he got whitey's standing ovation?
No mo' hate, then reparate.
No mo' hate, then compensate.

Every time the kid got to the chorus, the people who
could hear him, started joining him in the refrain.

No mo' hate, then reparate.
No mo' hate, then compensate.

This was not the first time this happened, and he
thought seriously of becoming a blues singer instead.
Without the hip-hop beat, the words to all his songs
sounded lame.

He saw the conference organizer heading his way. She was pushing through the crowd. When she finally reached him she said, "FourJ, we have to talk."

Jackson stood up and told the fans that he would be right back. Their moans and groans told him they were not too happy with his leaving. Some fans were standing there for over an hour.

"Wus Up?"

"The hotel manager told me a few minutes ago that the FBI is on the way over."

"What they want?"

"He didn't know, they wouldn't tell him."

"They ain't gettin in here, 'ya-no-what-um-sayin'."

"What are you going to do?"

"Call the media and see if you can get some satellite trucks over here," said Jackson.

The conference organizer gave him a funny look. He realized he had slipped into Standard English. He said, "Just go."

Jackson thought for a while. He could get some great publicity if he handled this right. Jackson rounded up his entourage, which included his older sister who was also his business manager, his two younger brothers and a cousin. When they were all together, Jackson said, "This is what I want you to do. Mingle with the crowd. Tell them that the FBI is coming to stop the conference, and they want to arrest me."

"Is the FBI really going to do that?" asked one of his brothers.

"How should I know. According to the hotel manager, the FBI is on the way over here for something. I don't know what it is, but this could be good for sales, maybe even another hundred thousand CDs, 'ya-no-what-um-sayin'."

They laughed at the fake urban talk.

"What I'd like to see is crowds barring each entrance. No violence but let's use a chant."

"What kind of chant."

"The one I've been hearing all frigging day."

The black FBI Chevy Suburban pulled up to the front entrance accompanied by a New Orleans police cruiser. The agents left the car, and a crowd burst through the doorway yelling, "No more hate, then reparate."

The agents and the police beat a hasty retreat back to their surrounded cars. A few minutes later, five more police cruisers arrived. Several satellite trucks were now on the scene. Jackson was watching from his fifth floor window. His cousin was rapidly clicking through the cable news and local channels to see if they had picked up the coverage.

"Here it is…Here it is!" yelled his cousin.

The reporter was saying that the FBI was here in an effort to arrest the rapper FourJ. She could hardly get the words out—the crowd turning up the volume on "No more hate, then reparate."

Jackson was disappointed when the news moved on to the story of the two persons of interest the FBI was looking for in the recent attacks. However, over the next hour, more channels picked up the demonstration at the River Park. The news stations were running snippets of some of the remarks he made over the last two weeks.

Jackson looked out the window and noticed that the FBI and police vehicles had cleared the area. He wondered what was coming next.

Five floors down, Alejandro had been washing pots and pans for the last two hours. He didn't realize just how hard a job this was. He was hot, sweaty and tired. About an hour ago, he watched the young chef he saw earlier, turn the heat down on the large kettle. Slowly the temperature was falling. Alejandro was becoming unsettled. He heard some of the kitchen help talking about the police outside and the commotion that was going on around FourJ. Alejandro hoped he didn't have to abandon his plan at this late hour. Still, the damn temperature was going down excruciatingly slow. After he cleaned each pot, he would check. Now it was at 180 degrees, still too hot for the ricin. He would wait until the temperature went down to 160 before he poured in the poison. He was surprised when the younger chef came over and stirred the gumbo and added the tapioca. Alejandro had heard the older man tell him to wait until the soup reached 168 degrees. Alejandro thought this young man isn't going to last too long in this job if he screws up the chef's award winning gumbo. The thought had barely left his mind when the man in black appeared again, his wrath directed toward the young chef.

"You ruined the Gumbo, you stupid ass. Who taught you how to cook? What an asshole... We don't have time to prepare another pot...Jesus, Mary and Joseph, I'm surrounded by idiots!"

The chef skulked away after the dressing down he received from his boss. Alejandro looked at the thermometer. The temperature was now down to 175 degrees. Alejandro didn't know how much more time he had. He couldn't wait until it reached 160, so when the temperature reached 170 degrees, Alejandro walked from the scullery. He had to wait a few minutes for some kitchen workers to clear the area. He carefully removed the top from the flask containing the ricin. He partially submerged the opening in the gumbo so not to send any powder into the air. He burned his fingers doing this. He flinched, almost causing a catastrophe for himself. He grabbed the large wooded paddle and then a high-pitched alarm sounded. Alejandro thought, *what the hell...?* The display read 168 degrees. He realized that the *sous* chef had set an alarm function on the temperature display to alert them when it was time to stir in the tapioca. He realized if the young chef hadn't screwed up, they might have caught him "red handed", so to speak. The silly pun reminded him of his burned fingers, but he smiled to himself, nonetheless.

Alejandro put the paddle down and headed directly to the locker room where he had left his street clothes. Ten minutes later, he was in the rental car on his way back to the airport.

Back on the fifth floor, FourJ was enjoying all the free publicity he was getting. So far, the FBI hadn't contacted him, and he knew nobody was going to get into the hotel anytime soon. His stomach was growling, and his brothers were complaining that they were also hungry.

Jackson said, "Order some food, and don't go wild with the room service again. Last time, I had a $2,000 bill from you assholes."

"Hey, they got gumbo. Says here it's free with any entrée. I want some of that."

Jackson said, "Yeah, get me some too."

30

THE GENERAL HADN'T HEARD from Alejandro since he phoned and told him that he was going ahead with the plan. He felt his decision not to tell Alejandro about how close the authorities were to arresting them was a good one. The general wanted this last attack to go forward and didn't want Alejandro to abandon it. After this, he didn't care what happened. There was a large quantity of ricin left in the airtight carrier that Alejandro had left on the plane. The general had given some to thought to using it on himself. He was dying and in constant pain from the cancer, but he thought that there were better ways to do away with oneself. The general had an automatic pistol in his bag that would be a better choice if it came to that.

The pilot was giving him updates on the news reports. They were running Alejandro and his photos every half hour. The pilot said that they were reporting that the fugitives were believed to be heading for New

Orleans. The general wasn't surprised that the FBI was so close. They hadn't done much to cover their tracks since they shut down the old plant. If he were serious about it, he would have told Barto to kill the Burke kid and the dumb bastard Juan. Instead, he sent Bartolomeo back to Bolivia.

Although he didn't care that the Americans knew they were behind the attacks, he didn't want the FBI to capture them. If they made it back to Bolivia, chances were good that the government wouldn't extradite him before the cancer killed him. But Alejandro's situation was another matter.

The general wondered what was going on with the repairs. Over an hour had passed since the technician had removed the faulty display from the aircraft's console. Not much activity had happened after that. When the pilot came back into the spacious cabin to check on him, he asked for the status.

The pilot told him that the work should take at least another two hours. The general wondered if they had that much time. Surely, the authorities must be looking for the plane. If they did find it, the general didn't know what the Americans would do. He held a diplomatic passport, and the plane belonged to the Bolivian delegation, so they might not come aboard immediately. Still, Alejandro had no cloak of immunity. Therefore, if they did come aboard they could arrest him.

His cell phone buzzed. The general figured it must be Alejandro. He was the only one who had the prepaid cell phone's number.

"Yes."

"It's done. I'm on my way back. I assume you're still at the avionics company."

"We are still here."

"I'm hoping we can leave as soon as I get there."

The general said, "I am not sure that is going to happen. They are not finished repairing the display."

Alejandro said, "I've have some bad news."

"What is it?" said the general figuring that Alejandro learned that the authorities wanted them.

"I'm listening to the car radio, and the FBI has our names."

"We heard about it on the television they have here. They are showing our photographs also. You must be discreet when you come to the hanger. Do not talk to anyone. Come directly to the jet. So far, no one has recognized me," said the general.

Alejandro said, "I'll see you in a while," then hung up.

The general took a couple of pain pills and nodded off. Alejandro woke him some time later when he entered the cabin.

"Sorry I woke you."

"It is all right."

"When I boarded, I saw that there's still a hole in the console. I guess we're not going anywhere for a while."

"Tell the pilot, I want to talk to him," said the general.

When the pilot came back on board, he said, "Nothing new on the news."

"We have a change of plans. We are not going to Washington for obvious reasons. We will go back to La Paz."

"Yes, general. I'll file a flight plan and request a new Diplomatic Clearance Number."

"How much fuel do we have?"

"We didn't burn much coming from Jacksonville, although I was going to have the tanks topped off at the FBO when we landed. But, I think we'll only have to make one fuel stop on the way back to La Paz. We have a light load, and we can do another 3,000 nautical miles before we have to refuel. However, I'll have to check the flight computer when the panel is working again." Then the pilot asked, "What about extradition problems?"

"Do not worry about it. Unless it has changed recently, the United States has an extradition treaty with every country in the western hemisphere."

The pilot came back a half-hour later. "I'm sorry general, I filed the flight plan but the FAA has closed the airport to all traffic, inbound and outbound until further notice. Also the request for the new DCN was denied."

A little while later, the pilot reported that the technician had re-installed the display. Since it was dark and the avionics company had to work on another aircraft, they needed the light in the hanger. They told the pilot that they would be pulling the jet out onto the tarmac.

Even though it was dark, there would still be enough light for the FBI to find them. The general thought they could leave the jet, but it would only be a matter of time before the FBI would catch up with them. They most likely had roadblocks set up near the airport by now. Their best bet was flying out.

The general felt the tug as the jeep pulled the jet from the hanger. As soon as they were clear of the door, he could see that the runway lights were off. Yet, the taxiway lamps were still lit. The general could also see that it was a clear night and a full moon was beginning to rise. This was good for flying but bad if you were trying to be discreet with a 30,000-pound jet.

Alejandro sat across from the general, so they could talk. "General, I'm thinking we don't have much time. Is it possible to take-off from a closed airport?"

"It is possible. However, I do not think either pilot would try it."

"So we're screwed."

"Alejandro, I have been giving this a lot of thought. I do not want the Americans to capture us. I am going to propose something to you that is dangerous and daring. There is a chance we may not make it back home alive."

Alejandro replied, "I don't want to spend the rest of my life in an American prison, so whatever you propose is fine with me."

"You and I are going to fly this jet out of here. Tell the pilots, I want to talk to them."

Alejandro found both pilots in the small galley that was located between the passenger cabin and the cockpit. "General Castillo wants to see you."

The two men went into the cabin. The general said, "Sit down."

After the two pilots seated themselves, the general began, "You know by now why the authorities want Dr.

Reyes and myself. And you probably could guess that I do not want the American FBI to arrest us."

The two pilots nodded their understanding, so he continued, "Here is what I want you to do."

The general told Alejandro to hand him his carry-on bag. He opened the bag and took out his 9mm semi-automatic pistol. He pulled the slide back to chamber a round. By the expressions on the two men's faces, the general could see he had their attention. He said to the pilots, "You will depart this aircraft. Alejandro will give you the keys to his rental car, and I would suggest you leave the area. The FBI will probably want to talk with you. Try to avoid that. If they catch you before you can get to the Bolivian consulate, you are to tell them that I pointed a gun at you and forced you to leave. Do you understand my instructions?"

"Yes, General."

"Get your belongings and leave now."

The two men wasted no time in departing the aircraft. When they were gone, the general had Alejandro close the plane's door and then join him in the cockpit. "You're going to learn how to fly a jet tonight," announced the general.

Alejandro didn't say anything so the general started his tutorial. "Before becoming sick, I took the controls of this aircraft seated where you are now. That is the co-pilot's seat. You do not need to know about all the instruments in front of you unless you are flying the jet from where you are seated. I have the same instruments in front of me, and I will be flying the jet. I know it looks complicated, but do not worry about it. Some say this aircraft flies itself. I have taken off and landed the Embraer, fourteen or fifteen times. Normally on a clear night like this it would not be a problem, except for there are no runway lights. With only two of us in the plane, we will need 5,200 feet to take off. Even without the lights, I believe the reflectors will guide us down the runway. It is now up to you whether we try it or not."

Alejandro didn't even hesitate. "Go for it."

The general smiled and then began the sequence that would power up the two Rolls-Royce jet engines.

31

FOUR HOURS EARLIER, Kerry using her FBI badge was the first one off the commercial airliner. In the gate area, she saw a women holding up a placard with her name. "I'm Kerry Sterling," she said as she hurried o-ver.

"I'm Special Agent Kathleen Rochelle, ma'am. I'll be your driver."

"Good, let's go."

The FBI vehicle was in a no parking zone near the terminal's entrance. The two women got in, and Special Agent Rochelle had them at the New Orleans field of-fice in twenty minutes. On the way, the special agent told Kerry that the FBI and local authorities had visited every location that was holding a conference and didn't find any trace of General Castillo or Alejandro Reyes. At first, the New Orleans police had left officers at each location in case the fugitives did turn up but a near riot at the River Park Hotel called them away. Special Agent Rochelle explained about FourJ holding off the FBI.

Kerry said, "That damn fool. For all we know, right now Reyes or Castillo could be poisoning their food."

When Kerry entered the FBI's building, the special agent in charge directed her to a conference room. The local FBI leadership was ready to give her an update. She appreciated that until she walked into the room and Nancy Noonan was sitting there. Kerry asked, "How did you get here so fast?"

"I took the Homeland Security Jet. Why did you fly commercial?" said Nancy with a grin.

This aggravated Kerry. She turned to the SAC and said much too abruptly, "What do you have for me?"

The SAC turned the meeting over to Peter Buonanno.

"Director, we've searched every hotel and conference center in the city and surrounding area except one and found no trace of Reyes or Castillo. However, we've determined that their jet did land here in New Orleans."

"Do you have the jet under surveillance?"

"No. We can't find it."

"What do you mean you can't find it?"

"We know it landed, and we know it didn't take off, but it's not on the tarmac or in any of the FBO's rental hangers."

"How does a jet disappear? For crying out loud."

Kerry was frustrated. She thought how hard could it be to find a private jet in an airport and said. "The air traffic controllers must know where the jet is. I'm sure they keep records and have tapes."

Peter said, "That's why we know they landed and didn't take off again."

"Unbelievable. Did you talk to the air traffic controllers personally?"

"There was a shift change. We haven't been able to talk to the on-duty ground controller. Supposedly he had the last contact."

Kerry looked at Nancy who had a smug look on her face. Nancy said, "How do you hide a jet?"

Since Nancy had now inserted herself in the conversation, Kerry abruptly changed the subject. "What's the story with the hotel that hasn't been searched?"

"The disturbance there hasn't abated," replied Peter Buonanno. "We haven't been able to get in yet."

"Do you have a plan?" asked Kerry.

Instead of Peter, the SAC responded to Kerry's question. "Director Sterling, we were waiting for your input before we decided to storm the hotel."

Kerry thought, *great*. If it turned into a disaster, she would be on the hook for the decision.

Nancy said, "I don't think storming the hotel would be a good idea."

For Kerry, Nancy's last statement made up her mind for her. If Nancy was against it, then Kerry thought, *I'm for it*. She said, "Let's plan the breach. We need to get inside the hotel to check it out."

"Do we have a layout?" asked the SAC. He directed his inquiry to Peter Buonanno.

"We have an old one. The hotel has done some extensive renovations over the last couple of years after Hurricane Katrina."

"Are the demonstrators letting people leave the hotel?" asked Kerry.

"So far the protesters haven't stopped anybody from leaving—only entering."

"I would suggest you contact the hotel management and see if they can come over here."

Peter said, "Will do."

While waiting for Peter, Kerry made sure they briefed the local FBI SWAT team on what may be coming. The SWAT team leader agreed that they would first try to negotiate with the protest organizers and then breach only if necessary.

Within an hour, the River Park Hotel general manager arrived with several other individuals. A special agent handed them visitor's badges and then led them into the conference room. Accompanying the general manager was the hotel's head of maintenance, front office supervisor, and executive chef.

Peter Buonanno started to brief them on what the FBI was planning when the man introduced as the executive chef pointed to the evidence board that was in the conference room. "I know that fellow," he said.

The executive chef walked over to the board, and pointed to the photo of Alejandro Reyes. "I know him."

"How do you know him?" at least three individuals voiced in unison.

"He's a new dishwasher. He's been at the hotel all day."

Kerry said, "Call over there right now. Tell them not to serve any food. Do it now!"

"When I left earlier, even though there was a ruckus outside, all the dining rooms were full," said the executive chef.

"Shut down the kitchen!" repeated Kerry.

Kerry then turned to Nancy. "You wanted something to do. Get Homeland Security to notify the hospitals and emergency rooms to expect multiple cases of ricin poisoning."

Nancy didn't argue and left the room already dialing her cell phone.

"Peter, we have to get in the hotel now," declared Kerry.

"We don't have time for any negotiations."

Kerry then turned to the SWAT commander. "Secure the hotel kitchen and apprehend Alejandro Reyes. Use whatever force is necessary to accomplish the objective. Do you understand?"

"Yes, Director."

"Okay, let's get over there."

Nancy insisted on riding with Kerry and her driver. On the way, Kerry called the deputy director to let him know what was going on.

When they arrived at the hotel, they could see that the protest outside was losing some steam. The temperature was dropping and the cold was having an effect.

The local police, already briefed on the operation, pushed the demonstrators away from the kitchen entrance without much effort. The SWAT team wasted no time. They had the kitchen secured and the entire staff pressed against the wall within two minutes.

Kerry looked down the line of people. There were 40 to 50 people and Reyes was not one of them. Peter's FBI team started interviewing the workers while showing them the photo of Reyes. One of the *sous* chefs said he saw the man leave about an hour before.

Kerry couldn't believe they missed him again and shouted, "He's got to be heading for the airport."

She then turned to her FBI driver and said, "Take me over there."

Nancy said, "I'm coming with you."

Peter told Kerry on the way out that there was already an FBI team at the airport. They were still searching for Castillo's aircraft. The driver asked Kerry where she would like to go when they arrived there. "Go to the general aviation facility."

"Nancy, when you landed with the Homeland Security Jet, did they have a passenger lounge in the building you entered?"

"Yes. It was quite nice. They even had a concierge who arranged a car for me."

"That's my best guess then," said Kerry.

Nancy said, "I'm going to have Homeland Security tell the FAA to shut down the airport."

Kerry thought that finally Nancy could be of some use. She listened as Nancy made the calls, surprised at how fast Nancy could navigate the bureaucracy. Within ten minutes, the FAA closed New Orleans airport to all inbound and outbound flights. Kerry watched as an airliner, ready to take-off, taxied away from the active runway and headed back to the main terminal area.

Kerry then heard a few riffs from an old Grateful Dead song. She realized it was Nancy's cell phone ring tone. Nancy answered and had a short conversation with the party on the other end. "That was the FAA. They said Castillo's pilot, tried to open a new flight plan from New Orleans to La Paz, Bolivia."

"That damn plane has to be here somewhere," said Kerry who was becoming more and more frustrated with their unsuccessful effort to find the aircraft. She called Peter Buonanno. "I want your agents to search every building big enough to hold an airplane. I don't care if it's designated a hanger or not. We know that jet is still here, somewhere."

"We're actually doing that now, Director."

"Okay, thanks."

Kerry who had photos of Reyes and Castillo took them inside the FBO. She had to do something; she was going crazy. She decided to take it upon herself to show the photographs to the workers inside the general aviation building in case someone had seen Reyes that evening. Nancy followed her every step.

About ten minutes later, she heard her cell phone.

"Director, I think we know where they are. We finally talked to the ground controller who was on duty when Castillo's plane landed. He remembered routing them along the taxiways to an avionics company located on the airport grounds. The name of the company is Apex Aviation Services."

"Where is it?"

"Director, Where are you now?"

"I'm at the general aviation FBO."

"It's southeast of you on the access road," said Peter "Let me give you the exact address."

Kerry listened and the relayed the information to her driver. "We're heading over there now," said Kerry.

"Director, hold on a second, we have some activity!"

Kerry heard Peter Buonanno giving instructions and then said, "Our helicopter has spotted Castillo's plane. Our pilot said it's moving slowly."

"Get someone to block the plane."

Nancy said, "I don't think you can do that."

"Why, for God's sakes?"

"I'm told that the plane has a Bolivian crest on the fuselage."

"So."

"That makes it the sovereign territory of the Bolivian government. It's like having diplomatic plates on an automobile. It's technically Bolivian territory."

"You're telling me, we can't stop this aircraft?"

"I'm saying you can't go onboard without permission from the Bolivian government."

"The hell with that."

"It's similar to when Air Force One is in a foreign country. It can't be boarded by officials of that country," said Nancy.

"Are you an expert in international law?"

"No. Are you?"

Kerry thought if Nancy hadn't said anything, she would have boarded the aircraft and dragged the two bastards out. She'd claim she didn't know. Once they had them in custody, the Justice Department could sort it out. Now she didn't know what to do. Kerry figured she better check with the deputy director even though she thought Nancy was a fool. She called and explained the situation to her boss who told Kerry he would call her back.

It took Kerry's driver ten minutes to find the company. There were actually four access roads along the south side of the airport. A continuous row of buildings fronted each of them.

By the time they arrived, the deputy director called. "Yes sir," said Kerry when she answered.

"Kerry, I checked with our liaison over at State. He told me that we can't board that plane without express permission from the Bolivian government. He's trying to get permission now. He also said if you attack the plane, it is considered to be an attack on the Bolivian government."

"So what are we supposed to do now?"

"Try to block the plane from taking off. But don't damage it."

"What do you consider damage?" asked Kerry.

"Kerry, don't screw around. I have six months until I retire. Do you understand?"

"I hear you, sir."

"The airport is shut down, correct?"

"Yes, sir."

"Set-up road blocks on the runways with emergency vehicles. Those assholes aren't in a helicopter. Castillo and Reyes can't go far. As soon as we get permission to board, then you can go and arrest them. Do you understand?"

"I understand."

"By the way, are you sure Castillo and Reyes are on-board?"

Kerry in the excitement of the moment, hadn't asked if Peter Buonanno had verified that both the general and Reyes where actually on the jet. Kerry said to the deputy director, "We haven't gotten close enough yet. We've only spotted their aircraft."

The deputy said, "Kerry, we've been here before."

"I know, I know."

"I've been handed a note from our director's secretary. They want me over at the White House situation room. Apparently, my call to the State Department set some wheels in motion."

Kerry thought she didn't need that kind of scrutiny in an ongoing operation.

The deputy director said, "Keep me in the loop. No, screw that. Keep this line open. I want to hear everything that's going on. Don't even think about arguing about it."

Kerry thought all this started with that idiot, Nancy Noonan.

Kerry said to her driver, "My phones tied up. Get me Peter Buonanno on your cell." The driver followed the instruction and handed her phone to Kerry. "Peter, I've been told by the deputy director that your agents are not to board or attack Castillo's plane. Do you understand?"

"What?"

"Do you understand?"

"Yes, Director. What do you want me to do?"

"Have the airport authorities place vehicles on the runway so the Castillo's plane is unable to take off."

"Yes, ma'am."

In less than five minutes, Kerry saw a number of e-mergency lights moving from different parts of the airport. Peter Buonanno called and told her that the FBI chopper pilot reported that all three runways were now blocked.

Kerry said to the deputy director on her open line, "We have all the runways blocked."

"How close are we to the airplane?"

"That's a problem, sir. The airport has restricted access. You can't just drive onto a taxiway with a private vehicle. We are looking for a way in."

The FBI driver handed Kerry her cell phone and said, "Director, it's ASAC Bounanno, he says it's urgent."

"Yes, Peter."

"They're on the move. There's an airport security vehicle following them."

"If we have the runways blocked they're not going far," said Kerry. "Find someone in the Apex Aviation that can tell us if Reyes and the Castillo are definitely on the plane."

"I'll do that now," said Peter.

32

ALEJANDRO AND THE GENERAL were sitting in the darkened cockpit waiting for the engines to warm up. The general had given Alejandro a laminated copy of a checklist. The general told him to start reading each item. Alejandro was in the process of doing that when he noticed emergency lights of numerous vehicles moving around the airport. He asked the general, "What do you think that means."

"They probably know we are here," said the general. "What is the next item on the checklist?"

As Alejandro told him, he looked at his father-in-law. Even in the low light, Alejandro could see he was in a bad way. His voice was still strong, but his body looked frail. Alejandro wondered if his father-in-law had the strength to do what they planned. However, there didn't seem to be a good alternative to what they were doing. Alejandro continued with the checklist until the general then said, "That is it for now until we start our takeoff roll."

The general changed frequencies on the radio. He told Alejandro he needed the latest weather update and most importantly the wind direction. The tower wasn't going to tell him which runway was active, so he had to choose one for himself. The general said, "Alejandro, New Orleans has three main runways but only two are long enough for the Embraer. Once we decide on the runway, then we must choose the direction. In other words, we have to takeoff as close as possible into the wind."

As the general was saying this, more emergency vehicles were heading in all directions. The general looked out and said, "They are blocking the runway that runs northwest to southeast and vice-versa. We cannot use the other runway because there is a strong crosswind. We would never make it. It is only 7,000 feet. We would not have enough airspeed and would probably run out of runway before the wheels left the ground. Nevertheless, it looks like they are blocking that too."

The general turned on the map light, which partially illuminated the cockpit. He looked at the airport diagram. After a minute, he said to Alejandro. "In Bolivia our air fields are not as good as they are here in the United States. We often had to make due with what we had. I am thinking we only have but one alternative and maybe a 50% chance of getting airborne. As you know, I am a dying old man, so it does not matter much to me. Again, this will be your decision."

Alejandro answered, "I told you before. I don't want to spend any time in an American prison. So do what you must."

The general pushed the throttles up enough to get the jet moving, then he made a right turn onto the taxiway heading southeast toward the north/south runway access. Alejandro thought he was going to try to takeoff in spite of the crosswinds and the vehicles he could see blocking the end of the runway. However, the general made a left turn onto a connector that led to the taxiway that served the main terminal used by the commercial airlines. The general said, we have some vehicles following us, I saw them when we made the turn."

When the general reached the main taxiway, he stopped the jet. "Alejandro, continue with the next section of the checklist. When you are finished, we will be using the taxiway to takeoff."

"Can you do that?"

"I think we will find out soon."

"Is it long enough?"

"On the airport diagram, it appears to be around 8,000 feet. The wind is coming from the northwest so as long as I do not hit anything, we should be able to take off."

"Can you see?"

"There is enough light coming from the main terminal. After we pass it, I will only have the taxiway lights. They have not shut those off. If there is something on the taxiway, we will probably hit it at over 100 knots."

Alejandro thought this is crazy. But again, there was no good alternative. When Alejandro didn't say anything, the general said, "You will have an important job to do."

"What do you want me to do?"

"The display to your right is your airspeed indicator. When it reads 160 knots, tell me."

"That's it?"

"That is all you need to do for now. Are you ready?"

"I'm ready."

The general gradually added power until there was enough thrust built up to begin the takeoff roll. He added more power until the jet was careening along the taxiway coming close to parked airliners as it passed the main terminal.

Alejandro was watching the airspeed indicator so he didn't see the right wing of their jet miss the tail cone of a Boeing 757 by less than four feet.

Alejandro yelled, "160 knots."

He knew right away that they left the ground and were now airborne. He looked over at the general who had a broad smile on his face. He hadn't seen that in a while. The general said, "Read the next section of the checklist, let us clean up this aircraft and get some altitude." The general raised the landing gear, retracted the flaps and trimmed the aircraft in order to reach the jet's peak performance. The aircraft quickly climbed to 14,000 feet when the general throttled back to conserve fuel. Alejandro's heart was still racing from their narrow escape but he managed a smile as he sat back and thought about his home in Bolivia. It was possible that he would see it again.

The FBI driver had parked the official vehicle in a spot where Kerry could see clear across the airport to the lighted main terminal area. She was talking with Peter Buonanno who advised, "We interviewed an avionics technician who recognized Castillo from one of the photos. He said the man was on the jet the whole time he was working on the display. He also said another man joined him a short time before the plane left the hanger."

"Are you convinced it was Reyes and Castillo?"

"Yes, and one of our agents observing the aircraft through binoculars, saw two men fitting the description of Castillo and Reyes when the cockpit lights came on briefly."

"That can't be right. Why would Castillo and Reyes be in the cockpit?"

"Director, that's what he told me."

"Is the jet still moving?"

"Yes. We have three vehicles following it."

Kerry wondered why Reyes and Castillo would be in the cockpit of a moving jet. She was mulling this over, looking out into space when she saw a fast moving object pass in front of the terminal.

"Peter, what was that? Something passed the main terminal at a high speed. It looked like a plane from over here."

"I don't know. I saw it too. Hold on."

When Peter came back, he said, "I can't believe it. The chopper pilot claims that Castillo's jet took off on the taxiway!"

Kerry threw up her hands and started banging on the dashboard of the FBI vehicle. She could hear the distant voice of the deputy director on the open line, "Kerry, Kerry are you there? What's happening?"

"Castillo and Reyes took off on the taxiway. They're gone."

"What?"

"They took off on the taxiway!"

Kerry heard the deputy director saying something. She couldn't hear much. The sound was muffled as if he had his hand over the phone. She could tell there was a lot of yelling and shouting though.

The deputy director came back on the line and said, "Agent Sterling, we have it from here."

Kerry knew the deputy director's misnomer of her title was a not so subtle reprimand. She wondered if the situation could get any worse. Then he said, "I need you back in Washington right away."

33

THE EXCITEMENT AND EUPHORIA of their narrow escape had started to diminish for Alejandro twenty minutes into the flight. They were now flying south over the Gulf of Mexico. Alejandro had seen the lights of several oilrigs as they passed over. The general was still flying the plane manually having not yet programmed the autopilot. The reality of their precarious situation was beginning to dawn on Alejandro; they had no place to go. Every country in South and Central America had extradition treaties with the United States. The jet they were flying had to stop once for refueling. They were going to need landing permission, and if they did land, there was no guarantee that the country would let them take off again. Alejandro didn't believe that their "great escape" on the taxiway would work a second time.

Alejandro looked at the general who seemed to be thoroughly enjoying himself. He thought he'd give the general a few more minutes of pleasure before he had to ask some hard questions. He was looking out the window. There was a full moon high in the sky—its reflection casting light on the water below. Alejandro decided not to disturb the general and wait until he spoke to him first. Then he saw something odd. It appeared to be a strobe light. He was trying to figure out what it was. It was coming closer. "General, there's a strange light here on the right of us."

"There are lights on our left also."

"What is it?"

"I believe they are fighter planes."

As the lights got closer, Alejandro could begin to see their silhouettes. The fighters were flying at the same altitude and matching the Embraer's speed. For the next few minutes, they came closer until their proximity reminded Alejandro of seeing military jets flying in formation. The general said, "They are navy fighters. I can tell by the shape of the tail fins."

"What do you think they're going to do?"

"They will try to contact us and request we turn around. When that does not work, they will try to intimidate us. After that, I do not know."

The general was almost correct. The navy fighters went right into intimidation mode. A third fighter came from below them and shot past the Embraer's nose in full after-burner. The jet wash rocked their plane violently. It seemed to Alejandro that the general had lost control, but the wings leveled again. "What was that?"

"That was the American pilots saying hello."

Alejandro couldn't believe the general was so calm. The general said, "I believe they want to play. Hold on, Alejandro."

The general turned the wheel to the right while pushing hard on the left rudder pedal. The Embraer turned on its side and dropped like a rock. Alejandro saw on the altimeter that they had lost almost a thousand feet in a matter of seconds. "It should take the navy pilots a few minutes to find us again. This time they may show more respect."

Alejandro said, "Should I go back in the cabin and see if I can find a leather helmet and a red scarf you can wrap around your neck?" As he said this, he noticed the navy pilots were back. The general said, "These men are good, much better than Bolivian pilots. I think I will harass this one on my left."

The general let the Embraer sideslip crowding the fighter. He kept inching closer until the pilot changed altitude. The general did the same thing to the fighter on the right. Suddenly both jets were gone. "You don't think they gave up?" asked Alejandro.

"No. They're setting up to engage. There is a minimum distance for a missile strike."

"You think they will shoot us down?"

"I don't know."

"Do you have a plan?"

"I'm trying to conserve fuel. We are now about 1,500 nautical miles from Caracas. La Paz is 1,650 nautical miles due south of there. The aircraft hasn't been refueled since it landed in Miami, which was two stops ago. According to the flight computer, we have 2,200 nautical miles worth of fuel in our tanks. You can do the mathematics."

Alejandro said, "I see."

"On the positive side, the current Venezuelan government is hostile to the United States, which is helpful to us. Nevertheless, we are probably as popular as the terrorist, Osama bin Laden, with the Americans. I'm sure the American government is putting pressure on the Venezuelans not to let us land there or if we do, to arrest you. Remember, I still have a valid diplomatic passport."

"What about Havana instead?"

"Havana to La Paz is well within the limits of the Embraer's range. Still, it's unlikely they will let us land there. They have an anti-hijacking agreement with the United States, and technically we hijacked this plane."

"So it's Caracas or nothing."

"It appears that way."

"What the hell was that!" yelled Alejandro as white streaks passed in front of their windscreen.

"Tracers from one of navy fighter's cannons," said the general.

"Are they trying to shoot us down?"

"No. They are back intimidating us again. If they wanted to shoot us down, we would be dead by now."

Alejandro watched the general start doing something with the computer and asked, "What are you doing?"

"Programming the auto-pilot, I have to use the lavatory."

"Are you kidding?"

"No."

"You're going to leave me here all alone?"

"Don't touch anything and you'll be fine," said the general.

The general got up from his pilot seat and fell down trying to leave the cockpit. "Are you all right?" asked Alejandro concerned that the general had badly injured himself.

"I forgot for a while that I'm a sick old man."

"But are you hurt?"

"I don't think so."

Alejandro helped the general into the cabin area. He sat him down and started examining him. "I was afraid when you fell, you may have broken a hip. It's common in…" Alejandro didn't finish the sentence.

"I think I'm all right," the general said with a smile. "By the way, who is flying the plane?"

If Alejandro had any doubt that what they were doing was crazy, the general's next statement cinched it. The general said, "I'm going to use the lavatory then take a nap. You go into the cockpit, and if you hear any buzzers or see any flashing lights, come back and wake me."

Alejandro, shaking his head, helped the general to the jet's small lavatory then went back into the cockpit. The moon would occasionally go behind a cloud and leaving only darkness. He hoped the weather would stay good until they reached Venezuela. Then all of a sudden, the jet rocked violently. He saw the flames from the fighter's exhaust in front of him. The navy pilots were harassing them again. Every ten minutes or so, the fighters would come from below. The jet wash would rock the Embraer. Each time the autopilot would bring them back to level flight. After awhile, Alejandro who was exhausted, became unconcerned and fell a-sleep himself.

He didn't know how long it was when he heard the loud buzzing sound. A light in center console display was also flashing rapidly. Alejandro went to get the general from the passenger cabin. He was moving so quickly that he banged his knee hard as he squeezed through the galley. "Son-of-a-bitch," he yelled in pain.

The general opened his eyes and asked, "What is wrong."

Alejandro said, "There's a problem—a buzzer and flashing lights."

The general asked calmly, "What time is it?"

Alejandro thought what difference does that make while he looked at his watch. "It's 1:30 AM."

"It's probably the autopilot. I set the alarm to go off when we were 40 minutes out of Caracas."

Alejandro realized he'd been asleep for almost two hours. "Help me up," said the general.

Alejandro helped the general back into the cockpit and pilot seat. He watched him enter something into the computer. The general then tuned one of the aircraft's two radios, dialing in a new frequency. "I am contacting Caracas approach control. We will soon know our fate."

The general switched his speech to English, the international language of aviation. Alejandro listened to the pilot lingo. The general and controller were speaking much too fast. Nevertheless, he understood the gist of the conversation. It sounded like they would not be landing in Caracas.

Alejandro asked, "What now?"

"We have enough fuel to make it to several other countries, and many of the larger Caribbean islands have runways long enough to accommodate us. Unfortunately, many of the airports close after midnight. We can't land without runway lights. And Caracas was our best bet, politically."

"So what I hear you saying is, we either crash or pick the country that has the nicest prisons."

"I am sorry, Alejandro. However, I believe you knew all along that it could come to this. We have killed many hundreds of people."

Alejandro looked at the general and sighed, "I don't want to spend any time in prison. I want to see my family again."

The general looked at him. They stared at each other for a time. "Are you sure, Alejandro?"

"Yes, sir."

The general didn't look away immediately. When he finally broke his gaze, he switched off the autopilot. "Alejandro, why don't you go back to the passenger cabin. I will join you back there in a short while."

As Alejandro got up from the co-pilot's seat, the general grabbed his hand and held it for a while. Then he said, "Go now."

The general retrieved his wallet from his pocket. He found the photo of his daughter and grandsons that he liked so much. He studied the picture for a time then he pulled back on the yoke to point the plane toward the stars and pushed back the throttles until there was near silence from the jet engines. The aircraft gained some altitude until the airspeed dwindled. When it was no longer able to keep itself in the air, it nosed over and plunged 14,000 feet—crashing into the sea.

Part II

Brian

&

Brother Lucas

34

BRIAN STAYED IN HIS BEDROOM most of the day. He was switching from one cable channel to another listening to the latest developments. Earlier that afternoon, while talking with his mother as she watched "her stories" as she referred to the daily soap operas, the network interrupted the show with a news bulletin. Brian froze when he saw the pictures of Alejandro and General Castillo. He almost didn't recognize General Castillo from the photo they were showing because he was much thinner in real life. He waited to see if they would show his photo also. They didn't. The reporter called them "persons of interest" in the recent terror attacks. The network wasn't giving much information so he went into his room to watch a 24-hour cable news channel. That's were he stayed for the next ten hours. Brian didn't leave the room to eat when his mother asked him if he was hungry. Brian wasn't hungry. He had severe heartburn. Several times during the day, he feared he was having an anxiety attack. Each time he took one of his the Kyri-Laison tablets. His medication didn't seem to be working as well as it should, and he swallowed three times the prescribed dose.

The news stations started reporting that the FBI had descended on New Orleans where they believed Reyes and Castillo were planning another attack. The news writers dropped the phrase "persons of interest" in favor of the term suspected terrorists. Bit by bit, the coverage began to tighten with a few facts slowly replacing the wild speculation. A profile of General Castillo began to emerge. Brian recognized much of the information from the internet research he did several months before. One network had the narrative of revenge as the motive for the attacks. Soon all the others had picked up the same story. The connection seemed to make sense because of the recent attack on the DEA training facility.

There wasn't much news until the story broke of the Bolivian jet taking off from a taxiway in New Orleans. There was a media frenzy around that piece of information. "How could the authorities who shutdown the airport let the terrorists escape," became the new narrative. Brian was hopeful. Maybe Alejandro would make it back to Bolivia. He had a lot riding on it. His spirits were dampened with the news that fighters from the United States Navy had intercepted the plane. Speculation now centered on whether the United States could or would shoot it down as pundit after pundit raised questions about diplomatic status and sovereign territory. This legal talk was becoming boring, and sometime after midnight, Brian fell asleep.

When he awoke early the next morning, the TV was still on. The news was that the jet that Reyes and Castillo had stolen had crashed in the Caribbean. At first light, the Coast Guard and the navy would be mounting a search for the wreckage. The navy pilots who had been following the plane reported that the jet aircraft was going at a high rate of speed when it hit the water. The crash would not be survivable to anyone on board.

Brian's primary emotion the night before had been anxiety. Now it was deep depression. He reached for his pills and took two. There would be no big payout or estate in Bolivia. He would not meet the young girl who wanted to be his friend. He had no job and his future looked bleak. He tried several times to reflect on positive thoughts. So far, the FBI hadn't arrested him. His Spanish language lessons were going well, and he had $92,000 hidden away. Brian thought that perhaps he could still go to Bolivia. He wouldn't be able to afford an estate, but maybe he could learn the language well enough to get a good job. Maybe he could find a way to sell the ricin. It must be worth a fortune to the right buyer. But how would he even find these people? Brian debated whether he should contact Xavier Batista, the person who originally recruited him into the methamphetamine trade. Xavier might know the right people. Maybe Xavier could set him up making crystal meth again. Too many thoughts were going through his mind. The Kyri-Laison was making him crazy.

For the remainder of the morning, he looked for things to do. He studied his Spanish lessons for a time. He played some video games until he was bored and then decided to check his email. Brian didn't check it everyday, so he liked to read it oldest first. The first message was from his high school class secretary inviting him and his classmates to their ten-year reunion. The reunion committee postponed it from the previous September because of the terrorist attacks. The new date was four weeks away. The location was the same but the theme was now Mardi Gras. Brian thought the last thing in the world he wanted to do was go to his high school reunion. His high school days sucked. He had few friends, and his classmates constantly bullied and mocked him. One in particular was the class secretary, a popular girl with a mean streak. It was in high school when he was prescribed the first of dozens of anti-depressant and anti-anxiety drugs that he used in the intervening years. The class reunion would have been bad enough when it was a barbecue last September, but Mardi Gras where everyone would probably act more obnoxious than usual would be too much. He definitely wasn't going.

The next email was from his sister, looking to borrow money from him again. Brian was running out of ways to say no. Occasionally, he would send her some cash. This was usually when his mother told him not to. His mother never gave his sister any money. Yet, she would send all she had to that abomination that she called a church.

Brian deleted the next eight emails that found their way through his spam filter. They were the usual offers for enlarging body parts, contest entry winners, new music, and phishing attempts to steal his identity. He wondered if anyone actually fell for this stuff. People seemed to him to be so gullible. That included some of his family members, namely his mother.

The last email was another one from the high school class secretary. The subject line was "DO NOT COME!" Brian thought, *what is this?* He read the message then slammed shut his expensive notebook computer. Hearing a crack—fearing he had broken the LCD screen—he carefully opened it again. To his relief, there was no damage. He thought, *that bitch.* The message from the class secretary said that the prior email message inviting him to the class reunion was a mistake. Perverts and felons were not welcome. Brian thought that maybe he might use some of the ricin on his former classmates. He didn't have many friends in high school. It would be nice to get back at those bastards who made his life miserable. And, all his tormenters would be in one spot. Brian remembered the deputy sheriff who slapped him in the back of the head a couple of weeks before. He'll probably be there too.

Brian was depressed again. His life was in the crapper. It was perhaps only a matter of time before the FBI found out about him anyway. Maybe he would attend his class reunion but not as an invited guest. This last thought made him feel better. All of a sudden, he was hungry. He asked his mother if she would make him some dinner.

Their dinner conversation took its usual form. His mother had given her monthly allotment away to the church again. A few years before his father committed suicide, he bought a large life insurance policy with the stipulation that the company would pay death benefits in monthly installments instead of in one lump sum. It was a good thing reflected Brian. By now, his mother would have given it all away.

"Brian, I need some money to pay some bills."

"You just got your check."

"I sent a donation to Divine Heart."

"How much did you send this time?"

"I don't want to argue about it again, Brian. It's my money."

Brian's mother belonged to the Divine Heart Unity Church, which he considered a sham. She would make him drive her to Saturday services every week. Brian believed that his mother suffered from agoraphobia, although she wouldn't admit it. The only time she would leave the house was to tend her garden or go to that monstrosity she called the cathedral. Since it was the only time she would venture out of their home, he went along with it. He would take her there every Saturday. What he didn't go along with, was the church bilking his mother out of all her money. She no longer had any credit cards. She used all her available credit, and the lenders refused to increase her limits.

Earlier in the week, Brian made a call to the church. He explained the situation, and asked them not to accept any more donations from his mother. Some functionary there told him that his mother had the right to spend her money the way she wished. If she chose to give it to the church, it would be a fine thing to do. Brian then called the insurance company, and after an hour of explaining things to four different people, they told him there was nothing they could do. They suggested he could hire a lawyer to gain guardianship over her. Brian wasn't going to do that. He had spent enough on legal fees trying to keep himself out of jail for that thing with the girl on the internet.

Tomorrow was Saturday so Brian asked his mother, "Do you still want to go to services, tomorrow?"

"Oh yes. I want to hear what Brother Lucas has to say about the tragedies."

"Ma, why do you want to listen to that guy? He's a fraud. All he wants is your money."

"Brian, DON'T SAY THAT!"

"Ma, do you think God would set it up this way?"

Brian himself was an agnostic but he could make a religious argument nonetheless.

"Brian, you have to have faith."

"Faith in what?"

"Faith in God!"

"No, you mean I have to have faith in the frauds who claim to speak for God."

"I don't want to talk about this anymore," his mother said as she stood up to go back and watch her Friday night reality shows. "Put the dishes in the dishwasher."

Brian was furious and took another pill. He didn't know what he would do if the medication quit working. He remembered how badly he felt as a teenager before they diagnosed him with severe depression. He supposed mental illness could run in a family. His sister, who he hadn't seen in years, was bi-polar and his father committed suicide when he was fifteen. His mother was a borderline agoraphobic and addicted to giving her money to that church. Perhaps tomorrow, he'll go talk to the church people in person while his mother is at services.

35

BROTHER LUCAS WAS STANDING all alone on the revolving stage of the immense cathedral after practicing the newly prepared sermon on why God works in mysterious ways. This was one of his favorite themes. He would deliver it four times, twice on Saturday and twice on Sunday. Brother Lucas expected the typical high turnout for both days. Tragedies were good for increasing church attendance, and there was a new one this week. Nevertheless, Brother Lucas couldn't remember any service in the last six months where a seat was available. He recently read a local Jacksonville newspaper article that he had the fourth largest congregation in the country. Brother Lucas didn't know how one could calculate that statistic, but he knew he had a huge following. His televised sermons now reached thousands of people every Sunday morning.

Brother Lucas looked over the empty cathedral. It was 7:00 PM, and he still had a lot to do. On the other hand, this was his favorite time to be in the glorious building, so he lingered there for a few more minutes. After almost two years, he was still in awe. It was a magnificent structure—in the shape of a giant pyramid, nearly 25 stories of gold colored glass. The tip of the pyramid was made of a crystalline material. It acted as a prism changing the sunlight into its spectral colors. As the sun moved, this light would filter across the different rows of parishioners and bathe them in a surreal glow. Many people told him they felt like they were at the end of a rainbow and would wait in line for hours for one of those special seats.

The edifice was unique. From his place in the center of the church, over five thousand seats surrounded him. The stage would rotate throughout the service. Large Jumbotrons, situated high up on each wall, carried his likeness as he spoke. He always found it amusing to see himself twenty feet tall as he talked to the congregation.

It was time to go. His sister Evelyn, who was also the church's office manager, was waiting for him with a pre-production DVD copy of the fourth iteration of his most famous sermon. This one should be special, Lucas thought. The production company shot it in front of a blue screen. They added backgrounds and special effects later. Evelyn had already viewed it and told him it was fantastic.

Lucas left the main structure and walked down the covered walkway to the office area. Three other buildings surrounded the large pyramid. They housed the food court, a movie theater, gift shops and the church offices. Evelyn was waiting in the office complex.

When he arrived, he saw that she was alone. The remainder of the office staff, now totaling fifty-two, had gone home for the day.

"Dad called about the tee shirts again," said Evelyn.

"Same thing...every time we add a new design he complains."

His father was a retired Unitarian minister who now ran the church's gift shop and other concessions. The commercialization of the ministry as he called it bothered him. The tee shirts bearing the likeness of the pyramid cathedral with various "God friendly" slogans always seemed to catch his ire. Lucas didn't have any problem with the shirts. This was a big revenue item. It would be common to see at least a thousand people attending the service wearing one.

"He's gonna go off when he sees the new hats," said Evelyn.

"Handle it, you're his favorite."

"Lucas, don't start with that."

Lucas Christopher Dodge was the middle child of the Reverend Samuel Dodge and his wife Ester. He grew up in St. Cloud, Minnesota and attended the University of Minneapolis. After he graduated with a degree in marketing and jobs hard to find, he took a position with a Toyota dealership in their new vehicle department. He did well. Lucas, as his younger brother referred to him, was a collector of people. He had many acquaintances but few friends. Lucas had the habit of telling people what they wanted to hear and promising to help them. He rarely delivered on his promises. Nonetheless, this trait seemed to work for him in the car business. It wasn't long before the owner offered him an assistant sales manager position. Lucas turned down the job. As he put it to his disappointed bosses, "I'm sick of freezing my ass off in Minnesota. I can sell cars anywhere." They asked him where he was going and he said, "I'm going to Disney World," and set out for Florida the next day.

Lucas wasn't in a big hurry and didn't make it a marathon driving experience, like the four other trips he made to Florida during his college spring breaks. He took many back roads along the way. While traveling these country byways, Lucas saw a multitude of small churches, some no bigger than a two car garage. Many had the three simple white crosses in front calling attention to their presence. There were also the pro-life billboards along the route. He found one that was particularly interesting to him. It said, "Abortion Stops a Beating Heart." He reasoned that it was probably true. Lucas didn't have a strong opinion on the subject one way or the other. He knew others did though. He was the son of a minister, however his religious convictions weren't that strong. As far as he was concerned, being a member of the clergy was a sure way to become poor. That is except for those televangelists. He admired them for being able to convince people to give up their hard-earned money. As a car salesperson, Lucas knew how difficult that could be.

On the third day of the trip, he was crossing the Georgia border into Florida when he saw that same sign again about the beating heart. He thought if someone could figure a way to bring the pro and anti-abortion people together, it could be lucrative. Lucas stopped for the night and stayed in a small express motel outside Jacksonville. He awoke in the middle of the night after dreaming about the sign.

Lucas didn't go to Disney World. The next morning while reading the local Florida Times Union, he saw an ad for auto sales people. The dealer was offering sign-on bonuses for experience, so he applied for the job. The Jacksonville Toyota dealership hired him immediately after management checked his references and sales history. He was there six months and became friendly with one of the other salespeople. His new friend, Ernie, was working to support his storefront church that he had started in a small run down strip mall. Since the dealership didn't open on Sundays until noon, Lucas would frequently attend his friend's small church. But, not too many others did. When it was slow at the dealership, sometimes Lucas would help Ernie prepare his Sunday sermons. One day Ernie asked Lucas if he could minister to his small congregation. Ernie and his wife had to be away for a family wedding. Lucas figured, why not.

The sermon he gave that day made Lucas one of the most popular preachers in the country and a millionaire twenty times over.

"Evelyn, where's the DVD?"

"It's in the small conference room."

Lucas walked in and the TV was on. The staff was in and out all day catching the news reports on the New Orleans terrorist attack.

"Do you think the threat is over?" asked his sister.

"I hope not. Tragedies are good for the God business."

"You know Lucas, you can be very irreverent at times. I'm telling you one of these days somebody's going to hear you."

"All right. Where's the DVD?"

"It's in the player."

His sister turned on the player for him and switched the monitor to DVD mode. They listened to the introductory music.

"I like the music," remarked Lucas. "Where did it come from?"

"I believe they said it was a jingle from an old Buick commercial."

Lucas supposed that was appropriate.

The video began with Lucas standing on the stage. Since the DVD was shot in front of a blue screen, they were able to have camera angles that couldn't be reproduced if the video was actually shot in the cathedral.

"Do you think they got the eyes right?" he asked his sister.

"Yeah, I think they look good."

Lucas paid particular attention to the appearance of his eyes. He wore contact lenses even though his vision was 20/20. He liked that glassy-eyed look that most television ministers appeared to have.

On the DVD, Brother Lucas began his famous sermon. It hadn't changed that much over the years. The message was the same, but now it took on a messianic quality.

"I'm sure you've all heard the old saying that God works in mysterious ways. If God had a question and answer session once a month, many of us would ask things like: Why do bad things happen to good people? What happens when we die? Is it Darwin or Genesis that's correct? Are we alone in the Universe? And to some of you, the most important question you need to know is…do dogs go to heaven too?"

The production company added a laugh track and Evelyn remarked, "I think the timing is spot on."

"I agree. It's much better than last time…much more subtle."

"Exactly."

The DVD continued…

"However, the greatest mystery of all involves an issue, which has caused more problems among families since brother fought brother in the civil war. There have not been many more contentious debates than about a woman's right to an abortion. Moreover, not since the civil war have people so vigorously disagreed about an issue with such varied opinions. In some cases, families and marriages have broken up over this matter.

However, this debate is less about the medical procedure than about the concept of when does life begin. This question is at the root of the issue. So let us try to answer that today. When does life begin?

The pro-life people say it's at conception. The pro-choice lobby claims the question doesn't matter. It's about the viability of the fetus. However, both concepts share one thing in common, they are subjective—both groups draw an artificial line in the sand.

If God gave us the answer to the question, when does life begin, it would sure make it easier for people of conscience to form an opinion on abortion as well as other weighty matters like embryonic stem cell research and certain forms of birth control.

Well I would submit to you that God did give us the answer. There is no real mystery here. When we ponder the question about when does life begin, we are not talking about life in general. We're not thinking about when the first organisms rose out from the primordial ooze. What we are talking about is when a human life begins, not so much in the biological sense but in the metaphysical.

I think most of us could agree, what distinguishes us from all other animals on earth is our soul. Our soul makes us human. So when do we get this soul? Some would say that the soul enters the body at conception. Others would say that the soul enters the body when a baby is born. Some would even say that the soul enters the body when the baby is viable, whatever that means.

We have a soul. We know that. We also know that God gives us this soul. God also decides when he wants to take it from us. I think we can reach an agreement on when the soul leaves the body. It's when we die. Yet, that begs another question. What is the definition of death? Is a person dead after the last cell divides in their body? Is the person dead when there are no brain waves? Is a person dead when they stop breathing? No. The general agreement is a person is dead after their very last heartbeat—after all the so-called heroic measures are taken. The time of death is recorded by the medical community after the very last heartbeat. There is some anecdotal evidence from those who have had near-death experiences. Some report watching from above as doctors worked on their body. Some say they followed the light. Some even say they saw other family members and friends who have died before them.

As I look at all of you, I see many heads bobbing in agreement. You've heard these stories."

At this point, the production company panned the audience and also spliced in a subtle music track. Lucas paused the DVD and asked Evelyn, "Do you think the music is too much?"

"No, no. Lucas it's good. It sets up the next shot... watch."

"The concept of the soul leaving the body at death is almost universal in all modern religions. The idea of death being after your last heartbeat isn't subjective. It's measurable through an EKG machine or a doctor's stethoscope, checking for a pulse or even from putting one's ear against another's chest. Therefore, I would submit that a human life ends after the very last heartbeat. I now see agreement on your faces."

The video changed to tight shots of individuals with angelic faces, their heads bobbing in agreement. "Are those real parishioners or professional actors?" asked Lucas.

"No they're professionals. The producer gave me a number of headshots to pick from. Those were the ones I chose."

"Did they use the blue screen?"

"I believe so."

"Looks realistic."

"I know."

Lucas pushed play and the DVD continued.

> *"Now if it is clear to us that the soul leaves the body after our very last heartbeat. Would it not make sense to believe that our soul enters our body at our very first? When the finger of God comes down and touches that tiny heart to start it beating—our Creator bestows on us our most precious possession—a gift that God gives to no other living creature, our soul. It's truly miraculous. Up to that point there were only cells dividing, like all other life on the planet.*
>
> *A heartbeat is precise. It's either there or not, no confusion, no controversy, no judgment calls, only the little miracle that God gives us. It's almost inbred in us that the heart and soul are connected in some special way. Poets and philosophers have written about the heart being the gateway to the soul. You've all heard people using such phases as the "it's the heart and soul of it."*

Lucas pushed pause again. "They edited my sermon!"

"Lucas, we talked about this and you agreed. That
entire trivia thing about the human heart isn't needed.
Just watch, and you'll see the passage flows better."

> "We make rules and boundaries for ourselves as
> well as others make them for us. Sometimes it's the
> government. Sometimes it's a group in which we be-
> long. Sometimes it's our religion. You would agree
> that without rules and boundaries, life would be cha-
> otic for most of us. We are happy most of the time
> when these boundaries are made for us that is unless
> we are a teenager."

Lucas noticed that the production company spliced
in a cutaway of people laughing at the remark. "Do you
think the teenager remark is that funny?" asked Lucas.

"Not when you've heard it 300 times. But if it's the
first time, I would think it would be humorous."

"I don't know."

"Do you want me to have them cut it?"

"No. But on the next iteration, let's revisit this."

The DVD continued...

> "For the most part, these boundaries make our
> daily lives easier. Then why is it that the concept of
> abortion is so contentious. Much of the argument has
> been about who makes the rules. Is it government, re-
> ligion or ourselves? It's a dilemma. Where do we put

that line? Since the Supreme Court ruling Rowe vs. Wade, the line is not zero abortions or unlimited abortions. Many states have set limitations, and the medical profession has weighed in on the matter. Naturally, the most vociferous would-be rule makers have been the women's and religious groups. Nevertheless, many of us have turmoil within ourselves. What rules and boundaries do I make for myself?

I've suffered this turmoil until I realized if I were a woman, I would never want to stop a beating heart. This would be my preference. But naturally, sometimes life intrudes, so exceptions must be made. I believe the normal exceptions of rape, incest and life of the mother are valid and appropriate. On the other hand, after a fetus's first heartbeat, I would also agree with one of our former presidents when he said, "Abortion should be safe, legal and rare."

I have no problem terminating a pregnancy before the first heartbeat. I believe the soul is not there. This leads me not to oppose stem cell research and things like the morning after pill, which to some is considered an abortion. For those who believe the line should be drawn at conception, what about things like in-vitro fertilization and other medical procedures? Could the soul exist in a test tube or Petri dish or a vat of liquid nitrogen?

On the other hand, there are those who would stop a heart from beating out of convenience with the rationalization that the fetus in not viable. Yet, the point of viability changes with every new pre-natal and pediatric medical advance. Both conception and viability are poor places to set the line for terminating a pregnancy. At the very least, they are imprecise, subjective and confusing. Sometimes they are even a moving target. When these conditions are present around any issue, most often contentiousness ensues.

Is it possible to bring everyone to my way of thinking? Of course not. Some people have a vested interest in their position on the issue. Religious leaders and advocacy groups many times have a stake on one side or the other. Some even have a financial interest in keeping the controversy alive. It's also been a recruitment tool for many political, religious and social organizations. Nevertheless, people are looking for a reasonable logical answer that they can believe and support without any consternation. I offer to them what was revealed to me in a dream, the concept of the first heartbeat as the answer..."

As Lucas watched himself tell the embellished story of his trip to Florida and the circumstances around his revelation, he though about what happened after he gave this sermon in Ernie's small strip mall church. The next Sunday twice as many people came. A person asked Ernie if Lucas could deliver the sermon again. Ernie hadn't heard it, so he agreed. Over the next few months, several churches in the area invited Lucas to do his sermon. Lucas accepted the invitations because he thought it might be a way to birddog some customers. Church had always been a good place to flush out car buyers. Lucas had a nose for that sort of thing. He was right. His customer base was growing while everyone else's at the dealership was waning. One of his customers who had heard Lucas speak owned a small publishing company and asked Lucas if he could make the sermon into a book. Lucas did what he was asked. The publisher then had some commentary added by a ghost writer.

At first, Lucas gave the booklet away free. He would stand outside churches and hand the small book to anyone who would take it. After awhile it became a favorite in the religious circles through word of mouth and the internet. When people started buying it, the publisher put some money into marketing the book. It went mainstream, eventually becoming a best seller.

The first heartbeat theme seemed to resonate with many people. Lucas was surprised how many people seem to embrace his hypothesis and how it came to be the basis for his church.

He started his own ministry called the Divine Heart Unity Church. He based it on the Unitarian philosophy that he grew up with. It was non-denominational. All faiths were welcome, including non-Christians. With the proceeds from the sale of his book, Lucas used some basic marketing principles including direct mail and radio advertising. He leased a large building from the owner of a defunct furniture store, which served as his church for the first twelve years. He would go to a local studio in Jacksonville to do his radio show. However, when the television people approached him, he wanted his potential donors to see him in a special place. Lucas hired an architect who he found out later had worked on the Luxor Hotel project in Las Vegas. When the architect first approached him with the pyramid design, Lucas thought the fellow was crazy. No religious place Lucas ever saw had taken that shape. The architect reminded Lucas about the pyramids of Egypt—how they still evoke to many, a sense of awe—a symbol of the afterlife. Lucas thought about it and eventually went with the architect's design. Lucas even had an oxygen system similar to the ones found in casinos installed to help his congregation stay alert and awake during the services.

When the massive cathedral was finished, his congregation and the public in general loved it. He built the structure along I-95 in an old orange grove fifteen miles south of Jacksonville. The cathedral was so special, it became a stop for many Florida vacationers who visited the area's beaches and attractions.

"What do you think?" Evelyn asked when the video was over.

"I like it," replied Lucas. "The fund raising hooks are more subtle. Tell the production company to rush five thousand copies. I think online business will continue to be brisk for the next few weeks because of the latest attack."

"Okay."

"Also tell Chet to move up the telemarketing campaign. Have him start it right away. Let's get the people in a giving mood."

36

IT WAS SATURDAY MORNING and Kerry Sterling was at her desk at the Hoover Building. She counted herself lucky that she still had her job. Now that Castillo's plane crashed, the media wouldn't be able to accuse the FBI of ineptitude for letting the fugitives get away. There would also be no long drawn out legal process. The attorney general would not have to negotiate extradition. Flamboyant lawyers would not turn the trial into a circus and indictment of U.S. policies, and the endless appeal after appeal would not take place before the country finally executed Reyes and Castillo. While closure of the story would not be immediate, the death of Castillo and Reyes would certainly hasten it, thought Kerry. This was good for her career. Kerry thought that the FBI did a good job in the investigation. But, timing, bad luck and most of all Nancy Noonan, interfered with the disposition of the case.

The taskforce was scheduled to meet in an hour to wrap things up. Kerry thought that the taskforce was a bad idea from the start. In fact, this is the only point that the deputy director conceded in her two-hour dressing down. Kerry thought her performance, while not stellar, was adequate and found the lengthy reprimand to be unfair. However as he told her, he had six months to go before his retirement. Somebody had to shoulder the blame, and it wasn't going to be him. Kerry knew that the Monday morning quarterbacks were still out in full force, and she vowed she was not going to give them the bullets to shoot her with. She would make doubly sure there were no loose ends before she closed the investigation.

Kerry spent the next hour reviewing the information then headed to the meeting room. When she walked in, she was surprised to see there were only six people there. Apparently, the membership had dwindled since there would not be many accolades to pass around. She would have liked it better if there was one fewer. She could do without Nancy Noonan who was back sitting at the head of conference table.

"Nice of you to join us," remarked Nancy.

Kerry looked at her watch. She was on time. Apparently, Nancy was still smarting from their argument after Castillo's plane took off on the taxiway. Kerry told her that if she hadn't interfered with the legal diplomatic bullshit, they would have stopped and boarded the plane right away. Of course, Nancy had a different take on the situation, and the fight that ensued between them was intensive and harsh. There was no dearth of name-calling and insults. They only stopped when the FBI driver got out of the car, and they both realized they looked bad in front of a subordinate.

Jeff said, "I think everyone is here whose going to come."

"Where do we begin?" inquired Nancy.

Matt looking back and forth at Kerry and Nancy offered, "My first inclination is to have this taskforce put out a final report that we all can agree upon. It will do none of us any good to snipe at one another in the media and the press. Can we agree on that?"

Everyone in attendance nodded his or her head. Matt continued, "I will be happy to write the first draft."

Kerry thought, *God Bless Matt Palena*. Nobody put up any argument so Kerry said, "I think we have to discuss some of the investigation's open items."

"What open items?" asked Nancy.

"We can't be positive that the attacks will stop with Reyes and Castillo. There may be others involved. The motel owner told us that three other people stayed there with Reyes. We believe we found one buried on the at the old plant. Two others, a Latino and an American are still unidentified."

Larry Simmons, the CIA member, who was still with the group said, "That's a hell of a loose end. Is it possible that there is more ricin out there?"

Jeff answered for Kerry, "I did some rough calculations when we determined the method they employed to process the castor beans into ricin. By the way, it was a patented process, but that's another story. Anyway, if the former owner of the castor oil facility was correct about the amount of waste mash missing, there could be five or six pounds of the poison still out there."

Kerry sighed audibly. "Are you kidding me?"

Matt said, "Kerry it could have been on the aircraft with Reyes and Castillo when it went down."

"But we'll never know since we can't examine the wreckage."

"You're right there."

Nancy interjected, "Wait a minute. I assured my boss that this mess was over. The inauguration is next week. She would like to keep her job in the new administration. So let's not go creating an assortment of problems. And besides, the public can't take much more of this."

Before Kerry had time to respond to Nancy, Matt interrupted and asked, "Kerry is there any evidence that the two unidentified individuals were actually in the plant?"

Jeff answered for her again, "Let me speak to that. We found two partial fingerprints; neither belonged to Reyes or Castillo."

"That's troubling," commented Matt.

"Come on now," said Nancy.

Kerry challenged her, "Nancy, we don't need more surprises. I'm not closing this case until every loose end is tied up."

Nancy changed the subject. "What's the latest body count from New Orleans?"

Matt explained, "We were lucky there. The kitchen staff only served twenty cups of the ricin-laced gumbo. Nineteen out of the twenty people who ate it, became sick. Thirteen died."

Nancy asked, "Was the rap singer one of them?"

"Yes he was."

Jeff Davis turned to Larry Simmons and asked, "Are we clear on the motive for the attacks. The press has been speculating that it was revenge. What's your take on that?"

"We did some more investigating. It is possible that the DEA may have had something to do with the death of the Castillo and Reyes family."

"Really?" exclaimed Nancy.

"It looks that way," answered Larry. "There was an informer who said that the DEA paid him for information about Castillo's habits and whereabouts."

"Can we believe him?"

"Who knows?"

"If that's true, why didn't they go after the DEA first? Why attack the political convention?" asked Kerry.

"I guess we'll never know the answer to that."

Nancy said, "All those people dead. I've been saying for the last twenty years that the war on drugs was a farce, and we should abolish the DEA. I know of countless cases of abuse I could tell you about. I was thinking of writing a book about it. Maybe I will now."

Kerry without trying to hide the sarcasm mumbled, "We would expect nothing less."

Matt asked, "Can we wrap this up. I'd like to get back to Atlanta this evening."

"What do we want to do about the five million dollar reward? Two hundred thousand leads came into the FBI hotline," said Kerry.

"Did anyone point us to Castillo or Reyes?" asked Larry.

"We're still sorting through them. But I don't believe that any civilian gave us enough information to claim any part of it."

"I say we rescind it," said Nancy.

Trying to avoid an argument between the two women, Jeff said, "Why don't you run it by the deputy director and see what he wants to do."

That seemed like a reasonable idea to Kerry. There was no further discussion about it. Matt said he would send them a draft of the final report as soon as possible. He would begin working on it right away on his flight back to Atlanta. Everyone agreed not to talk to the press again until they reviewed Matt's report. To Kerry's relief, there was no talk about the taskforce ever meeting again. However, they did schedule a conference call in four weeks time.

37

BRIAN WAS SITTING IN THE CAR waiting for the
services to be over. His mother would give him the all
the details of Brother Lucas's sermon. Brian detested the
man almost as much as he did his former classmates.
Lately, he was thinking more and more about how he
could exact revenge on those classmates. He hadn't seen
most of them for years, but those miserable days in high
school still weighed heavily on his psyche. He was sure
that he would not be taking the expensive Kyri-Laison
if they hadn't tortured him everyday in school. This
thought brought to mind his two most pressing problems. He needed more of the drug and the money to
buy the expensive pharmaceutical. He was taking five
times the prescribed dose on a daily basis. Each pill cost
him almost five dollars apiece. He was now taking fifteen tablets a day. Adding to this cost was the doctor's
visits. Many physicians were leery to prescribe the drug
because of its adverse side effects. To get multiple pre-

scriptions, he had to visit numerous doctors, some as far away as Orlando. He was currently on the patient list of six different providers. It was an expensive habit, and he had to find some way to pay for it. At this rate, he would be spending more than $30,000 over the next year on the drug. It was also costing him another $5,000 a month paying his and his mother's bills. He reckoned it wouldn't be long before most of the $90,000 was gone. He didn't want to abandon the thought of moving to Bolivia. He needed to make some money.

When he was working for Alejandro Reyes, it wasn't a problem. Before that, cooking crystal meth gave him a good income. Occasionally he would purloin some of the meth and sell it on the street to add to his wages.

Brian contemplated cutting back on his medication. He knew his dosage had increased to dangerous levels. Doctors lectured him frequently about the adverse side effects. They wanted to make sure he could recognize them if they occurred. So far, Brian hadn't noticed any of the problems associated with the drug, like paranoia, periods of intense euphoria and sociopathic tendencies. Still, he did question his judgment from time to time. Impaired judgment was another reported side effect. He thought he should watch that more closely.

The problem now was how to pay for the drug. He faced the same dilemma as before. Nobody wanted to hire him because of his criminal record. He didn't want to go back into the dangerous and risky crystal meth business. If they caught him, he could go to prison. He would also have to contact Xavier who was the only person that could link him to Alejandro. Brian contemplated these things while he waited in the car. He decided to take the chance. Later he would go looking for Xavier. That may be his only alternative.

It was almost time for the church services to be over. His mother would be one of the last people out of the building. She wouldn't leave her seat until all the parishioners were gone. Brian waited until almost everyone left. Then he walked up to the entrance where his mother was waiting and escorted her to the car. They did their normal Saturday food shopping routine, and then Brian brought her home.

After dropping off his mother, he went looking for Xavier. He spent most of the day searching the normal haunts. When not finding him, Brian thought maybe it was a sign that hooking up with Xavier wasn't' such a good idea. However, there was a meeting of the therapy group that night. He thought that maybe Xavier would be there. Brian was no longer required to attend so he hadn't been to the meetings for some time.

Brian bought himself a quick meal and headed over there. He found Xavier Batista in the parking lot sitting in his pick-up truck. Brian knocked on the passenger window. Xavier looked surprised to see him and signaled him it was okay to get in.

"I thought you would be long gone by now," observed Xavier.

It was obvious to Brian that Xavier had heard about Alejandro and linked him to the attacks. Brian didn't even bother asking him about a job making crystal meth and instead went right to the idea of selling the ricin.

"I have some of the stuff," said Brian.

"On you now?" said Xavier looking like he was going to jump out of the truck. The media attention had made proximity to ricin seem akin to radiation. "No, no, no," answered Brian. "I need a place to sell it."

"What's that got to do with me?"

"I thought you might know someone."

"Are you crazy? I don't want to get involved with that. Besides how much could you get?"

"I'm sure to the right buyer, maybe a half million."

"Are you bullshitting me?"

"No," Brian answered, seeing he now had Xavier's attention.

Xavier was quiet for a while and then said, "I might know some people. They trade guns for drugs. I could ask around. I want a sample."

Brian thought about this. There was no way he was going to give Xavier any ricin. The guy might kill himself. It wasn't safe. Then Brian thought about the small testing vials. He could give him one of those. Brian explained about the vials.

"How much ricin do you have?"

"Two pounds," Brian answered. He had more than that but he thought he'd hold some back. He didn't want to give up the delicious notion of attacking his former classmates...not yet anyway. "I can get the ricin while you're in the meeting," offered Brian.

Xavier agreed to wait for him in case he was late returning. Brian immediately headed over to the storage locker. He had 24-hour access. What Brian didn't know was that Xavier, instead of going to the meeting, followed him.

While he was in the storage facility, he rubbed the outside of the glass vial with a solution known to render ricin harmless. He had taken some supplies along with a brand new hazmat suit from the old plant when he left. He had stored everything in the locker.

Brian went back to the meeting place and saw Xavier waiting in his truck. Brian thought that maybe the session ended early. He gave the vial to Xavier with instructions on how to handle it. When he was satisfied that Xavier understood the danger, he left the man in the parking lot.

Brian didn't feel like going home. He rode around entertaining wild thoughts about how he could dose his former classmates. He supposed most people had fantasies about killing. Of course, only a few went through with it. Brian knew he was partly responsible for the death of many hundreds of people. He knew he could have quit making ricin any time he wished. The veiled threats hadn't scared him. It was the money and the chance of a new life that kept him at the old plant. After a while, he wasn't even afraid of being caught. It was only when he saw Alejandro's photo on television, did the fear come back, although it was short-lived. Now he was back taking chances again.

Brian began second-guessing himself. His decision to bring Xavier into the picture might not have been wise. He didn't know if he could trust him. The authorities may have a reward for those involved in the attack, and Xavier may want to collect it. However, since the general and Alejandro were now dead, the FBI would probably not be as diligent in pursuing the case.

Brian chased the negative thoughts out of his head and tuned the radio, stopping at a hip-hop station. They were playing a tribute to FourJ who was a victim of the latest attack in New Orleans. Brian didn't feel any empathy for him or the other victims who died. It was not in his nature anymore. Perhaps he *was* suffering from adverse side effects of Kyri-Laison and becoming a sociopath. He would have to do some research on the internet when he went home.

Brian started playing different scenarios in his mind about how he could poison his former classmates. His job working with Alejandro was in the "back room" behind the scenes. He didn't have to be creative. All he had to do was follow a formula someone else created. Alejandro was the one with the big ideas. Brian knew it would be a challenge for him. He wasn't imaginative; he was analytical. That's why he chose biochemistry as a profession. Brian decided that he would put a plan together anyway. Whether he could make one good enough, he didn't know. If he did, would he have the wherewithal to carry it through? It was a test for him. Brian thought it would be fun.

38

BEFORE BRIAN WENT HOME, he took a ride by the hotel that would be hosting the reunion. It was near the airport and business people used it for meetings and small conferences. On the weekends however, it would cater to an assortment of weddings, reunions and other social events. Brian parked the car in the large lot. He didn't see any security personnel patrolling around, but there were a number of video cameras mounted high up on light poles. They were stationary, and from his vantage point, there appeared to be a number of blind spots.

Brian walked into the large atrium. There was a bar in the lobby overlooking an indoor pool, so he sat down and ordered a non-alcoholic beer. He preferred rum to beer, but he didn't want the police to stop him for a DUI. He wasn't taking any chances after the narrow escape with the sheriff's deputy. He looked around and could see some of the meeting rooms. However, none looked large enough to accommodate a reunion or wedding. Nevertheless, a steady stream of people exiting a hallway told him that there must be more rooms in back. It was Saturday night, and there seemed to be a great deal of activity at the hotel.

Brian finished his beer and looked for the men's restroom. On his way, he passed a number of large rooms filled with people. There was at least one wedding still in progress. He could see three entrances that served the hotel's conference area in addition to the way he came in. Brian wondered if Alejandro had gone through the same process when he explored his locations. Brian reasoned he probably did. Brian left the hotel by way of the north entrance and walked to his car.

On the way home, he thought again about how he might do it. The reunion was still three weeks away. He would need to think of something. The idea of filling salt shakers wouldn't work again. He wondered if there was anyone left in America that was salting his or her food. Homeland Security had banned the sale of balloons—as if anyone would try that again thought Brian. He smiled thinking about how much opposition Homeland Security took for that decision. That government agency wasn't at all popular with the mothers of America and their children.

As he understood from the news reports about the New Orleans attack, Alejandro had put the ricin directly into the food that was cooking. That wouldn't work for him. He had no idea how commercial kitchens operated. Condiments other than salt seemed like the best bet. He could always soak the small packages of sugar substitute in a solution of ricin. If he were careful, it would be almost undetectable. However, that gambit would work better for a morning meeting where most everyone was drinking coffee.

By time Brian arrived home, he had come to the realization that this wasn't going to be easy. He didn't sleep well that night. Since he was wide-awake, he began going over in his mind again how he could use the ricin. Airborne attacks were out of the question, and skin and eye contact was largely ineffective. It had to be ingestion. He had three weeks to come up with something. The reunion was the Saturday before Mardi Gras. Brian thought it was probably why the bitch and her friends picked it as a theme. Maybe he could use that somehow. Brian got up, turned on the light and started writing. Sometimes this helped his thinking process. He thought Mardi Gras is known for drinking, partying, beads, making a lot of noise, and acting stupid. He himself went one year with a graduate student group. He had a good time. Brian looked at the little cardboard horn he kept on his dresser. It was a memento from that trip. Brian thought about the horn. Maybe there was an idea there. Tomorrow he would go to a party store and check it out. He fell asleep with that thought in mind.

The next day he headed out to a large discount store that had a section for party favors. He saw similar horns and noise making devices and bought a sampling. The whole bill was less than ten bucks so it wasn't a problem. Once home again, he turned on his stereo with the sound just below his mother's tolerance level and began playing with the noisemakers and other paraphernalia.

The best bet seemed to be the things called blowouts. They were coiled paper ribbons that changed into a foot long tube when you blew into them and then snapped back to a coiled shape again. They've been around for years and were a favorite at children's birthday parties. He saw people with them in New Orleans at Mardi Gras, and he remembered they called them *serpentins*. Brian noticed that when he was playing with them, he would consistently blow them out several times in succession, and he would always take a breath in between each blow. He reckoned this was perfect. If he treated the plastic mouthpiece with ricin, he could possibly a-chieve inhalation as well as ingestion. They would also be easy to tamper with. He could dilute the ricin with a weak solution of citric acid and swab the entire inside of the plastic mouthpiece. The citric acid would probably add a slight lemony taste, which may activate the person's saliva glands.

Brian's mother made him lunch and remarked about how good a mood he seemed to be in. Brian was happy. Although he only had the germ of a plan now, he had figured out the hardest part. The rest of the afternoon, he put together an outline of all the elements that had to be in place. Brian was back in his comfort zone. From now on it was an analytical exercise—a systematic progression following a fixed formula. Now Brian was confident he could do it. There was only one critical element that could be problematic. How would he get the blowouts into the room? He didn't have any doubt that once they were there and a person had a drink or two, they would use them. It would be a statistical certainty that the most obnoxious of his former classmates would use them first. Brian calculated that he would need approximately 200 of the favors. His graduating class at the private school he attended was less than 250 students. Not all would come but there would be spouses. To be safe, he would need three hundred. He thought that could get costly. Brian did an internet search for online stores that sold party favors. There were plenty. One in particular could custom print the blowouts and gave 72-hour express service from the time of ordering. The store also accepted wires from check cashing establishments. Brian thought this was perfect. He would have his high school name and class year printed on the blowouts. He would have them shipped to a personal mailbox he rented. He used the mailbox so his mother didn't know what magazines he was reading. They also accepted packages and forwarded mail.

Brian spent the rest of the day perfecting the plan. When he was done, he looked it over. He could make this happen if he wanted. He realized this was the first time in his life that he felt in control. He had power. If he decided to kill, there was nothing they could do. Their lives were in his hands. This felt good. It was better than the Kyri-Laison. The constant dull ache that lurked behind his forehead was gone. His body felt strong. He was high.

39

FOR THE NEXT SEVERAL DAYS, the good feelings didn't diminish. Even his mother's constant nagging to go out and find a job didn't ruin his mood. Brian liked feeling this way. He didn't want it to stop. The idea of killing the bastards that made his school days miserable gave him an intense feeling of well being. Brian decided he was going to do it and nobody could stop him.

Instead of using his name, he opened an online account with the party favor supplier under the name of his high school class secretary. He decided against using his personal post office box as the shipping address. It would be too easy to trace back to him. He opened another P.O. box in a different part of town, again using the class secretary's name. He ordered the merchandise that night. The entire order including the custom printing and priority shipping came to less than $85.00 and arrived four days later.

The company did an excellent job. Brian was sure his former classmates would use the blowouts. He now had less than two weeks to prepare, so he immediately set about the task of gathering everything else he needed. He found the citric acid at the health food emporium, the plastic sheeting and other materials at the home store. His plan called for renting a motel room to do the work. Using his home was out of the question. He had no privacy there. Brian reasoned that there would be plenty of motel rooms available near the beach. Tourist season in northern Florida didn't begin until late March. On the other hand, he realized this was not a benefit but a problem. It would look suspicious for a young man to be all alone in an empty motel for a number of days. Surely, some employee would get curious. He realized he would have to go to Orlando where the season starts earlier. While he was thinking this through, Brian was stuck behind a slow moving recreational vehicle. This was annoying him until he realized that could be just the thing he needed. Using an RV as sort of mobile laboratory would be perfect. It would afford him the privacy that he needed, and cleaning it up after would be easier because of the materials they used in construction. He remembered seeing a large billboard advertising RV rentals along I-95.

Brian drove to the interstate and traveled along the highway until he saw the sign. He made note of the location and went directly to the RV dealership. When he inquired about renting a recreational vehicle, they told him the only requirements were a valid license, a credit card and he had to be over 25 years old. Brian spent the next twenty minutes looking over the rental fleet. He decided on a 32-foot fun hauler. Besides having a kitchen and sleeping accommodations, it had a small area in back similar to a garage where one could carry a motorcycle or ATV. This was perfect. When he was through, he could hose out the area. Brian arranged to pick up the RV the next day. The salesperson said he could leave his car there for the three days he was renting.

The next morning, Brian went to his storage locker to get the ricin and the other items he would need to protect himself. As he lifted the heavy padlock to insert the key, he stopped cold. There were deep marks on the hasp. It looked to Brian as if someone tried to cut the lock off with a bolt cutter. They didn't succeed because Brian had purchased the kind that bikers use to protect their expensive motorcycles. He looked at the bottom. There were scratches as if someone attempted to pick the lock. Brian panicked. He got into his car and drove away from the self-storage facility. The authorities must be on to him. For the next two hours, he drove around checking his rearview mirror every minute or so. He even stopped his car several times looking for helicopters and other aircraft. Nobody was following him. He figured maybe it was somebody trying to break into the locker and had nothing to do with the ricin. After a-while, he convinced himself that this was the case and summoned the courage to go back to the storage facility. Still, to be sure, he waited in his car for another half-hour. When he finally removed the lock and opened the metal door, he looked around. Everything was how he left it. Nevertheless, he didn't waste anytime removing the items he needed. He called the RV dealership and told them that he would be a little late but to hold his reservation.

When he arrived later, the sales representative went over the operation of the RV's systems. He then had Brian drive around their large parking lot for a while making sure he could handle the big vehicle. The sales person pronounced him qualified. Brian didn't waste any time in transferring the contents of his car to the RV. Nobody seemed to be paying him any attention. He thought this was probably a common occurrence. When he was done, he drove to a recreational vehicle park near St. Augustine. It was about half full so he figured he wouldn't attract any attention. It took him some time to navigate the large vehicle onto the pad he was assigned and about another hour to make all the hookups. He wished he'd paid more attention when the sales representative went over the RV's systems with him. When he finally had everything working, he set up his lab. Before mixing the solution, he grabbed one of the new blowouts. When he tried it, he noticed two things. The mouthpiece had a dime size diameter, which would take longer to swab. The second thing he noticed was when he stopped blowing the paper tube, the re-curling motion would force air into his mouth something akin to an asthma inhaler. Brian decided it would be easier to drop a small measure of ricin into the four-inch long plastic mouthpiece after he un-curled the paper tube a bit. The ricin would be more lethal this way.

He did his best to measure small amounts of ricin into the *serpentins*. It was difficult at first because the ricin powder was much finer that expected. It was the residue from cleaning the jet pulverizer. He knew he used much too much. Each blowout had enough ricin in it to kill ten people even though it was barely noticeable to anyone looking for it in the tubes. When he was finished, he calculated that he had used less than an ounce of ricin from his stash.

Brian carefully repackaged the blowouts in the plastic bags that originally held them. He spent the next day walking around the RV Park, not doing much of anything except going over in his mind the plan for getting the blowouts into the reunion area. That was four days away. He returned to the RV dealership and unloaded everything into his car. He started back toward the self-storage facility and decided not to go back there. Next to the RV dealership was a similar establishment. Brian went in and rented a smaller storage unit in the climate-controlled section. It had deadbolts so it didn't need a padlock. The clerk issued Brian two keys for which he had to leave a deposit. This was fine with him. However, there wasn't 24-hour access to his assigned locker. Brian didn't think this would be a problem.

After he loaded the unit, he headed home. Brian was feeling productive, so he thought he might try again to get his mother's donation money back from the Divine Heart Unity Church. He made the call and was unsuccessful. A church worker blew him off saying he would have to talk to the office manager. This made Brian a little angry. He thought that he would make a personal visit to the church office manager some Saturday, while his mother attended the service. But, he wasn't going to try it this Saturday. He needed to focus entirely on the reunion.

40

BRIAN DID HIS BEST to keep himself busy the remaining two days. It was hard. Finally Saturday came, and he began to make the final preparations. He didn't bother to take any of his medication. Brian didn't feel like he needed it. This was a good omen—maybe even the start of a new life, he thought.

After a quick trip to the rented storage area, he had the blowouts in his car. Now he was getting nervous.

When he arrived at the hotel, he went into the lobby to see if he could find some indication of where the reunion would be held. There was a TV monitor, scrolling the party's name and the location. He made note of it then walked through the atrium area to find the function room. The reunion was in one of the larger spaces. He looked in and saw that there were at least thirty round tables, all bare. Brian counted eight seats at each table. It was still early in the afternoon so he decided to come back later.

About 4:30, Brian returned to the hotel. This time he didn't use the atrium entrance. There was one closer to the conference area, which was unlocked. He ventured over to the meeting room. Now the lights were on, and someone had begun dressing the tables. Brian went out to his car and removed the large box, which contained the blowouts.

Once back in the room, he took out the ten plastic bags and placed them atop the tables. He hoped that whoever was readying the area would get the idea that the blowouts should be part of the table setting. He would return in a while and give instructions if needed. Brian hoped that wouldn't be necessary. He didn't want anyone to describe him later. He thought that perhaps he could phone-in the instructions. Yet, that would also leave a record. Brian left for a second time. All this waiting was driving him nuts, but he refrained from taking his medication.

He returned just before six o'clock to find the room transformed. There was a centerpiece on each table in the shape of a mini parade float filled with beads. Three more strands hung on each chair back, and a mask sat on each seat. At each table setting was a blowout carefully arranged as if it was a piece of silverware. *Excellent*, thought Brian as he moved further into the room. He was surprised. Three youngish women who had not been visible from the doorway were hanging something on the back wall. One was on a ladder, and the other two were holding a banner of some sort. Brian quickly ducked back out. He didn't know if they saw him or not. In those few seconds, Brian recognized two of them as the secretary and president of his high school class. He was only there for an instant so they probably didn't notice. If they did see him, they might not recognize him. He gained 45 pounds over the last ten years mainly from the medication. However, the sheriff's deputy who stopped him only weeks earlier, knew who he was. Still, that was after staring intently at him for several minutes. Then the realization came to his mind, *so what if they did see him, they would all be dead soon. Dead people don't give good descriptions.* Brian smiled at the joke he made to himself.

Later that night, it was hard for Brian to concentrate on anything. By 9:00 PM, he was pacing around the house, his mother chiding him each time he walked into the living room. He wanted to know what was happening at the reunion. Keeping himself away from there was hard. He told himself that Alejandro would never go and put himself at risk. However, Brian finally gave in to the urge. He knew it was risky. But, he only needed to sneak a peak.

On the way over, he remembered about the masks he saw on the chairs. He stopped at a discount store that he thought would carry them. He didn't have any luck. If it were closer to Halloween, there would have been tons of them. He asked a clerk about masks, and she directed him to the toy department where they still had a few. It took him a while but he found a Zorro set which had a mask, hat and small rubber sword. It cost him forty bucks, which he learned later would turn out to be a waste.

When he arrived at the hotel and walked to the entrance, he didn't even have to go in. Through the glass, he saw that a service bar was setup outside the function room. There was a crowd of people standing there waiting to order drinks, and a number of them were harassing each other with the lethal blowouts. He congratulated himself. He'd done it.

Brian supposed it was silly, but he was watching the cable news from the time he arrived home. He knew it would take hours before the symptoms became apparent and the authorities suspected an attack. Nevertheless, he didn't sleep at all that night. He wanted to hear the first bit of breaking news.

It wasn't until 11:00 the next morning that the first reunion story hit the newscasts. Then there was a tidal wave for the remainder of the day. The public was in an uproar. Homeland Security had assured them that the threat was over with the death of Alejandro Reyes and General Castillo. Now there was another attack. It became a media feeding frenzy. Recriminations were flying and politicians of both parties were calling for the resignation of the Director of Homeland Security. She was a holdover from the last administration who the new president hadn't yet replaced. The administration was less than a month old, so the president didn't have to shoulder any of the blame. What made it worse was that the death toll from this attack was unusually high. While the attack in New Orleans only killed thirteen people, nearly 300 people had already succumbed since early morning.

The pundits were saying that the latest attack made no sense at all. Neither the revenge nor the racist theories held up. The assault was on a room full of predominately white people who had no obvious ties to the government. The media was reporting that the authorities were baffled. This was giving rise to irrational fears. There were even reports of food riots as well as other anti-social behavior in some areas.

All this Brian took in with a sense of glee. He was powerful he thought. He could do anything he wanted now. He had over two pounds of the poison still left. However, the nagging feeling that he made a mistake by telling Xavier about the ricin tempered some of this enthusiasm. The FBI reinstated a five million dollar reward for the arrest and conviction of the perpetrators. There was a good possibility that Xavier might turn him in. This was a loose end, and he would have to address it. Brian started making a plan.

41

KERRY WAS EXHAUSTED. She'd been awake since four in the morning after taking Matt's call. It was now almost midnight and she was in the FBI lab. Jeff Davis had confirmed that it was indeed the same ricin, which was responsible for the previous attacks.

"I told you this wasn't over," said Kerry.

"Kerry, come look at this," said Jeff who was standing in front of a display monitor connected to a microscope. "What do you see?"

"The grains, or what ever they are, look a lot smaller on the left than the right."

"Good eye. The particle size of the ricin on the left is one-third the size of that on the right. Still, it has the same chemical signature. This is almost unbelievable," said Jeff.

Kerry asked, "What's the significance?"

"The smaller the size, the more lethal it is if it's inhaled. That's probably why we're seeing such a high fatality rate in the last attack."

"Oh, man."

"Kerry, we have to catch these people soon."

"Really?" said Kerry. "I have an idea. Why don't you put your girlfriend on it, she has a good understanding of law enforcement."

"I know this is going to break your heart but Nancy Noonan has resigned from Homeland Security. She sent me a text a little while ago."

"It's her own fault. We all agreed not to talk to the press until we put out the final report. She and her boss spent the last three weeks grandstanding on how THEY were instrumental in stopping the attacks."

"Kind of takes the FBI off the hook," responded Jeff.

"Yeah. Their little publicity grab put Homeland Security right in the cross-hairs of the media."

"Kind of reminds me of 'Good job, Brownie'," reflected Jeff.

Kerry laughed at Jeff's last remark. It was late, and they were both getting punchy.

Jeff said, "Speaking of the media, they're right about one thing. The attack on a high school reunion doesn't make sense."

"I agree. It doesn't fit any of our scenarios. It resembles a random or opportunistic attack, more than part of a larger conspiracy."

Jeff nodded and observed, "At first glance, it looks almost accidental like the problem we had with the hotspots after the convention attack. But the ricin was definitely planted in those party favors."

"We're sure of that?"

"Absolutely sure."

"This sucks. We have nothing to go on."

"Maybe the reward offered will turn up something," said Jeff.

"I don't know. It didn't do much the first time except to tie up agents running down false leads. We still have over 100,000 to process, and I'm sure five million bucks will bring every nutcase and crazy out of the woodwork again."

"I guess your right. You've got nothing."

"Thanks a lot."

"The ricin you found doesn't give us any more information?" asked Kerry again.

"No. It's the same but processed slightly different. But the origin of the party favors might shed some light because they were custom."

"What do you mean? I was told you can get those blow-out things anywhere."

"Yeah, but these were printed with the high school's name and the class year. Somebody had to special order them."

"Tomorrow I'll have Beverly Ruddy find out if the hotel catering staff provided them or who brought them in from the outside. Do you see any indication of where they were made?"

"Where is everything made now-a-days?"

"China."

"Yeah, but they could've been printed here."

Four days later, Kerry Sterling called Beverly Ruddy to get an update and to congratulate her on her promotion to Assistant Special Agent in Charge of Counterterrorism. Kerry was instrumental in getting Beverly promoted from Supervisory Special Agent to her new role. She liked the way Beverly responded to the events in and around Jacksonville. After they spoke for a while, Kerry asked about the investigation.

"We were able to find twenty-four individuals who were part of the graduating class that didn't attend the reunion. Four of the "no-shows" had misdemeanor records, and there was one gentleman who had a felony conviction."

"What was the conviction for?"

"The person pleaded out to lewd, wanton and lascivious behavior. The subject was caught up in a child predator sting. Apparently it was a plea bargain."

"Was there any violence involved?"

"No. He didn't get that far. No actual meeting took place."

"What did the interview report say when you're agents talked to him?"

"I actually went to his house and spoke to him personally. We're short-handed down here, so I did the interview in place of one of my agents."

"What do you think?"

"He's kind of a weird guy. He seemed nervous when I first identified myself. Then he settled down."

"What did you make of that?"

"My take was that Burke is doing something, but it probably has to do more with his old habits involving young girls. You know those people don't change."

"Why didn't he go to the reunion?"

"He said he wasn't popular in high school and didn't feel the need to see any of his former classmates."

"Did you believe him?"

"I believe him about not being popular. But he didn't exhibit much animosity toward his former school mates though."

"What about the other interviews?"

"It was a dead end. Nobody knew anything." Then Beverly said, "On another topic, we talked to the hotel people about the party favors. They said they hadn't supplied them. They were brought in from the outside the day of the attack. Of course, nobody saw anything."

"Were there any security cameras?"

"There were some in the parking lot. The footage is almost worthless. There were too many blind spots, and the camera angles made it difficult to discern individual faces. If we know who we're looking for, then it may help later."

"Did you talk to any of the survivors?"

"As you know, there weren't too many. Whoever did this was smart. He or she knew it would be hard to resist playing with those party favors. We talked to three people who were there."

"Did they see anything out of the ordinary?"

"Oh, they certainly did. Almost everyone there were wearing masks. The theme was Mardi Gras."

"I see your point."

"Bottom line… we don't have anything."

"What's the story with the tip line?"

"As you can imagine we were bombed with callers. Five million dollars is a lot of money. Our office has almost eighteen thousand follow-ups."

"That's totally unworkable," declared Kerry.

"Tell me about it, Director. We have every special agent in the office following up on the calls. Nobody is working on anything else."

Kerry said, "I have a theory. Let me run it by you."

"Okay."

"I don't think this is random. Since the attack was so close to the old castor oil plant, that can't be a coincidence. We have two unknown subjects who were mentioned by the motel manager that we haven't found. I'm thinking that maybe Castillo and Reyes hired some local help."

"Director, I think that would make sense. We know that Castillo was involved in the drug trade and may have used some of his local talent. I'm told that making ricin is not much more complicated than making crystal meth."

Kerry said, "Maybe you should get the people at the DEA down there to shake some bushes and see what flies out."

"I'll do that."

"Okay, that's it for now."

"Thanks again for recommending my promotion," said Beverly.

"You earned it. Now earn it again."

"Yes, Director."

42

BROTHER LUCAS WAS FINISHING HIS SERMON
on why bad things happen to good people. This latest
attack was close to home for many of his parishioners.
Some even knew several of the victims. Someone told
Brother Lucas that one of his own flock was killed in the
recent Jacksonville attack.

When Lucas finished speaking, he stood there as the
music played. All the songs he selected were uplifting.
The congregants would stand and close their eyes while
holding a slightly cocked fist in the air. It reminded
Brother Lucas of someone holding a beer mug. This a-
mused him. The people would clench their fists in time
to the music supposedly representing the movement of
a beating heart. Lucas didn't know how this practice began but it became part of the ritual. Brother Lucas cap-
italized on this by selecting music in the sixty to eighty
beat per minute range, which coincided to a person's
normal heartbeat. He had huge speakers installed. They

lined the cathedral providing a low level of bass, which completed the audio metaphor. The sound and vibration was designed to create the impression of being inside a human heart. Lucas thought it was actually quite moving, although somewhat contrived.

As the music continued, Lucas looked around. The church welcomed members of all faiths. He had a true ecumenical congregation. There wasn't a cross displayed anywhere in the cathedral. Some of his parishioners belonged to other churches as well. That's why Lucas held services on both Saturdays and Sundays. He once commissioned a marketing study to determine his target audience for his telemarketing and other promotional campaigns. He learned that the typical adult member of his church leaned toward a pro-life stance, and for many, the concept of the first heartbeat solved a moral dilemma. Those torn on the subjects of embryonic stem cell research and more aggressive forms of birth control like the morning after pill, could now feel comfortable supporting those stands and still be pro-life. Although these issues were not the official position of the pro-life establishment, most of the institutional funding for his church came from pro-life organizations who thought that Brother Lucas's theory was a step in the right direction. He appreciated their money, if not their position.

After the service was over, Brother Lucas walked to his normal greeting spot, which was right outside the gift shop. There he would converse with his "brothers and sisters" as he liked to call them. While he chatted, he kept an eye on the table piled high with his new DVD. He liked that. This was the best one yet. Besides the famous sermon, it contained commentary from scientists, theologians and even celebrities. As usual, sales were brisk. The title of the DVD was "God's Mysteries" but Lucas knew it was the first heartbeat theory that the people wanted to embrace.

When the crowd near the gift shop thinned, Lucas went back to the church offices. There was a meeting of church elders every Saturday afternoon. For his church that meant his family. No outsiders were responsible to develop church policy. As usual, his father did most of the talking. Evelyn told Lucas that the meeting would be short today. She said there wasn't much on the agenda. This made Lucas happy. He didn't feel like hearing his father grouse about his fund raising practices.

Evelyn said, "We're having a problem with the son of one of our women parishioners."

"Let me guess," said Lucas. "He wants his mother's money back."

"That's correct."

"Haven't we discussed this before? We don't need the money bad enough to bring us negative publicity. Isn't that right Dad," said Lucas trying to curry favor with his father. "For a lousy couple hundred dollars…"

"Lucas, it's $170,000 dollars," interrupted his sister.

"Who are these people?"

"The mother's name is Emily Burke. The son is Brian Burke."

"What do we know about them?"

"As usual we do a thorough background check on all our heavy hitters to give more info to the telemarketers in the special unit."

"Yeah, yeah?"

"The remarks section on the direct marketing system says that the mother is a widow who receives monthly proceeds from an insurance policy. The check arrives around the eighteenth of the month. So that's when the telemarketers call her for a donation," said Evelyn.

"Do we get something every month?" asked Lucas.

"I'm thinking you're taking advantage of that poor woman," interrupted his father.

Both Lucas and Evelyn ignored him. Then Evelyn said, "We did a background check on the son after the fifteenth time he called us. The man's a jerk."

"Did we find anything?"

"Yeah, he pleaded no contest to a sex crime. He's on the sexual predator database. It seems he likes little girls."

"What an asshole," said Lucas. "Obviously we're not going to give the money back."

"What do you want to do?" asked Evelyn.

"I think you should put in a call to his mother telling her he's harassing the church, and it would be difficult for us to allow her and her son to worship here."

His father said, "You can't do that."

"Why can't I?"

"It's not right, that's why. You were taught better."

"Okay, what do you want to do?"

"Threaten the little prick not his mother."

"You got that Evelyn?" said Lucas laughing.

Evelyn, who was also laughing, changed the subject and asked, "Dear brother, what do you want to do a-bout the oxygen system?"

"Did it break down again?"

"It was the flow controller."

"I thought they were going to put in a new digital one."

"They did. They're saying that contamination from inside the pipes is interfering with the sensors as it passes through the controller."

"So what do they want to do?"

"They said an inline filter would help. I told them to do it."

"So what's the issue?"

"Nothing, I'm only telling you about it."

"Fine."

His father said, "I told you that oxygen system was going to be a problem when the architect suggested it."

"I know you told me, Dad. But so far, I haven't seen anybody fall asleep in my church."

"Don't be a smart-ass. You know that only happened once or twice when I was preaching."

"You mean once or twice a Sunday. Don't you?"

"Lucas stop," said his sister.

"Are we done here, then?" said Lucas anxious to get to the driving range. The weather was beautiful.

"We're done," said his sister.

43

IT WAS SATURDAY. Brian hated Saturdays. First, he had to take his mother to church and then they went food shopping. This meant his mother sitting in the car while he searched for the items using her convoluted list. Then she would criticize him for purchasing either the wrong item or wrong size or not using the coupons she gave him. Brian noticed that men hardly ever used coupons, and he was embarrassed handing them to the clerk. He couldn't see why it mattered to his mother, anyway. He paid for the groceries himself. That was the routine, and he was depressed.

For Brian it was a bad week all around. The high he felt from attacking his classmates had all but vanished after he received a visit from the FBI woman. As soon as the doorbell rang, and he saw the official looking car, Brian believed it was over for him. Xavier had turned him in to the authorities. He'd been surprised when his mother opened the front door to see a women standing there alone. He heard her say that she had some questions about the reunion and would like to talk to him. He thought that if they were coming to arrest him, surely they would have sent more people. She stayed about 15 minutes. It was obvious to him from her questions that he wasn't a suspect. However, the encounter told him that he had to deal with Xavier and quickly. But first, he had to take his mother to church and then to the store. He told himself, *that's right Brian keep your priorities straight.*

Brian couldn't believe the reunion had only been two weeks ago. It seemed like much longer. Now he didn't know what to do with himself. He knew he was suffering from acute anxiety. Brian measured the intensity of the malady by the number of pills he swallowed.

"Brian, aren't you ready yet?"

"It's only seven o'clock. The service doesn't start til' ten."

"You know I like to sit in the special seats," said his mother.

His mother always insisted that they get to the cathedral two hours ahead of time. He would wait in line with her. She wouldn't talk to anybody but him. When they finally opened the doors, he would escort her to her "special rainbow seat" and then go wait in the car until the service was over at noon. The crazy part was that she wouldn't let him go to the grocery store while he waited. They argued about this all the time. He suspected that she worried about having a panic attack and wanted him close by. She refused to see a doctor about her condition. One time he slipped her one of his Kyri-

Laison tablets. He put it in her food to see what would happen. It turned out nothing happened. The medication didn't affect her at all.

Brian drove the six miles to the pyramid and waited with her in line as usual. It particularly bugged him this Saturday because the day was cloudy. There would be no rainbows in the church, but she still made him wait in line. At 10:15, the doors opened. He got his mother seated, then headed for the parking lot. Instead of listening to his MP3 player, he took out his notepad and started jotting down the things he had to do. On the top of the list was Xavier. It was obvious to Brian that the FBI was getting close. He saw on the news that they reinstated the reward. So, in his mind, it was now only a matter of time before Xavier turned him in. The other day he found his father's pistol that he kept for protection. Brian didn't know too much about guns, but his father had taken him to the range a few times as a child. He remembered he didn't like the place. It was noisy and smelled of cordite. Trying to poison Xavier would be out of the question and using any other weapon would probably turn out badly. Xavier, although smaller, looked like he could handle himself. Brian decided that he would shoot him. He would take his father's gun to the range and practice. He would get familiar with the weapon.

The next item on the list was money. Even if Xavier didn't turn him in, the FBI would never stop looking for the attackers. Eventually, he would show up in several of their databases linking him in several ways to the crime. This would eventually make him a suspect. He knew he hadn't covered his tracks as well as he should. The plan was to go to Bolivia, which obviously hadn't worked out. Brian didn't have a backup plan. The bottom line: he needed money now, and he knew exactly where to find it.

Brian left the car and walked directly to the church offices. Once there, he told the receptionist he wanted to talk to someone about getting his mother's money back. The receptionist asked him his name and told him to have a seat. It would be a few minutes.

"Hello, are you Brian Burke?" asked a middle-aged woman a short time later.

"Yes I am."

"My name is Evelyn Dodge. I'm the office manager. How can I help you?"

Brian explained why he was there while the woman listened patiently and didn't interrupt. She appeared friendly and didn't seem offended or surprised at what he wanted.

"I see, Brian. Is it okay if I call you Brian?"

"Sure."

"Well Brian what you're asking for, isn't going to happen,"

Her tone was anything but friendly now. This surprised him.

"Let me put in to you this way. Your mother has been a friend of this church for a few years. You're not impoverished from what I can see, and it's her money to do with what she wants. Now I'm familiar with your case. You've called here many times harassing our staff.

Up to now, we've been patient but our patience is wearing thin."

"So you're saying that you're not going to give my mother's money back?"

"Let me ask you something, Brian. Has your mother ever asked for her generous donations to be returned?"

"You don't understand…"

"No, Brian. You don't understand. Your mother gave us the donations out of the goodness of her heart, and I don't see where that is any of your business. Your sister hasn't called asking us to return your mother's money."

This last statement alarmed Brian. How did the office manager know he had a sister? Could this be a subtle threat, he wondered. Brian didn't have to ponder that question for long.

"Brian, here's what we're going to do. If you do not stop haranguing my staff, I'm going to ask that Brother Lucas ban you and your mother from the church. You can call it an excommunication if you would like. You and your mother would be our first."

Brian was stunned. The only time his mother left the house was to come to this place.

Evelyn walked right up to him to get within inches of his face and said in a low voice, "Brian you're not dealing with little girls here. If we ban you—and you decide to come anyway—we will call the police and have you arrested. Brother Lucas may take it upon himself to explain to the entire congregation why it is that you and your mother are no longer welcome. We have many little girls who come here to worship with their parents, which have to be protected from sick perverts like you."

Evelyn said the word pervert so vehemently that she sprayed saliva in his face. Brian didn't want the police to arrest him. This woman was serious. He turned a-round and left without saying another word. The office manager had shaken him badly. He needed to walk it off, and he needed his medication. He took two pills and swallowed an antacid tablet along with them.

Brian walked around for about twenty minutes. He hadn't calmed down much from the ordeal with Evelyn Dodge. The Kyri-Laison hadn't kicked in. But, Brian didn't want to take anymore. After a few more minutes, he started to feel better. The exercise was helping. He was now in an area that visitors didn't frequent. He was walking past a smaller building behind the pyramid. It looked to him to be a maintenance structure of some kind. It was likely this was where the building's HVAC and other mechanical systems were located. Behind this small structure was a chain link fenced enclosure with a large gate. There were white plastic strips intertwined between each link. To a passerby, the contents of the area weren't visible. On the other hand, if one walked closer to it, they could see what was in there. That's what Brian did. What he saw surprised him.

The ten-foot gate door was unlocked. Brian looked around, didn't see anybody so he went in. There were twenty-four large gas cylinders attached to a manifold. Brian knew by the tanks' green color and the chrome valves that they contained medical grade oxygen. The manifold led into a flow controller with a digital read-out. Brian walked closer. It showed oxygen was flow-ing. He looked around. There was a box lying near the fence. He picked it up. It was the packaging for a filter. He studied the apparatus. Apparently, someone had added an inline filter to the system. It was serviceable by turning off a valve and opening a cover. Brian didn't turn off the valve but he did open the cover. A latch at each end held the filter in place, which could be opened or closed by hand without any special tools. Brian put the box down and left the area. The services would be over soon, and he had to meet his mother at the front entrance.

His mother would be one of last people out. Brian wasn't disappointed. He waited almost fifteen minutes and watched 5,000 people leave before his mother appeared.

They did the normal Saturday grocery shopping and then headed home. Brian was quiet. He was wondering about the oxygen system he saw. His medication was apparently working, and he wasn't scared or anxious anymore. If fact, he was now angry at the way that women had treated him. The last bitch that treated him that way was dead. The thought made him feel good. Maybe it was time that Brother Lucas and Evelyn, the office manager, learned some respect. The thought of attacking the Divine Heart Unity Church gave him the same thrill as he got when he contemplated the attack on his high school classmates.

Thoughts started pouring into his head. The thieves weren't going to give his mother's money back. Instead, they were going to embarrass her and call the police on him. Brian decided he had to stop them. He gave little thought to the innocent people that also attended the

church. It seemed to Brian that they were willing ac-
complices in the church's thievery. They were the en-
ablers. Like his mother, they sent money to the church,
no questions asked. He would never get his mother to
stop giving her money away...that is, unless there was
no Brother Lucas or the Divine Heart Unity Church.

44

BY THE NEXT MORNING, Brian Burke had worked himself up so much so that he was now obsessed with attacking Brother Lucas's church. Those bastards were not going to give his mother's money back. Their threat to banish his mother from the church or embarrass her would be devastating. She would never leave the house.

He was running scenarios through his mind about how he could do it. So far, the only thing he knew for sure was that he would have to hit on a Sunday when his mother wasn't at the services. As he thought about the different options, there appeared only two choices. He could target the food court, but he had no information that Brother Lucas or the bitch Evelyn ate there. On the other hand, he could attack inside the pyramid. He finally decided against the food court idea as being too impractical. He knew the key to assaulting the church had to come from the HVAC system. He had to learn more about it. He decided he would use a ruse on the contractor who installed it to get more information. The day before, Brian noticed there were stickers on some of the oxygen equipment. He bet it was the same company that installed the air conditioning system. However, he didn't remember the name of the company.

Later that afternoon, Brian drove to the cathedral. The parking lot was almost empty. He parked near the few cars that were there so as not to attract attention. Nobody was around, so he walked behind the building to the fenced-in area. The gate was still unlocked. After he entered the enclosure, Brian found three stickers all with the same name. The sticker contained a telephone number and a web address along with the company's name. Brian decided he would look the company up when he arrived home. Before he left, Brian spotted the box that previously contained the filter. He picked it up and took it with him. He hoped that maybe it could be helpful.

After he arrived home, he looked up the HVAC contractor on the internet. He found it was a large concern with several offices. The company did work in many of the larger cities including Las Vegas. When Brian read Las Vegas, it sparked something in his mind. He remembered reading about how some casinos pump pure oxygen into the gambling areas to keep people alert and awake. Now he knew what the church was doing with the oxygen cylinders. Brian decided to give the company a call the next morning.

His mother was all excited at dinner. She read in the TV section of the newspaper that 60 Minutes would be interviewing Brother Lucas that evening. She was chattering about it the whole time they were eating. Brian getting tired of the Brother Lucas talk grunted, "Ma, don't you get enough of him on Saturdays?"

"Brian, if you came in and listened to the service once in a while you'd see."

"See what, another guy with his hand out?"

"Brian, you know that's not true."

"How much did you send him this month?"

"I told you before that's none of your business. Come watch the show with me. You'll see. Listen to what he says."

Brian agreed reluctantly. He knew it was the practice of the show's producers to have on popular preachers from time to time. However, these were usually soft interviews. The show's producers presumed it was not in their best interest to make their advertisers unhappy by hard-balling members of the clergy. Therefore, it would usually be a puff piece. Brian didn't expect any revelations to come out about Brother Lucas or his fundraising.

The show started with another segment. It was a story on steroid use in professional sports. This time it was hockey. Then it was time for Brother Lucas.

Brian's mother was excited. "Brian, Brother Lucas is on!"

The interviewer, a new woman on the show with a British accent asked, "Where did you come up with the first heartbeat theory?"

"I prefer not to call it a theory. It was a revelation that came to me in a dream. It made sense right away," stated Brother Lucas.

A voice-over reiterated the first heartbeat theory to the audience for those people who weren't familiar with it.

"How come you don't allow heart transplants?"

"Sally, every religion has its own special doctrine. For some there is mandatory church attendance. Others have rules regarding which foods you can eat and when you can eat them. We don't do any of that. Nevertheless, to answer your question, we believe the heart is God's gateway to the soul."

"Is it true that some people died because they refused to let the doctors transplant a new heart?"

Brian wondered, maybe this wasn't going to be easy interview.

Brother Lucas replied, "Well Sally, I've heard those stories but I don't have any personal knowledge that they're true. I don't believe our position is that radical. Look what other religions do. Jehovah Witnesses frown on blood transfusions and Christian Scientists believe in seeking medical attention only as a last resort."

"Let's talk about your church's stance on abortion."

"Okay."

"You say that it's permissible to have an abortion in the weeks preceding the first human heartbeat?"

"We do not consider that to be an abortion."

"So you don't a have a problem with embryonic stem cell research or the morning after pill."

"No we don't."

"What about after the first heartbeat. Should abortion be made illegal?" asked Sally.

"Not in my personal opinion nor is it our church's position. Let me put it this way. We agree with Bill Clinton who said, 'abortion should be safe, legal and rare'."

"How would you define rare?"

"Rare would certainly include rape, incest or the life of the mother being in jeopardy. In my opinion, it could also include other circumstances, which would create a severe hardship for the mother or the family. Let me make another point. I'd like to address this comment to those vehemently pro-life people. Trying to make abortion illegal is counter-productive. It serves only to galvanize your opposition."

"I missed that, can you explain that a little further?" asked Sally.

"Let me start with a frivolous example. Take the use of tobacco. There are restrictions on who and where you can use it, but it isn't illegal. If you try to make it illegal, I believe more people would actually smoke cigarettes. Smokers would put up a better fight for their rights. Yet, what tobacco's critics have been able to do is make it almost shameful to smoke. Children beg their parents not to smoke cigarettes and companies discourage hiring smokers because of higher health insurance costs. It's my belief there are many people in your audience who now believe that smoking a cigarette in public is far worse than getting an abortion."

"So your advice to pro-life organizations is stop trying to have Roe v. Wade overturned."

"Yes."

"Let's go back to your one heartbeat theory again. What accounts for the popularity of your message?"

"It's a good middle ground for most people. It's far less subjective than the pro-life stance that human life begins at conception or the pro-choice notion of viability. Our position gives people better direction. In other words we say, don't stop a beating heart. We think most people can relate to that. There are many in your audience who don't like abortion but don't want to make it illegal either. We offer them a comfortable stance."

The next part of the interview was a guided tour of the Divine Heart Unity Church's cathedral and some positive interviews with parishioners heaping praise on Brother Lucas.

Brian was beside himself. The interviewer didn't ask one question about their fundraising tactics or the lavish lifestyle of Brother Lucas or the Dodge family holdings. He said as much to his mother.

"Brian, hush up about that," she said. "Don't ruin it for me."

"Ma, you know that first heartbeat theory is load of crap."

"Don't use that language."

Brian was ready to leave the room. However when the program returned from commercial, Brian found he was a little too quick on the draw in his criticism for the interviewer. She asked, "Some people have criticized your church for its fund raising practices. How do you respond to that?"

"Can you show me one religious organization that doesn't raise funds? Most of the donations to us go to programs like our coronary care unit facilities and other places to help people. Our church is committed to charitable works."

"How much have you spent on this magnificent cathedral and the other trappings?"

"Sally, I don't really know. That would be a question for our church elders. They take care of such things."

Brian had enough. The last few answers were obvious lies. He had read a number of tabloid stories about Brother Lucas and his family. The articles reported on their lavish homes in Florida, Minnesota and the Virgin Islands. Brian wished that 60 Minutes had interviewed him. He could tell Sally what's her name about Brother Lucas's fund raising practices. Maybe they could help get his mother's money back.

A strange thought hit Brian. As notorious as Brother Lucas seemed, it was nothing compared to what he had done over the last six months. He bet that if they ever interviewed him, the show's ratings would be triple that of Brother Lucas.

This made Brian smile. He decided then that nothing would stop him from attacking the Divine Heart Unity Church. It will be bigger than anything the general or Alejandro had accomplished. It would be even larger than the political convention attack. Yeah, he was going to do it…that was for sure.

45

ON MONDAY MORNING, Brian called the contractor, Nationwide Climate Control Co., and the receptionist put him through to the sales department. Brian told them he was the project manager for an environmental research firm that was building a laboratory in Florida. They were interested in oxygen system for their hyperbaric studies. Brian mentioned that Lucas Dodge had highly recommended their company. The sales person told Brian that a subcontractor did the oxygen work at the cathedral, and they could better answer his questions. The sales representative gave Brian the number and told him to give the subcontractor her name as a reference. Brian thanked her then made the call.

It turned out that a casino contracting company installed the oxygen equipment. After several questions about the system, they transferred Brian to their project manager who would have the details that he needed.

The man's name was Jimmy Haskel, and he liked to talk.

Mr. Haskel told Brian that the oxygen system worked two ways. It had an automatic mode. Carbon dioxide sensors would start the flow of oxygen when the CO2 reached a certain level. There was also a manual override. Brother Lucas had a button on the podium where he could start the flow of oxygen on demand if he needed. Once the oxygen left the tanks, a console would control the flow to the building, mixing it with outside air until it reached thirty percent saturation.

"It sounds like a sophisticated system. I'm not sure we need all that for what we're planning," said Brian.

Jimmy Haskel explained, "Well the original design wasn't as complicated as it is now. I probably shouldn't be telling you this, but we added the manual override after we installed the system. Brother Lucas wanted the ability to start the system on demand."

"Did you make any other modifications?"

"We recently added a filter system. Although in my opinion, I don't believe it was necessary."

"Can you say more about that?"

"I'm going to be frank with you. You didn't hear this from me."

"Okay."

"We told the architect that the oxygen system was not large enough to handle the volume of the pyramid. Similar systems, like those we've installed in casinos, are only in the gambling areas away from any large atrium. You've been in the cathedral?"

"Yes I have."

"It's huge."

"So what's the complaint?" asked Brian.

"They think there's something wrong with the controller because they're using so much oxygen."

"The architect won't admit to them that he made a mistake, so we've been adding fixes to the system. We disabled the automatic controls, and now it only works from the podium."

"So if Brother Lucas doesn't push the button, no oxygen will flow into the cathedral?"

"That's correct. We also installed boost pumps to the air handlers. They're actually industrial strength fans similar to what fire departments use to evacuate smoke from a building. So when someone pushes the button on the podium, the entire volume of air in the building is exchanged within twenty minutes while also increasing the oxygen level."

"What does the filter do?"

"Nothing really. The architect insisted that we install it. His theory is that something is contaminating the sensors thereby giving false readings to the controller. Of course, that's baloney. The system doesn't work that way. Bottom line, eventually we'll have to install a larger system. Although from what you've told me about your project, your requirements will be simpler and much less expensive."

Brian said, "I have one more question. You said that Brother Lucas could manually start the system by pushing a button on the podium. How does he stop the system?"

"The system stops automatically when the oxygen level reaches thirty percent."

"So he can't stop it if he pushes the button again."

"No. You would have to access the controller console for that."

Brian thanked Jimmy Haskill who said he would be emailing Brian some information. Brian told him that he would review it and be in touch as they moved further into the planning stages of his project.

Brian thought about what Jimmy told him. It would take twenty minutes or less to administer the ricin once Brother Lucas pushed the button.

Brian thought, *this is perfect. Brother Lucas would poison his own flock.* This was turning out to be surprisingly simple. He would use the superfluous filter as a container to hold the ricin. He bet it wouldn't take much effort to modify it for that purpose.

Brian had the box. He looked up the brand name and model number on the internet. The search turned up dozens of companies that carried them in stock. They were heating and air conditioning supply companies, and several were in the local area. Brian thought about ordering the filter online but the companies he found only took debit or credit cards. He didn't want to create a paper trail so he thought about acquiring a pre-paid card under an assumed name. Brian wasted three hours before he concluded it was no longer possible to obtain debit or credit card either anonymously or under a false name. Since the 9-11 attack, congress passed legislation banning the use of anonymous credit cards. The financial institution issuing the card now had to verify all personal information including a social security number. This was alarming to Brian. If he had to run, these new requirements would make things much more difficult for him. He decided he would use cash, but that meant he would have to show himself at the supplier's place of business. When the FBI discovered the filter was the source of the ricin, they would contact the local companies that sold them. Brian decided he wasn't going to make it that easy for the FBI to find him. He decided to go to Orlando or farther south to purchase the filters.

By 8:00 PM, Brian had returned home from his trip to Orlando with three filters. He purchased them for cash, and he was surprised at how inexpensive they were. He guessed that Jimmy Haskell, knowing that they were of little use, didn't choose to install anything that needed to be robust.

The next morning, Brian went out to the detached garage behind his house. His father had used it as a workshop, and there were plenty of tools. Brian had no idea what most of them did. But, he was sure he could find something that could take the filter apart. He reflected that it was a good thing he bought three of them. A few hours of trial and error had destroyed one. The second one he was able to take apart and load it with baking soda. He tested it with the blower side of the old wet/dry vacuum cleaner that his father kept in the garage. The system worked great. Now all he had to do was figure out how to get the ricin into the remaining filter without exposing himself to the poison. There was no way around the fact that he would have to pour it into the filter's core chamber. There would be dust. He would have to perform the operation while wearing a hazmat suit. He would also need a clean environment. It would be difficult, if not impossible to decontaminate the garage. The structure would be useless for long into the future.

The solution was to use an RV again. Although, he hadn't used the hauler area of the RV he rented previously, he noticed that the sides and floor were made of diamond plate. He could clean it with a pressure washer after he was done.

Brian decided to reserve an RV that he could pick up the next day. He then went to the new self-storage area to retrieve the ricin and other items he would need to keep himself safe. He put all the items in the trunk of his car.

That night, Brian went looking for Xavier. He had his father's automatic pistol. If the opportunity presented itself, he would shoot him. It seemed easy enough to Brian. In the movies, an assassin would walk up behind the victim, shoot him once in the head, and then calmly walk away. The only problem was that he couldn't find Xavier. He returned home after midnight, unsuccessful in his attempt to kill the only person who could link him to the reunion attack.

The next day, Brian picked up the RV and found a location to park it for the night. This one was in Lake City, which was a considerable distance away. It was a big fishing area, so it wasn't unusual to have tourists camping there in early spring. The operation to transfer the ricin to the filter went smoothly. He used over a pound of ricin. He wrapped the filter in a heavy plastic bag used for storing clothing items. Brian forced the air from the bag creating a vacuum. He knew he was safe as long as air didn't leak back in. Then he squeezed the filter back into its box. He thought about how he was going to install it into the oxygen system without the use of the hazmat suit. That was going to be tricky. He decided he would buy a cheap poncho. They had them for sale in the office when he checked-in to the RV Park. Apparently, they were popular with the anglers. The ponchos only cost a few dollars and took up little room while still folded in their package.

Before leaving the RV Park, he availed himself with the self-service washing area that campers used to rinse down their trailers and boats. He let the big vehicle dry for a while and then checked-out.

Brian returned the RV to the dealership and put the remaining ricin and filter in the storage locker. He planned the attack for the next Sunday. However, he concluded he could change the date easily if needed. Now all he had to do was wait. In the meantime, he would go looking for Xavier again.

46

XAVIER BATISTA WOKE UP to the sound of glass breaking and footsteps. He reached for the small pistol he kept under his pillow. Then he felt the unmistakable feeling of a cold metal gun barrel thrust into the back of his neck.

"Get up you piece of shit!"

Flashlight beams hit his face from all directions as hands grabbed him and threw him on the floor. Some-one put a knee on his shoulder as someone else pulled his arms together and slapped handcuffs on his wrists.

"Didn't you hear us knock?" said one of the men.

"Screw you."

The DEA agents pulled Xavier to his feet. "Put your face against the wall."

"What's this?" said another agent finding Xavier's pistol.

"Looks like a gun to me."

"Yep, sure looks like a gun."

"Raul, are parolees supposed to have guns?"

"Don't think so. Somebody might be in big trouble, huh?"

"Hey scumbag, do you have any other weapons in the house?"

"Screw you."

"Is that the only English you know, dickhead?"

"I was born here you racist bastard."

Agent Raul laughed and said, "Marty, he must know you."

Marty gave Xavier a flick behind the ear.

"Hey man, that hurts."

"Then watch your mouth."

For the next hour, Xavier heard the agents taking his house apart. He had over a pound of crystal meth and about $30,000 in cash. It didn't take the searchers long to find it. They let him get dressed and then took him out to a vehicle. After a short ride, Xavier found himself at the local office of the DEA where they handcuffed him to a table leg.

Marty introduced himself formally to Xavier. "I'm Special Agent Frist."

Xavier said, "You don't mind if I call you Marty?"

"Not if I can call you dickhead. Tell us about the dope."

"I'd like to call my lawyer," said Xavier.

A couple hours later, Xavier's lawyer arrived. The door was open so he could see his attorney talking to the DEA agents. Then his lawyer came into the interview room.

"You still have a balance on your account," mentioned his attorney.

"I sent you a check, man."

"It must be in the mail then, huh?"

"You charged me $17,000 last time. What do I still owe you, $300 bucks?"

"Actually it's $500.00 now. I left home an hour ago."

"Quit busting my balls."

"Xavier, you had two guns and over a pound of crystal meth at your house. That was stupid."

"Tomorrow I was moving it to another place. I only had the dope there one night."

"You know if all their paperwork checks out, you're going to jail for a long time."

"How long?"

"Counting the parole violations, I'm thinking twelve years."

"Holy shit!"

"Maybe I can get it down to eight if you plead out," explained his attorney.

Xavier thought for a while. "Let me ask you something. Can I still collect a reward for something even though I've been arrested?"

"As long as it doesn't have anything to do with the crimes you're charged with now," answered his lawyer. "Why, what do you have?"

"I know who did the ricin attack in Jacksonville."

Xavier noticed the lawyer had a skeptical look on his face. "You know who did the attack?" uttered the lawyer.

"Yeah."

"There's a five million dollar reward for that information. If you're not bullshitting me, I might be able to get you off on these charges too. I want to let you know up front my fee for negotiating the reward is 30%."

Xavier's lawyer left the room to talk to Marty who was standing with a number of other agents. He heard the agents laughing. When his lawyer returned, he told Xavier that they didn't believe him. There would be no deal.

Xavier said, "I can prove it."

"How?"

"I've got a sample of the ricin."

"You have a sample?"

"Yeah, the guy who made it said he had two pounds of the stuff and wanted to know if I could sell it."

"Listen to me Xavier. When the agents come in to talk to you, tell them that you refused to have anything to do with the ricin. You only took the sample, so the fellow would stop bugging you. Stick to that story. Do you understand?"

"Yeah, I got it."

Xavier's lawyer left again and this time didn't return for almost an hour. When he did, there were eight people with him. Some were in plain clothes unlike Marty and the others in SWAT gear who earlier raided his house. "These men would like to talk with you," indicated his lawyer.

"Mr. Batista, you told your attorney that you may have some information about the recent terrorist attack in Jacksonville?"

"I know who did it."

"And you're willing to share this information with us for a reduced sentence."

"No man. I don't want a reduced sentence. I want no time in prison."

"Mr. Batista, that isn't going to happen," said a man with grayish hair.

"No jail time or no name," said Xavier.

"Let me confer with my client," mumbled his lawyer.

Xavier declared, "I'm not doing any time."

The man with the gray hair then said, "I guess we're through here."

"I got a sample of the ricin."

The men stopped and turned around. "Your lawyer told us that you had a sample but you got rid of it. You still have some of the ricin? Where is it, and where did you get it?"

Xavier's lawyer said, "Tell them what we discussed."

He told them using the exact words that his lawyer suggested. "Don't you know it's illegal to possess ricin? We can add twenty years to your sentence."

Xavier's lawyer said, "Don't listen to that."

"I'm not, here's the deal. I'll give you the ricin if you drop the weapons charges. If it checks out, then I'll give you the guy's name when the all the charges are finally dropped and I get the reward."

The man with the gray hair said, "We don't have anything to do with the reward—that you'll have to negotiate with the FBI and Justice Department. We'll be back to talk to you later."

The man with the gray hair was the Special Agent in Charge of the DEA's local field office. He called his counterpart at the FBI's Jacksonville Field Office, and they had a discussion. A short time later, ASAC Beverly Ruddy showed up at the DEA office to talk with Xavier Batista. Beverly introduced herself to Xavier and his attorney.

"I'm told you know the name of the person who attacked the high school class reunion three weeks ago."

"Yes I do."

"I'm also told you have a sample of the ricin?"

"Yes."

"How much do you have?"

"I would say it's less than half a gram in a tiny glass jar."

"A tiny glass jar?" asked Beverly.

"The guy said it was a testing vial," added Xavier.

"How do you know the individual who gave you the ricin?"

"I don't want to go into that right now."

"Let me be frank with you, Mr. Batista. In the last six months, we have over one hundred thousand people that claim to know the names of the terrorists. Many of them make the same claims you do. They have samples of the ricin, which turns out to be nothing. Why would I believe that you're not wasting my time? You have to give me something."

Xavier conferred with his attorney who nodded his assent. "I was the one who introduced the guy to Reyes. But I didn't know what they were planning at the time."

"Not enough," said Beverly who stood up to leave.

"The guys a biochemist," said Xavier.

Beverly sat down again. "Tell me when you introduced him to Alejandro Reyes. I need the exact day."

"It was in late May."

Beverly thought the timing was right. "You have to tell me more."

"There wasn't much to it at the time. I saw the guy once more after that."

"Did he talk about what he was doing?"

"No, but he said he had a job that he had to commute over an hour back and forth everyday."

"Does the man live in Jacksonville?"

"Yes he does."

"And he had to commute over an hour to work every day."

Beverly who made the trip to Fargo, Ga. many times, thought that if the man did live in Jacksonville, it would be over an hour commute. "If you knew the identity of the perpetrator why haven't you tried to collect the reward before this?"

"I did. I called the hotline and gave them the information. They gave me an I.D. number and everything."

"What was the I.D. number they gave you?" asked Beverly.

"Do you think I'm stupid?" laughed Xavier.

Beverly knew that they still had thousands of leads to examine from the hotline. Eventually they may check out Xavier Batista's information, but if there was still ricin out there, another attack was possible. "All right, Mr. Batista this is what I'm going to do. I'm going back to confer with my superiors, and if they agree, we will have the Justice Department drop the weapons charges when you deliver the sample of ricin."

47

KERRY STERLING WAS IN HER OFFICE, frustrated and angry. They had nothing. Reinstating the large reward hadn't produced any tangible leads. Kerry had the forensic team reexamine the old castor oil plant in Georgia. They found a bottle cap buried in the back, which had a partial fingerprint. Jeff told Kerry that they were using special software to join the two partials together hoping to get enough information to point to a suspect. Unfortunately, over 20,000 people had fingerprints with similar characteristics.

Kerry thought when they started comparing lists in the database maybe it would help. However, she didn't hold out much hope. Therefore, when Beverly Ruddy called and told her Xavier Batista's story, Kerry immediately went to the Justice Department to get an agreement for a possible plea deal. Unfortunately, the DEA wasn't cooperating. They agreed to drop the weapon's charges but not the possession with intent to sell, no matter what Batista told them. Almost a pound of crystal meth was a big bust that they didn't want to plea bargain away.

Kerry called Beverly and told her to go ahead and get the ricin sample from Xavier Batista. If it checked out, she would go to the Justice Department and threaten to shoot them if that's what it took to get a name. Kerry thought to herself that bureaucrats and turf wars were going to ruin this country.

Later that day, Beverly called back and told her that they had retrieved the sample from where Batista hid it and had flown it by helicopter to the CDC lab in Atlanta to save time. Dr. Palena was testing it to see if it was indeed ricin. Kerry held her breath for the next few hours.

The call came from Jeff instead of Matt Palena. Jeff was all excited. "Matt called me a few minutes ago. It was ricin, and he said that although they have to do more tests, it appears that it's the same as Castillo and Reyes used in the original attacks. However, it's different from the recent attack in Jacksonville. We know this because of the particle size."

Kerry asked, "What do you think?"

"Matt said the ricin was in a vial that was probably used for testing in the machine we found in the pond. I know I don't have to tell you this Kerry, but you have to do whatever it takes to get the information from this Batista person."

"Thanks, I'm calling the deputy director now."

Four hours later, the Justice Department having pressured the DEA agreed that everything was on the table with regard to Xavier Batista's deal. Kerry immediately informed Beverly to have Batista transferred to the FBI's custody. In the meantime, she would be flying down to Jacksonville, this time using the FBI's executive jet.

When Kerry arrived, she found Xavier Batista eating a sandwich and talking to Beverly. Kerry walked in the interview room and Beverly said, "Mr. Batista, this is Assistant Director Sterling of the FBI. She has the authority to make a plea deal with you. She also has the authority to recommend you receive all or part of the reward for your information."

"She can give me the reward?" said Xavier with his mouth full of food.

Kerry said, "Yes. I can recommend you get the reward if your information leads to the arrest and conviction of the person who was responsible for the recent Jacksonville attack."

"Where is your attorney, Mr. Batista?

Beverly answered, "He called and said he would be here…"

As she was saying this, his attorney walked in wearing a tuxedo.

Xavier said, "Fancy."

"I'm going to the ballet with my wife, so we have to have this wrapped up by 7:00 PM or the FBI will be investigating my murder," said the attorney.

Kerry reflected—it was Saturday night. Other people had lives, unlike herself. Maybe on the way back, she would stop in Atlanta to see Matt.

The attorney spent some time looking over the plea deal and had Xavier sign it. "Xavier, go ahead and tell your story. Do not leave out any details and tell the absolute truth. Do you understand?"

"Yeah, man."

When Xavier gave the name Brian Burke, Kerry saw the surprised look on Beverly's face. It took a half hour for Xavier to tell all that he knew, with questions from both Kerry and Beverly confirming many of the details. When he was through, Beverly removed Xavier's handcuffs, and he was allowed to leave. Kerry watched him and his lawyer high-five each other in the parking lot probably discussing the five million dollar reward.

"We need a warrant for a search of Brian Burke's residence," declared Kerry.

"I believe we have enough, but finding a judge on Saturday night might be problematic. But I'll get right on it," said Beverly.

Beverly was right. It was after midnight when she finally found a judge who issued a search warrant. If it were up to Kerry, she would have broken down Brian Burke's door right then. However, both women agreed that they had to be cautious because of the ricin. They would need the special FBI team equipped to deal with terrorist threats. The possibility existed for exposure to hazardous materials. Kerry reckoned that it would take at least until 8:00 AM to properly organize the raid.

At precisely 8:01 on Sunday morning, sixty-five federal agents descended on the home of Brian Burke. They entered the premises with lightning speed. A number of agent's were dressed in hazardous materials gear, looking like spaceman. Brian Burke's mother began screeching from the sudden intrusion. Her arms were flailing in all directions. It took three people to subdue her, dislocating her left shoulder and breaking her wrist in the process.

The FBI search of the residence and property found neither Brian Burke nor the ricin. In the meantime, paramedics had sedated Mrs. Burke. She was in no shape to tell them anything. The agents methodically examined each room in the residence. They also searched the adjacent garage where they found remnants of some kind of filter as well as the packaging material from the manufacturer. They located Brian Burke's notebook computer in his bedroom. An FBI analyst began using a special piece of software to recover Burke's web browsing history. They transmitted this information to the FBI lab at Quantico where Jeff had a team of analysts examining the websites to determine if a pattern existed.

In Burke's bedroom, they also found a hand drawing of some kind of system with notes. An agent used his camera phone to transmit this information to Jeff Davis.

While the search of the property was proceeding, other agents—with the help of the NSA, were examining Burke's email and phone records. This search turned up an attachment containing an engineer's drawing of an oxygen system installed at the Divine Heart Unity Church a few years before. The contractor who had installed it, sent the attachment to Brian Burke.

Kerry now back at the Jacksonville field office was coordinating the information with the help of Beverly

Ruddy. On the speakerphone were both Jeff Davis and Matt Palena along with a specialist at The Centers for Disease Control who knew all about HVAC and indoor environmental management systems. It was he, who was now speaking. "If I was to guess and mind you it's only a guess, this Burke character is planning to modify the church's oxygen enhancement equipment." "Is it possible that the ricin could be delivered through the church's oxygen system," asked Kerry.

"Quite effectively, I would say. Because of the boost pumps, one could efficiently disburse the ricin powder to all areas of the main building within several minutes."

Matt said, "Kerry, if it's the same ricin that was used on the high school reunion, this attack would be devastating. Thousands would die within a few hours."

Beverly exclaimed, "It's Sunday morning. The church will be filled to capacity. I've been in there. The place is huge. My guess it would seat five or six thousand people."

Jeff asked, "We have no idea where Burke is now?"

"No. He wasn't at the residence but we think we just missed him. There were dishes on the table. It looked like two people had recently finished breakfast."

Kerry declared, "We have no choice. We have to e-vacuate the church now!"

"I'll inform the local police and try to contact the church directly," said Beverly.

"We need to find Brian Burke," said Kerry. "Also, Matt if you can inform the local hospitals to be ready to accept cases of ricin poisoning, I'd appreciate it."

"I'll do that."

"Beverly, wait a minute," said Kerry.

"Tell the local authorities we need a chopper in the air near the church."

"Will do."

"I'm on my way over there. Can you get me a car and driver?"

"Director, you can ride with me."

48

EVELYN DODGE WAS LISTENING to Lucas give his sermon. On Sundays, it was her job to monitor the telecast. It was going out to hundreds of thousands of people who were listening to her brother. She had the volume turned low. It was the third time she was hearing this particular homily. Lucas had delivered it twice the day before and would deliver it twice today. She always listened to each day's sermon. Lucas would vary it enough to keep it interesting to those people who attended more than one service on a weekend. Evelyn surmised that these people were probably also the biggest contributors. While she was listening, Evelyn was doing her other work. She was examining the daily revenue entries on the church's accounting system when her phone buzzed. The receptionist told her that someone from the FBI was on the line.

"They say it's an emergency," said the worried receptionist.

"Okay, put them through."

"This is Evelyn Dodge."

"What is your position there?" inquired the caller.

"I'm the Divine Heart Unity Church's office manager," said Evelyn who was already getting impatient. She had work to do.

"My name is Beverly Ruddy. I'm Assistant Special Agent in Charge of the Counterterrorism Division at the Jacksonville FBI Field Office. We have reason to believe that there is a possibility of an attack on your church."

Evelyn wasn't going to fall for this. The church had its share of nutcases calling on a regular basis. She said, "I'll be sure to tell Brother Lucas about the attack," and then she hung up.

Her phone buzzed again, and the receptionist said it was the FBI again. "Muriel don't bother me with this anymore. It's another crank call."

Two minutes later, Muriel came running to her desk. "Ms. Dodge, it is the FBI! They gave me a number to call back and I did. It was the FBI Field Office, and they put me right through to Special Agent Ruddy. She's on line two, right now."

"Hello."

"Listen to me carefully. If you hang-up on me again, I will have a uniformed officer there in 30 seconds to arrest you. Do you understand?"

"Yes Agent," squeaked Evelyn now shaken with the sudden turn of events.

"I want you to evacuate the church. There will be a team of police officers there to assist you. Again, do you understand?"

"Yes, ma'am."

"We don't want to start a panic, so wait until the officers arrive to assist you. Is that clear?"

"What's this all about?"

"The officers will tell you when they get there."

"I need to know."

"Do what I tell you. Is there a service going on right now?"

"My brother is giving the sermon."

"Is there some way you can get a message to him without alarming people?"

"Not really. He speaks from the center of the cathedral. He is in the middle of five thousand people."

Evelyn heard the sigh from the agent who then said, "Wait for the officers."

Evelyn didn't have to wait long. Four uniformed police officers entered her area along with someone in plain clothes. The person in the suit showed her his FBI identification. He said, "I need someone here who can shut down the air conditioning system."

"That would be Peter. He knows about all the mechanical systems here."

"Where's Peter now?"

"I sent him to the bank night deposit drop box with yesterday's receipts."

"When will he be back?"

"Ten or fifteen minutes, I would think."

"Does he have a cell phone? Can you call him?"

"I'll try."

Evelyn called Peter on his cell phone, and he said he was stuck in traffic. Apparently, there was something

going on. The police had the road blocked near the cathedral. Evelyn told the agent what Peter told her.

"What kind of car is Peter driving?"

Evelyn informed the agent who told the state police
to find Peter's car in the traffic jam.

"Do you know if the oxygen system is in use today?"

"You know about our oxygen system?" asked Evelyn
who thought that was a secret.

"Is it being used today?" repeated the agent.

"I don't know. My brother has a button..."

"We know about the button. Has he pushed it today?"

"I don't know."

Evelyn listened as the agent called his boss with an
update. They talked for a while, and then he asked her,
"Have you ever heard of a man named Brian Burke?"

"Oh, yeah. We're familiar with that gentleman. He's
a real piece of work. He's been harassing our staff for
six months."

The agent repeated to his boss what she had just told
him, and then handed her the phone. Beverly Ruddy on
the other end said, "Tell me what you know about Brian
Burke."

"He started harassing us with some phone calls. He
was unhappy that his mother had been generous in her
donations. He wanted us to return the money."

"Did you?"

"No we didn't."

"Did that upset him?"

"You bet. We had to threaten to call the police, if he
didn't stop harassing us."

"How much did his mother donate?"

"Over $170,000."

"When was the last time you talked to him?"

"It was about three weeks ago. I think it was on a Saturday."

Beverly asked Evelyn to return the phone to the special agent. She listened as they talked for a few more minutes. It appeared to Evelyn they hadn't yet found Peter.

"We don't know for sure that Brian Burke is on the property and if he intends to attack the church today. As we told you, we don't want to start a panic. What is the best time to give Pastor Lucas a message?"

"He calls himself Brother Lucas."

"When is the best time to give Brother Lucas a message without alarming the congregation?"

"As soon as he finishes giving his sermon, there's a music interlude that lasts usually about twenty minutes. During that time, I can give him a message."

"When will he be through with the sermon?"

"Hold on," Evelyn said as she turned up the television's volume and listened. She had heard the sermon twice already and thought it would be about another ten minutes or so. She told the agent who asked. "On a normal Sunday, how long does it take to empty the cathedral?"

"At least fifteen minutes, maybe longer."

The agent helped her create the terse message for her brother. Evelyn waited until the sermon was finished and the music started. She walked down the long aisle, swaying with the beat so not to attract too much attention. She could see her brother watching her. As she approached, he walked down the four stairs from the stage. He kissed her on the cheek and smiled while he whispered in her ear. "What's wrong?"

Evelyn smiled and whispered back. "It's bad." She then handed him a note, which said, "THE FBI SAYS DON'T USE THE OXYGEN!"

"I already did," he muttered.

49

WHILE EVELYN DODGE WAS GIVING the message to her brother, the FBI and local police were frantically searching the parking lot for Burke's car. There were three parking areas, which could hold up to four thousand cars. Automobiles filled most of the spots. The authorities were riding up and down the rows with a description of Brian's car and his license tag number. Unfortunately, the car registered to Brian Burke was a white compact, which looked like half the vehicles in the huge lot. In addition, many parishioners parked so they would be facing out. That way they wouldn't back into the traffic flow trying to exit the crowded parking area. Since Florida was one of the states that didn't require a front license plate, searching for Burke's car was not as easy as it seemed. This necessitated some agents walking between the rows while their partners drove up and down the aisles.

Kerry had decided to stay with Beverly Ruddy. They were in communication with the agents on the ground as well as the helicopter in the air. They were now sitting in a traffic jam because state and local police had setup roadblocks near the cathedral in an effort to find Brian Burke. Beverly was chastising herself for not giving clear direction to the local authorities on what she wanted them to do. Even with the siren and flashing lights of the FBI official vehicle, they were making slow progress.

The two women were getting a play-by-play of what was happening on the ground at the Divine Heart Unity Church. So far, nobody had seen Brian Burke or his car. Kerry was starting to think it was a false alarm.

Except for the special agent who was working with Evelyn Dodge all the others were using the push-to-talk mode of the cell phones to communicate.

"This is Casey. I've spotted the subject's car!"

"Where?"

"Row 16, half way down."

Beverly called the chopper pilot. "Do you see anyone walking in the parking lot?"

"There's hundreds of people walking around," advised the pilot.

"Casey, is anybody in the car?"

"I can't tell. The windows are tinted. Wait a minute. Someone's getting out. I have the subject in sight."

Kerry told Beverly, "Tell them to be careful, he may have the ricin on him."

"Casey, wait for back-up before you apprehend the subject."

"He's walking away, through the rows."

"Is he carrying anything?"

"He has a box and a gym bag?"

"What's the box look like?"

"It's rectangular about two feet long."

"He has the filter with him!" exclaimed Kerry

Casey said, "I'm going to drive around and intercept him in the next row. Shit…"

"What happened?"

"I hit a car backing out."

"Anybody hurt?"

"I'm not sure."

"This is New Orleans all over again," sighed Kerry Sterling.

Beverly Ruddy contacted the chopper pilot. "Look for someone carrying a box and a gym bag."

"Roger that."

Beverly turned to Kerry, "We're almost there."

Kerry said, "Get all your agents out of their cars. Do a foot search. Have them seal off the entrances to the cathedral and find the building holding the ventilation equipment. That's were he's headed."

Brian turned around when he heard tires screech and then a thump. Somebody got whacked he thought. He'd seen more than one accident in this parking lot as everyone usually tried to leave at once. Brian kept walking. He didn't have too far to go. His medication was finally working after he took four tablets. The whole morning he'd been doing nothing but waiting, his anxiety growing as it got closer to the time when he would install the filter. He was up since six and left the house at a little before 8:00. He went to the storage area to find that it didn't open on Sundays until nine o'clock. After he retrieved what he needed, he went directly to the cathedral. He had been sitting in the parking lot for the last two hours.

Brian looked up when he heard the helicopter flying low overhead. He didn't think much of it and continued heading for the enclosure. When he reached it, the gate was unlocked as he expected. Brian looked around and then opened the gate. As a precaution he brought a padlock so he could lock himself in. That way a maintenance worker or one of the security personnel that he'd seen patrolling the grounds wouldn't surprise him.

From the gym bag, he removed the poncho and industrial grade rubber gloves, which would reach to his elbows. Then he removed the respirator and put it on making sure there was no gap between the hood of the poncho and the edge of the rubber seal. As he was doing this, he looked up. The helicopter seemed to be hovering right over his head. He stared at it for a while and then went to the controller console.

"I've got him," said the helicopter pilot, who was flying the Bell Jet Ranger. An FBI agent had the door open and was strapped in the opening.

"Where is he? What's he doing?" Beverly asked the pilot anxiously.

"He appears to be putting on some rain gear," said the agent who was hanging out the helicopter's back door. "He's gloving up and he's put on a mask."

"Find out where he is," yelled Kerry.

Beverly hailed, "Where is he?"

"He's in a small fenced-in area in back of what appears to be the maintenance building. I can see the fans on top of the condensing units."

"Are there any agents nearby?"

"I can see three people running his way. They're almost there."

"Thank God," declared Kerry.

Brian looked at the console's display to make sure the oxygen was flowing. Apparently, Brother Lucas had pushed the button. Brian carefully removed the filter from the box and placed both on the ground. Next, he grabbed the shut-off valve. It was a single rubber covered handle—unlike a faucet—all the way off to all the way on, was less than a 180-degree turn. He closed the valve. He opened the filter compartment, unsnapped the two latches and removed the element. As he did this, he looked up. The helicopter was still there. Now a door was open, and it appeared someone was staring at him using binoculars.

Brian panicked. As he ran to the gate, he could hear footsteps. He could see men running toward the area. Brian knew he was caught. Then a strange feeling of calm came over him. He walked back to the filter compartment, removed the plastic bag from the ricin-filled element and installed it between the two latches. He heard shouting as people were trying to get through the gate. Brian closed the two latches, replaced the cover, reached for the valve and then...his heart stopped.

EPILOGUE

IT TOOK THREE HOURS for the authorities to determine that no ricin made it into the cathedral. Brother
Lucas along with his parishioners used the time to pray
for their deliverance. The only casualties that day were
Brian Burke and his mother.

The medical examiner did an autopsy on Brian and
determined that he had suffered massive heart damage,
most likely resulting from an overdose of the medication he was taking. A short time later, the FDA ordered
that Kyri-Laison be taken off the market because of its
acute adverse side effects.

Emily Burke, who had been traumatized during the
raid on her home, never recovered and is now institu-
tionalized in a mental health facility. Her monthly insurance stipend now goes to pay for her care. Ironically,
Brian Burke got what he wanted. Her money no longer
goes to the Divine Heart Unity Church.

Brother Lucas's stock has risen in the religious community. People called it a miracle that Brian Burke's last

heartbeat came before he was able to attack the church-goers. Brother Lucas's television ratings are the highest of all the televised clergy. There is talk of building a second pyramid cathedral outside of San Diego.

Bartolomeo Sanchez made it back to Bolivia, and with the help of a ghostwriter, he authored a best sell-ing book. Bartolomeo knew the whole story, as he had been one of the bodyguards on the night the DEA raid-ed General Castillo's residence. Bartolomeo became a rich man from book royalties and later from selling the movie rights to a major studio.

Nancy Noonan, riding on the wave of publicity as the story of the attacks unfolded, also wrote a book. This one was critical of the DEA. In her book, she also covered her role in the investigation. She gave the im-pression that she was instrumental in the identification of the General Castillo and Alejandro Reyes. She claim-ed that she was able to do this in spite of the FBI's lack of cooperation with Homeland Security. Her book be-came a best seller and ignited a passionate debate about the effectiveness of the DEA's war on drugs. Legislation is pending in congress to decriminalize marijuana, co-caine and methamphetamine. Nancy, who enthusiasti-cally supports these measures, is also considering a run for congress.

Dr. Matt Palena, still works in Atlanta for the Centers for Disease Control. He spends most of his time investi-gating ricin hotspots that still plague many areas of the country.

Both Jeffrey Davis and Kerry Sterling took a leave of absence from the FBI to work as consultants for a major motion picture studio. The big budget movie about the ricin attacks will use many of Hollywood's A-list stars. Kerry is happy with the actor the studio chose to play her. She is the tallest of Hollywood's elite. The films producers are shooting much of the movie in northern Florida.

On the political front, the opposition party won landslide elections to take control of the government. However, their popular "get tough" law and order stance with the public is starting to wane. The polls show that the president, who was injured in the first attack and defeated later in his reelection bid, will return to be his party's nominee.

Conspiracy theorists continue to write articles and books about the true nature of the events. They point to everybody from white supremacy organizations to the Taliban as being behind the attacks. A popular notion is that General Castillo and Alejandro Reyes never existed. To date, nobody has been able to find the wreckage of General Castillo's plane, which adds fuel to some of the speculation.

THE END

About the Author

Rob DiGiacomo, before writing Last Heartbeat was the author of the critically acclaimed thriller, Lap 121. He also wrote numerous non-fiction articles that appeared in various trade magazines and newsletters. Rob spent his early years growing up in New England and attended the University of Rhode Island after serving in the United States Navy. He moved to Florida in 1989 and now resides in the Tampa Bay area where he's working on his next book.

E-mail him at: author@LastHeartbeat.com